There Was A Soldier

Based on a true story

David Muir

Hoddamdale Books

Author's Note: What follows is based on actual occurrences and real people. Although much has been changed for fictional purposes, it must be regarded in its essence as fact.

This book is dedicated to my
mother and to her parents

Explanatory Notes on the Text

Short time breaks are represented by new lines; longer breaks by a large asterisk. Where a short time break occurs at the head or the foot of a page, a smaller asterisk is inserted to denote such a break.

It is hoped that the context of German dialogue is sufficient to understand its English translation.

Some of the Scottish characters speak in a regional dialect characteristic of a relatively small area in the southern part of the county of Dumfries and Galloway (where the Muir family come from). The dialect of other Scottish characters, who come from outside this area, does not usually necessitate as much 'translation'.

A glossary is provided overleaf. However, it is hoped that once the reader has 'tuned in' to the dialect and becomes used to it, its context will give meaning without resorting to frequent reference to the glossary.

The glossary is, of course, not intended to be as comprehensive as a Scottish dictionary. Rather it aims to include most of the common words spoken by some of the principal characters.

Glossary: Scottish dialect to English

a'	all
a'bdy or a'body	everybody
a'reet	alright
ain	own; e.g. on your own
ah (as in "pizz<u>a</u>")	I
ah'm; ah'll; ah'd	I'm; I'll; I'd
awe (as in "or")	oh
aye	an expression of affirmation
alane	alone
awfy	awful
bits	boots
chanty wrassler	a shifty person; a chancer
dain	doing
dae (as in "t<u>ea</u>")	do
daes (as in "f<u>izz</u>")	does
deid	dead
din	done
ee (as in "t<u>ee</u>") or ye	you or your
ee'll; ee've	you'll; you've
efter	after
fa (as in "p<u>a</u>t")	for
fettle	to set about (someone)
fi (as in "f<u>i</u>t")	(also for) for
fin	find
fri	from
gaen	gone
garn	go, going
greet	cry (tears)
hae; haen (as in "h<u>ay</u>")	have; having
iss (as in "hi<u>ss</u>")	me or us
ken	know
lift/lifted	steal/stolen
ma (as in 'h<u>a</u>t")	my
mair	more
maun (as in "Marne")	man

(the) moran	tomorrow
(the) moran's moran	the day after tomorrow
nae (as in "Dis<u>ney</u>")	no
havenae; disnae	haven't; doesn't
wouldnae; wasnae	wouldn't; wasn't
isnae; wullnae	isn't; will not
dinnae; couldnae	don't; couldn't
naebdie	nobody
na or nah	(also for) no
no	not
noo (short, as in "wh<u>o</u>")	now
ony; onything	any; anything
oor	our
oors	ours and hours
oot	out
ower	over
piece	sandwich
pit	put
schuil (as in "skill")	school
starving	(feeling the) cold
si (as in "t<u>i</u>ck")	too
stane	stone
tae (as in "tea")	to
(the) day/night	today/tonight
telt	told
weel	well
whee or whi	who
whit	what
wi	with
wid	wood
wid	would
wis	was
wull	will
yissed	used (as in "used to")
yersel	yourself

Prologue

An Ending and A Beginning

'Is that you, David?'

'It's me, Mum,' I replied from just inside the front door of my mother's ground floor flat.

I looked in on her before going into the kitchen. 'How are you today?'

'Oh, all right I suppose.'

'I'll just put your shopping away,' I said.

I re-wrote the date of each of her ready meals in large print on their cardboard sleeves, put them in the fridge and put the kettle on.

I heard my mother shuffle her walking frame along the passage from the living room to the bathroom.

She should be back in her usual place by the time I finish this.

I found a space on her cluttered chair-side trolley for a cup of coffee and a plate of ginger biscuits, placing my coffee on the edge of her unused dining table.

'Well, I've got some news, Mum. I know someone who can look for his war record.'

'Who's that?'

'I used to work with him: Pete Payne. He is an expert in ancestry research. You never know, he might be able to find something.'

'What do you plan to do?' she asked.

'Write it as a novel.'

'Why a novel?'

'It'll be based on fact though. We've got precious few of those, so the plan is to write it as a novel based on what I know. Even if Pete doesn't come up with anything, that's what I'll do. There'll be loads of research to do about the war anyway. So, if Pete comes up with something, I can use it.'

'I'm looking forward to reading it.'

'It could be a long job, Mum, what with the research. You'll be the first to get a copy though.'

Chronic glaucoma and cataracts had curtailed my mother's ability to read many months ago.

I'll read it to you, Mum.

My mother didn't live to hear me read the story to her. Jean has gone, but her family gave me a story: this story.

Davey's Story

Scotland Needs You

'Undo your shirt please.'

The stethoscope felt cold on Davey's chest as the army doctor listened to his breathing.

'You can button up now. Stand there please.'

'Five feet five inches,' the doctor announced, entering the measurement on a form.

'Now your weight.'

Davey watched the doctor slide the counterweight.

'Ten stone exactly.'

More form filling.

'Turn to face the chart and read what you can see.'

Davey dutifully read down the chart.

'Over there. Take this with you.'

'That's almost it,' said the soldier reading down Davey's form. 'Kate your next of kin?'

'Aye, sir.'

'And one child?'

'Correct, sir.'

'The army needs to know your next of kin. Just a precaution you understand.'

I can guess why.

'Read the declaration and sign the form, here,' said the soldier, pointing with his pen before handing it to Davey and turning the form around.

Davey read the attestation and signed in the space provided.

'Here's your rail warrant. Take this form with you to Berwick-upon-Tweed and report to the barracks. There is a train from Lockerbie at ten in the morning. Change at Edinburgh. Good luck, Muir. And thank you for volunteering.'

Davey pocketed the form, made his way through the throng of recruits in Annan Town Hall and breathed air free of sweating bodies.

That wasnae si bad. Easy medical.

'It's Davey, isnae it?' said a voice behind him.

'Aye,' said Davey, eyeing the owner of the voice, recognition slowly working through his mind.

'Ah'm Hamish. Ah havenae see ee since we left the schuil.'

'Hamish! Good tae see ee. Ee've been in?'

'Aye, that ah have. Ah missed the earlier recruiting. Away working.'

'Me tae.'

'Where're ee heading?'

'Back tae the Fechan,' said Davey.

'Ah'll walk with ee.'

The two men set off along the lane to Ecclefechan.

'Declared fit?' asked Hamish.

'Aye. Yersel?'

'Aye. The medical wis easy enough.'

'They wrote doon ma tattoos,' said Davey.

'Why?' asked Hamish.

'Dinnae ken,' Davey lied. 'Said ah wis on the short side, but fit enough.'

'Ye were the smallest kid in oor class,' said Hamish.

'And picked on.'

'Ah remember … a big kid. Whit wis his name?'

8

'Er, Wullie something,' said Davey.

'A'wis picking on ee.'

'Until ee clattered him. Left iss alane efter.'

'Oh, aye. Ah remember,' said Hamish with a laugh.

'And ee were the daftest in the class,' said Davey.

'Ah wasnae any guid at the schuil, Davey. Larking aboot ... Ah wis guid at that.'

The two former school friends walked on for a while without speaking.

'D'ye remember Kate?' said Davey.

'Aye. A bonny lass.'

'We're wed,' said Davey.

'She always had her eye on ee, Davey. Ah'm no surprised.'

'We have a bairn, Marion.'

Hamish grinned and gripped Davey's shoulder.

'There's the Kirtelbridge Road. About half-way,' said Hamish.

'Did ee recognise a'body else?' asked Davey.

'Na. Did ee?'

'Naebdy. A few o' the lads fri the Fechan hae volunteered. Already left. Why'd ee volunteer?' asked Davey.

'Awe, no entirely sure. Fed up wi working on the fairms. It'll be a hell of an adventure, Davey. There'll be good crack. It'll no last long. Better pay than ah get noo. Yersel?'

'My faither-in-law's an engineer. He's volunteered already. Kate disnae want me tae garn. It's oor duty though, isnae it?'

'Ah'm looking forward tae haing some laughs.'

Hamish isnae taking this seriously.

'Have ee ever been tae Berwick?' asked Hamish.

'Na.'

9

'Well, first time for the baith o' iss, then.'

Davey and Hamish parted company near Ecclefechan.

'Ah'm off tae catch a train hame tae Lockerbie.'

'See ee at the station the moran then,' said Davey.

'That's it. We've signed up. Nae garn back noo,' said Hamish.

'Aye, reet enough. Duty calls,' said Davey. 'Tae Berwick then.'

Davey lifted his uncle's Navy kit bag. It felt bulky.

'Whatever have ee put in here, Kate?'

'Socks, pants, shirts, and yer work jacket. The long heavy one. Ee'll need it this winter.'

'We'll be getting army kit.'

'Aye, but ee dinnae know when. Ah've given yer bits a clean. They'll be the best tae begin with. And there's a piece in the side pocket.'

Davey sighed. 'Dinnae make such a fuss, woman.'

'Ah'll make a fuss if ah like. Ah dinnae ken how lang ee'll be gaen. Have ee got ee papers frae yisterday?'

'That's twice ee've asked,' said Davey, patting the top pocket of his jacket.

Kate jiggled Marion.

'She's getting heavy,' said Davey.

'Aye. Have ee got everything?'

'Aye. Ah'm ready.'

Davey leant over Marion and kissed Kate on the cheek. It tasted salty.

Their eyes met.

'Ah hae tae garn. Dinnae fret, love.'

Kate nodded slowly.

'Look efter yersel,' she said. 'Write soon.'

'Ah'm nae much for the writing.'

'Aye, but ee'll write me.'

'Aye, ah wull.'

'Ee'd best be garn.'

Davey sat on a kitchen chair, put his boots on and shouldered his kit bag. He held his arms out, took Marion and carried her into the street.

'Goodbye, wee un,' he said, stroking Marion on the nose.

Marion responded by poking her father in the eye.

'Ouch!'

Davey handed his daughter to Kate.

'Ah'll away,' he said, rubbing his eye.

Marion buried her face in her mother's shoulder, crying quietly, as if she understood.

'Hush, it's a'reet,' said Kate.

Davey and Kate looked at one another, neither moved or spoke for a little while.

'Dinnae miss the train,' said Kate.

Davey stopped halfway up the hill that led out of Ecclefechan, turned and waved. Kate waved back. He stopped at the top of the hill, waved again. Kate held Marion's tiny arm in the air.

That's iss away then.

Getting Ready for the Fight

Slow-moving lines of men snaked across the parade ground of the barracks in Berwick-upon-Tweed towards a row of tables. A soldier ordered Davey and Hamish to join the end of one of the lines.

There must be hunnerds here.

There was little talk amongst the new recruits as the lines shuffled forwards.

Eventually Davey's turn came.

'Name.'

'David Muir.'

The soldier glanced at Davey and added his name to a list.

'Papers,' he said, holding out a hand.

Davey pulled his attestation form out of his top pocket and handed it over.

'Next of kin?'

'My wife, Catherine.'

'And you have just the one child?'

Davey nodded.

'*Robert Burns* and *Scotland the Brave*. Two tattoos.'

Davey nodded again.

The soldier signed below Davey's signature and added the form to the pile on his table.

'Welcome to the King's Own Scottish Borderers,[1] Private Muir. You go back through the archway onto the field and report there.'

Hamish caught Davey up as they left the parade ground and made for the tented area opposite the entrance to the barracks.

'Noo we ken whit the tents are fa,' said Hamish. 'It looks like a holiday campsite.'

Soldiers organised the recruits into roughly alphabetical order before assigning them to a tent. Davey and Hamish ended up in adjacent tents.

Each tent accommodated four men. Single bunks covered with planks of wood and a thin mattress filled with wood shavings took up most of the space.

Davey put his bag on the unoccupied bunk and sat down.

'Hello, I'm Davey Muir.'

Hells bells, that's hard.

'Ah'm Murray. Ah wonder how lang we'll be here?' 'Nae idea,' replied Davey.

'Ah'm Cameron,' said the man next to Murray.

'Ah'm Fraser. They call iss Paddy at hame,' said the other occupant.

'Paddy? Where's hame?' asked Cameron.

'Belfast.'

'Belfast!' the other three cried in unison.

'Aye. My folks moved from Glasgow when ah was wee. Nice kit bag, pal. Where'd ee get it?'

'Ma uncle was in the navy,' replied Davey.

Still got his Scottish accent.

---

[1] Usually abbreviated to KOSB.

The men sat on their bunks, eyeing one another cautiously, aware that getting to know each other had been forced upon them.

Cameron broke the uneasy silence and asked the others what they did before they enlisted.

'Worked in quarries and coal mines,' said Davey. 'Away from hame, mostly.'

'Ye must be tough for a small maun, if ee dinnae mind me saying so,' said Cameron. 'Sounds like hard work.'

'Aye, Ah'm used tae it.'

'Builder's labourer, me,' said Cameron.

'And me,' said Fraser.

'Junior clerk tae a solicitor in Dumfries,' said Murray.

He could fin it tough.

'Ah did hear that we'll be here for a day or two,' said Cameron, a comment that gave vent to questions with few answers.

'When dae we get some food?'

'Will we get some leave?'

'Ah wonder whit the training'll be like?' said Murray.

'Awe, no si bad,' suggested Fraser.

Murray's worried tone put an end to the men's immediate concerns and reminded them why they had volunteered.

A blast from a bugle shook the recruits out of what remained of a fractured sleep. Davey woke and left the tent just as a soldier marched out of the archway, raised his instrument to his lips for the second time and marked the start of his first day in the army.

14

When he had uncovered his ears, Davey asked the soldier where he could get a wash.

'Through that door, private. Make sure you shave. You always have to shave in the army, no matter what. The canteen is through that door, opposite the washrooms.'

'Thanks, er, corporal.'

Davey took advantage of using the washroom before everyone else. He stripped to the waist, had a thorough wash and shaved. He could smell the scent of home on the towel that Kate had packed.

She's given iss yin o' the best towels.

Breakfast comprised bread and jam, streaky bacon and strong tea. Davey didn't spot any familiar faces on the long table where he took his tin tray and sat down to eat.

The recruits were barely given time to finish before an NCO banged an enamel mug. The noisy chatter died down.

'Breakfast will be over in ten minutes, men. Return to your tents, take off jackets and caps and put on sturdy footwear. Then come back to the parade ground. You must be there by eight-thirty.'

'I've only got my ordinary shoes,' said the man opposite Davey.

'Me too,' said several others.

Ah think ah ken whit's coming.

Davey returned to his tent, carefully folded his jacket, stowed it in his kit bag and shoved the bag underneath his bunk.

It's a bit chilly. This thick shirt should dae.

The other three came in together.

'Ye were up early,' said Murray.

'Only just,' replied Davey. 'Ah wis standing next tae the bugler when he let rip.'

'Why nae jacket?' enquired Cameron.

'Ah reckon we've got a march on,' suggested Davey. 'Have ee fellas got spare socks?'

'A march! Already. We've only been here for five minutes,' said Murray.

'If ee've got 'em, put on two pairs of socks,' suggested Davey.

The others rummaged in their battered suitcases while Davey relaced his boots.

'We should be garn,' said Cameron, glancing at his watch.

Regular soldiers of the KOSB organised the recruits into ranks along one of the long sides of the parade ground. An officer stood on a dais in the centre and addressed the assembled men through a megaphone.

'Welcome to the King's Own Scottish Borderers. And thank you for responding to the call for volunteers. From now on, you are subject to army discipline. Listen, look and learn the rules quickly. Training will begin very soon and will last several months. Good luck, men.'

Short and sweet.

Another officer took the place of the first.

'You will be sent for training in the south of England. Yesterday, you arrived here as civilians. In a few months you will be turned into soldiers ready to serve your country. Trains will be leaving early in the morning.'

An early introduction to discipline and stamina followed immediately.

Just as ah thought.

NCOs organised the recruits into groups of sixty, in ranks of three. Davey found himself positioned in the third rank of the first group out of the barracks; Hamish was in the row in front of him. A drill sergeant accompanied Davey's group, marching briskly alongside. Another soldier brought up the rear.

The remaining groups marched around the parade ground until it was their turn to begin their first march as soldiers of the KOSB.

Davey's troop left the barracks through its imposing stone arch, turned left along the Parade in front of the ranks of tents and marched into the centre of town. Another left turn took them down Church Street, then Hide Hill towards the walls of the town. Shoppers and residents of Berwick stopped and watched the ranks of men dressed in their everyday clothes march along the middle of the road.

They must be yissed tae this sight.

Men in shirtsleeves, braces on show, capless and hapless in their ordinary shoes, strived to march in step in response to the relentless shouts of the sergeant.

'Keep in step. Left right, left right,' he called out whenever the rhythm of their step faltered.

'Better. That's better. Keep it up. Left, right, left right, left …' intoned the sergeant. 'Left turn.'

Davey winced as the wind whipped at his face as the streets of the town gave way to its ramparts. The North Sea chilled the eastern fringes of Berwick, even in September.

The men marched along the town's defences towards the barracks. Davey marvelled at the scale of the granite buttresses between the edge of town and the grey sea beyond as he tramped along, his boots chiming with the rhythmic step of the men around him.

We're almost in time noo.

The wind from the sea relented a little as the men turned away from the ramparts in anticipation of the end of their first march as enlisted men. They were in for a disappointment: the drill sergeant ordered them to keep marching past the inviting entrance to the barracks.

'You've only done a few miles, men,' he bellowed. 'Faster next time.'

Davey tried not to look at his tent as the men began their second circuit.

We could be in fi a few o' these.

Each group completed five circuits of the town's walls before they were allowed to return to their tents.

Davey felt pleased: his boots had served him well. The march hadn't taken as much out of him as his tent mates. All three were lying on their bunks, moaning about how tired they were and how their feet ached.

'Bloody hell, that wis awfy,' said Cameron. 'And this is just oor first day.'

'So much for easy training,' observed Murray.

'Where'd ee get those boots from, pal?' asked Fraser.

'Quarry work,' said Davey.

'Ah wish ah had boots like yours,' said Cameron. 'This marching lark is nae much fun in ma shoes.'

'Surely we'll be getting army boots soon,' said Murray.

'Aye, ah hope so,' replied Cameron.

Davey took off his boots and made a cursory inspection of his feet before he too stretched out on his bunk.

Ah'll need tae keep a close eye on ma bits.

'Form up in ranks at the back along the road,' ordered an NCO as he put his head around the entrance to Davey's tent.

Davey shouldered his kit bag and the others carried their suitcases and lined up. Hamish stood a few ranks ahead.

This will take iss as far fri Kate as ah've ever been.

After one day, Davey felt different, glad to be part of a famous Scottish regiment, waiting to march through Berwick with pride and with purpose born of duty – they were going to war.

As the men marched along the Parade and up Castlegate towards the station, they drew the attention of women and girls who shouted encouragement and blew kisses. Some of the new recruits blew kisses in return and shouted their thanks.

A bit different from oor march yisterday. They ken where we're away tae.

Davey thought about Kate as he marched. He didn't return the smiles and waves of the girls.

Men climbing in and out of compartments, looking for pals or seeking out loved ones who were waiting to see them off exacerbated the chaotic scene at the station. Soldiers from the barracks eventually got the carriages of the long train organised. Davey spotted Hamish and waved frantically.

Hamish dodged the futile efforts of a corporal urging men to get aboard, skipped out of line and joined Davey without drawing attention to his change of position.

'Ah've lost track of ma tent pals,' said Hamish.

'Come in wi iss,' said Davey.

Davey, Hamish and the others from Davey's tent settled in a vacant compartment; they were amongst the last to board. A sixth man leapt in moments before a soldier slammed the carriage door shut. He barely had time to sit in the vacant space opposite Davey before the train shuddered into life and slowly crossed the river Tweed to begin its journey south.

'Well, that's it. We're on oor way,' announced the stocky man sitting opposite Davey. 'Ah'm Angus.'

The train stopped twice, at Leeds and Leicester, where trestle tables lined the platform, offering buns that were past their best and stewed tea. The men arrived at Bordon weary and still hungry after their long journey to Hampshire.

A short march took the new troops of the 7th KOSB to the camp where they were accommodated in the barracks of the Royal Engineers.

Davey, Hamish, and Angus were billeted separately from Cameron, Fraser, and Murray.

An intense regime of daily physical training, squad drill, and long marches commenced immediately at Bordon. Most of the men were ill-prepared for such punishing training.

'Ah didnae think it wid be this hard,' moaned Hamish after a particularly long march. 'The last time ah did ony PE was at the schuil.'

'That was only ten miles,' quipped Angus.

'Well, it felt like twice that,' said Hamish, as he flopped onto his bunk.

'When dae we get proper bits?' said Hamish. 'Ma shoes are falling apart.'

'We've no seen a rifle or onything like that yet,' said Angus.

'Ah reckon they're getting us fit before the real training,' suggested Davey.

'Ah can't wait tae learn how tae fire yin,' said Angus, holding an imaginary rifle.

'Ye left-handed too?' said Davey.

∗

King George V inspected the troops in November, after two months initial training. The battalion paraded without rifles or uniforms: the men had none at that stage.

'Why is he King of Scotland?' whispered Hamish as the men waited to begin their march past.

'Did ee nae dae weel in history?' murmured Davey.

'Ah telt ee, ah was nae guid in the schuil.'

The ranks of men marched past the King, saluted on the 'eyes left' command, and continued across the parade ground on the order 'eyes front'.

How'd he get a' those medals?

'Well, that was a waste of time,' said Angus when the battalion had been dismissed. 'Ah'd rather dae PE than stand aroon fi oors waiting on His Majesty.'

Hamish lay on his bunk. 'We must have looked a shambles in oor worn oot jackets and trewsers.'

Lee-Enfield non-firing, drill-purpose rifles were issued at the start of the day's squad training after parading for the King.

The weight of the weapon felt awkward held in Davey's right hand by his side. He instinctively wanted to hold it in his left.

Davey watched the drill sergeant transfer his rifle from its side position with the butt on the ground to his shoulder and back again in response to his own commands.

On the left fi marching.

The sergeant demonstrated the drill several times before instructing the men to do the same.

'Shoulder arms,' he shouted. 'Two, three, four.'

'Change arms. Stand at ease.'

'Again. Shoulder arms. Two, three, four.'

The static drill continued over and over again, until Davey's arms ached.

The order to 'stand easy' came as a relief.

Davey flexed his aching left shoulder. At least it felt more natural to hold a rifle with his left hand.

'Now we march with 'em. Attention! Shoulder arms. By the left, quick march. Left, right, left, right …'

Davey's troop made several circuits of the parade ground, with the drill sergeant shouting marching orders. The orders to 'halt' and 'stand easy' came at last.

'Ground arms,' spelt the end of Davey's first practice in holding and marching with a drill weapon.

'Report to the firing range at oh nine hundred hours,' said the sergeant.

Hamish was in his usual position: lying on his bunk. Angus was shirtless and vestless, rubbing at the reddened skin on his shoulder.

'How's yer shooder, Hamish?' said Davey.

'Bloody hurts,' he replied. 'And ah've got a blister on baith palms. Whit's the point of a' this drill? We dinnae need it when we're in the fight.'

'It's tae teach us discipline,' said Angus. 'Didn't ee realise?'

'Aye, of course ah did. But no for weeks on end. We've done nothing else but march aroon and dae endless PE.'

'And dig trenches,' said Davey.

'Ah did enough labouring before joining up.'

'It'll be over eventually,' said Angus. 'We'll be sent ower soon. Can't wait tae get stuck in.' Angus made a lunging motion.

We're baith left-handed at that tae.

Davey stood next to Angus and Cameron and watched the dozen or so men lying on their fronts on the firing range. Two corporals moved along the row of prone men, adjusting the position of hands on rifles. One of the corporals had demonstrated how to hold a rifle firmly into the right shoulder, how to operate the bolt and use the sight before firing a few rounds at one of the white cardboard targets placed in front of a grassy bank some fifty yards away.

Could be awkward moving the bolt.

Each man fired three rounds. The noise was a shock, making Davey's ears ring.

Whit's it garn tae sound like holding yin?

Davey noticed how the weapon thrust into the shoulder of the man immediately in front of him.

'Firmer, private. Pull back slightly with both arms.'

The instructors continued to make adjustments before the next three rounds were fired.

Davey took up a position next to Angus when their turn came.

'Two lefties,' observed one of the corporals. 'Have either of you fired a rifle before?'

'No, corporal,' replied Davey and Angus together.

'Try the other shoulder.'

'It disnae feel right,' said Angus.

Davey tried to hold his rifle against his right shoulder.

'Me neither, corporal.'

'Well, do what feels right then.'

Davey waited for the order to fire his first round. The barrel felt hot. He gripped the butt, pulling it firmly into his left shoulder, and lined up the sight with his target.

Whit bit lines up wi …

'Three rounds … fire!'

The first round shook the rifle and slammed it into his shoulder. Davey adjusted his grip and tried again.

That felt better.

After three more rounds, targets were retrieved. Davey had made five holes in his.

'Probably just your first round missed, private,' said the corporal. 'Not bad for your first effort.'

Cameron had done particularly well. A cluster of holes around the centre of his target attracted attention as his target was passed from man to man.

One of the corporals reloaded a rifle while a new target was set for Cameron. Everyone watched in anticipation. Six more holes in the centre confirmed Cameron's skill.

Cameron beamed to a round of applause.

Davey and Angus discussed their first experience using a service rifle, while Hamish lounged on his bunk.

'It's fine when the end of the barrel is resting on something,' said Angus. 'Ye can use yer right hand tae operate the bolt, just like the others.'

'Aye, but it could be awkward otherwise,' said Davey. 'Ah cannae see how we can swap ... na, we cannae use oor left hand tae pull back the bolt.'

'Wull ee no stop blethering,' said Hamish. 'Ah'll get ee both a left-handed rifle.'

'Great idea,' said Angus. 'We'll ask when we get uniforms this afternin.'

Obsolete uniforms of tunics and trousers were issued later that day, replacing worn out civilian clothes.

'Just as well,' said Angus. 'Ma trews are din.'

'Mine too,' said Hamish.

'Whit dae we dae for jackets?' said Davey.

'Ah dinnae ken,' said Hamish. 'We've got these thick tunics. Perhaps that's it?'

'Still nae bits, then,' said Hamish. 'Ma shoes have almost had it. Look at these holes.'

'Aye, mine are no sae bad,' said Angus. 'They'll no last much longer though. Ah'll be barefoot efter the next march.'

Davey guarded his precious work boots carefully. He tied them to the underside of his bed when he was not wearing them and slept with them underneath his pillow.

They should last for a few more marches.

*

The dreary winter of 1914–1915 accompanied the battalion's largely outdoor training regime. The cold didn't trouble Davey, but Hamish relied on constant encouragement to keep going. Davey worried about his pal's fitness and willpower. He would need to watch over him all the way to France.

Lord Kitchener, the Secretary of State for War, inspected the battalion on a frosty morning on nearby Frensham Common in mid-December. The men were smartly turned out and were fitter and stronger than when they arrived. The previous four months of basic training had hardened muscles. They were ready for war but lacked any first-hand knowledge about how it would be fought when they got to France.

Despite learning and practising how to dig them, life in trenches and trench warfare were beyond Davey's imagination.

David Muir, 14387 KOSB, 1915

The original (sepia) photograph was taken some time during the first six months of 1915.

Leave of Absence

'It'll cost ee a week's pay, Davey.'

Davey stood with his back to the stove. The draughty hut let in a bitter wind, carrying the promise of worse weather in store. 'Ah've got tae see her before we garn over.'

Hamish lay on his straw-filled mattress and stared at the ceiling.

'Kate's expecting another bairn. Ah must garn.'

'Have ee no tried for special leave?' asked Hamish.

'Nothing daein. Ah'll hae tae risk it.'

'Ah still think ye're barmy. It's a long way to the Fechan. Garn AWOL is a serious offence.'

'Ah'll tak ma punishment. They willnae chuck iss oot o' the army will they?'

Hamish sighed, swung his legs off his bunk and put his shoes on. 'C'mon, we've got a lang march just noo. Best get ready.'

Davey and Hamish left the hut and lined up next to one another on the parade ground. The keen wind carried a stinging rain.

'This is garn tae be a miserable march,' muttered Hamish as their unit formed up and set off at a brisk pace.

'We're getting fitter though,' observed Davey. 'Can't ee feel a difference from when we first got here?'

'Ye're fitter than me. How did ee get so strong?'

'Coal mining,' replied Davey. 'Near Newcastle, before the war. Bloody hard work. Then working in a quarry down near the Solway Firth.'

'Quiet in the ranks,' yelled Sergeant Gibson. 'Save your breath, Private Muir. Let's step up.'

'Ah'll away the night,' whispered Davey. 'If onyone asks, ye dinnae ken whit ah'm up tae.'

'That includes whispering, Muir.'

'Sorry, sarge.'

Davey packed socks and pants in his kitbag, turned up the collar of his tunic and slipped unseen out of the hut of sleeping men.

Instead of taking his chances at the main gate, he made for the southern edge of the camp away from the barracks where the training grounds edged a wood. Davey worked his way along the barbed wire fence in the pale moonlight until he found what he had seen during training: a farm gate in the boundary fence.

Davey scaled the gate carefully, holding down the slack barbed wire that spanned its uppermost bar.

There's bound tae be a path efter a gate.

He pictured the large map mounted on the wall of the camp's post office. The main road from Guildford that passed the main gate of the camp lay to the north-west.

Davey followed the wide path until it left the wood and emerged in a farmyard. He took off his boots, crossed the yard and took what he hoped would be the farm track to the main road.

Davey's heart jumped at the sound of barking dogs. He sprinted along the side of the track, leaving the canine alarms to their duty.

They're no following.

He reached the road, panting for breath. He turned left and walked quickly away from the farm entrance, his feet damp from his dash in wet grass.

A finger post at a cross roads confirmed that he was on the main road from Guildford to Portsmouth.

Davey sat on the edge of a milk churn stand just beyond the crossroads, put his boots on and set off at a brisk pace.

The station at Bordon is tae risky.

A right turn in a town named Petersfield set Davey on a route towards Winchester.

Aboot fifteen miles. Ah should be there by daylight.

Davey reached the eastern outskirts of the city just as it was getting light.

He'll ken.

A tall man in a white apron busied himself placing advertising boards outside a bakery.

'Depends on where you want to go, soldier,' he said in reply to Davey's request for directions. 'We've got more than one station.'

'I'm wanting a train coming from Southampton,' said Davey, 'going north.'

'Then it'll be Cheesehill. Pretty much straight on from here. There's signs as you get nearer the centre of town. You turn left when you reach the river.'

'Thanks. Can ah get something fi the journey?'

'Come on in.'

Davey bought two plain rolls and a large slice of fruit cake.

'That's yesterday's cake,' said the baker, putting Davey's purchases in a brown paper bag. 'It'll be good for a day or two yet.'

Davey put the bulging paper bag in the top of his kit bag.

'On leave?'

'Aye.'

'Good luck, soldier.'

'Thanks,' said Davey as he hoisted his kit bag over his left shoulder.

A walk of twenty minutes from the baker's shop took Davey to the station. The clock in the small ticket office showed seven thirty. He had less than an hour to wait for a train to Birmingham.

'Don't you have a rail warrant?' asked the elderly man behind the glass.

'It disnae cover this part of the journey,' replied Davey.

The man hesitated, frowned and looked at Davey through half-closed eyes. 'That'll be ten and six to you, soldier,' he said before handing Davey his ticket and change. 'Cross over to Platform Two. The eight twenty.'

The throb in Davey's feet denied him the opportunity to catch up lack of sleep.

'Don't stare,' said the woman sitting opposite, scolding her daughter.

'It's a'reet,' said Davey, smiling at the little girl.

'Are you on leave?'

'Aye.'

32

The little girl averted her gaze, snuggled into her mother's side and closed her eyes.

The throb reduced to a tingle. Drowsiness overcame Davey, helped by the rhythm and clatter of the train.

He woke in Oxford. The mother and daughter were gone. A large woman, nursing a basket on her lap, returned his gaze.

Oxford station slid past the window.

Tae late tae garn back.

The timetable boards at Birmingham railway station showed a Glasgow train leaving at ten minutes past two from Platform 7.

It'll be dark when ah get hame.

Davey found a bench and ate his rolls and cake. He resisted going to one of the station tea rooms; there would be more questions about leave. Instead he made do with a long drink from a water fountain.

His ticket cost him eighteen and six.

That's a month's pay spent the day. Kate'll no be pleased.

Davey spent the long journey from Birmingham to Ecclefechan staring out of the window or dozing. He avoided lengthy conversations, his mood dulled by an unrelenting feeling of unease. He heart beat stronger than normal the closer he came to the end of his journey.

Ah've got myself intae bother.

The station clock at Carlisle showed just after ten o'clock. Forty minutes and four stops found Davey standing on Ecclefechan station watching the red light of the guard's van receding towards Lockerbie until darkness and silence announced his home-coming.

Davey slung his kitbag over his shoulder, sighed deeply and crossed the footbridge, leaving the deserted station to await his return. The familiar short walk along the Carlisle road filled him with apprehension. Guilt mingled with doubt set his pulse racing, accompanied by tightness in his throat as he entered the High Street.

Davey knocked on his front door, the tapping of his knuckles echoing along the deserted street.

He was on the point of knocking again when Kate opened the door. Her hand flew to her mouth, suppressing an intake of breath.

'Whit are ee daein here? Ee didnae tell iss ee were on leave.'

'Can ah come in?'

Kate stood aside.

'Ah'm no on leave.'

'Whit! Have ee deserted?'

'Of course not. Yer postcaird said ee were expecting. Ah had tae see ee.'

'Ma God, Davey. Yee'll be in so much bother.'

'Ah ken that. Ah had tae take the risk. There's no leave yet, so ah had tae come.'

'Sit doon, sit doon,' said Kate. 'It's late. Have ee eaten?'

'No much.'

'Yer a daft bugger, Davey Muir. Daft and foolish. Have ee gaen soft in the heid? Whit'll they dae tae ee when ee garn back?'

'Ah dinnae ken. Ah'll tak ma punishment.'

'They might throw ee oot.'

Davey shrugged. 'Ah hope no.'

'This is the daftest thing ee've ever din.'

'Aye, so ee keep saying.'

'How much wis yer ticket?'

'Aboot a month's pay.'

Kate shook her head.

'Ah'll carry on sending ee postal orders when ah next get paid,' said Davey. 'Nae mair train tickets.'

'Just see that ee dinnae. Anyway, ah'm fine, as ee can see. Ah'm glad tae see ee, but ah'm worried aboot whit ee've din.'

'Sorry, Kate.'

'Aye, well ... wait there. Ah'll mak some tea. Would ee like a scone?'

Davey recounted the events of the day over cups of tea and tatty scones. Kate listened without interruption, her countenance unsmiling and stern, her head shaking slowly from time to time.

Davey licked the last of a few crumbs from his fingers. 'Grand scones, as usual. Ah've missed 'em.'

'Well, ee're here noo. Ee'd better stay oot o' sight the moran.'

Davey nodded. 'Ah can get a guid night's sleep.'

'And ee can garn back the moran's moran,' said Kate, pointing at Davey. 'Ah'd make ee garn in the moran, but ee need tae rest. Ah dinnae suppose another day wull mak a difference.'

'It might,' said Davey. 'Ah dinnae ken the going rate for garn AWOL.'

Davey spent most of the next morning in bed, getting up around mid-day. Marion's face lit up when she saw her father come into the kitchen.

'Dinnae tell a soul ee saw me,' he whispered as he bounced Marion gently on his lap.

She smiled at him, burbling happily.

'Aye, Daddy wull come again soon,' he said, keeping up the pretence.

'Ony idea when that'll be?' said Kate.

'Nae idea. Ah'll send a caird.'

'Whit happens next?'

'Mair training and then we garn ower tae France.'

Kate took Marion. 'Time for a sleep, wee un. That's when we'll worry, Davey, when y'eel be ower there.'

'Ah, dinnae fret. They say it'll be ower within a few months. Ah might no have tae fight or onything.'

'Whit time's the first train tae Cairle in the moran?'

'The first train's down at six thirty. Ah'll leave by the back before it gets light. Can ee mak me a piece?'

Davey slid out of bed while it was still dark, collected his clothes from the chair in the corner of the bedroom, lit a candle in the kitchen and got dressed. Kate had wrapped a piece, some tattie scones and homemade ginger biscuits in brown paper. He packed his food parcel on the top of his kit bag, put on his tunic and buttoned it to the neck.

Kate came into the kitchen, rubbing her hands together. 'That's ee away, then.'

'Aye, ah'm away.'

'Ah might not see ee again before ee garn over,' said Kate, her eyes glistening.

Davey drew Kate to him, hugging her tightly until her sobs subsided. 'Dinnae fret, Kate. Ah'll be a'reet.'

Kate pulled slowly away, wiping her eyes on the back of her hands.

Davey shouldered his kit bag, opened the back door, hesitated then turned to face his wife.

The look between Davey and Kate lingered in the chill candlelight, their eyes finding each other, unwilling to let go.

Davey turned away, stepped into the yard and closed the door behind him. He used familiar paths across the field behind the terrace of cottages to make his way to the main road, then turned right for the short walk to Ecclefechan station.

The train to Carlisle drew up in a cloud of noisy steam. Davey was the only passenger waiting at the otherwise deserted station.

Naebdy at the ticket office.

The train had no corridor, so his lack of ticket would go unnoticed.

Davey's knowledge of the local train timetable hadn't let him down. He changed at Carlisle for a train to Birmingham and purchased a ticket.

The Birmingham train had a corridor, which gave Davey the opportunity to stretch his legs and for inspectors to check tickets.

Just as weel ah've got a ticket this time.

Davey eat his cheese piece and two tatty scones while he waited at Birmingham station for the two fifteen train to Southampton. A large group of soldiers gathered, stretching two or three deep along the platform near Davey's bench.

Ah wonder where they're off tae.

He put what remained of his food in the top of his kitbag, slung it over his shoulder and approached the line of men. 'Where are ee off tae?'

'Southampton,' replied the soldier on the end of the line. 'You?'

Grand.

'Winchester.'

'That's near Southampton, isn't it?' said the soldier to the men standing nearby.

'Yeah, but we don't stop there,' said another. 'Why d'ya want to know?'

'Ah'm late returning from leave,' said Davey. 'Ma warrant has run oot.'

'Oh yeah.'

'Aye.'

'You're in a spot then, mate.'

'Aye, ah ken that.'

'Is that a Scottish accent?'

'Aye. Ah'm with the King's Own Scottish Borderers, oot o' Berwick-upon-Tweed,' said Davey. 'Could ee help us oot?'

A group of soldiers gathered around.

'How d'yer mean?' said one.

'Er, if ah came in with ee, ah could save on the train fare.'

'What d'yer think, fellas. Do we help out a fellow soldier?' said another.

'That we do,' came the reply. 'Wait with us,' he said. 'We'll get you into our compartment.'

'That's guid o' yee. Thanks very much,' said Davey. 'Is this yer train?'

Davey was ushered into the first compartment of the first carriage without drawing the attention of the NCOs further along the platform. The station clock read ten minutes pas two; he would be in Southampton in a few hours.

At least ah'll be back the night.

A sergeant slammed the door without a glance inside.

'You're in, mate. The serge didn't notice you over there. I'm Stan.'

'I'm Davey.'

'George.'

'Ken.'

'Mitch.'

'H.'

'Where're ee a' from?'

'We left base at Cannock this morning,' said Stan. 'We're with the Staffs.'

'Are ee going over from Southampton?'

'Yeah,' said Mitch. 'By the look of your uniform, you're still training.'

'Aye. Ah volunteered a couple of months ago. We're still waiting for kit.'

'What're yer doing off base?' asked Ken.

'Ah went tae see ma wife,' said Davey. 'She's expecting.'

'Without permission?' said Ken.

Davey hesitated before replying. 'Aye.'

'Tell 'em that,' said Stan. 'You might get a light punishment.'

'Strictly speaking, going AWOL amounts to desertion,' said George.

'But they'll know ah haven't deserted when ah get back the night,' said Davey.

'Even so, expect a severe telling off and some sort of punishment,' said George. 'They might even chuck you out.'

'Nah,' said Stan. 'What happened to that bloke in the hut next to us? He was late back from leave. What did they do to him?'

'He got a fine and extra duties,' said George.

'I've never heard of anyone being slung out for going AWOL,' said Stan. 'Cheer up, Davey. You'll just get a fine and jankers.'

'Jankers?' said Davey.

'Extra duties, like George said. Menial tasks. Cleaning and suchlike.'

'Whatever it is, a'll tak ma punishment. It'll have been worth it ti see ma wife.'

Davey took the bag of biscuits out of his kitbag. 'There might be only enough for one each,' he said, offering the bag around.

'Yer wife makes good biscuits, mate,' said H.

'Good luck, Davey,' said Stan. 'Good luck,' echoed the others.

'Tak care o' yersels ower there,' said Davey. 'And thanks for hiding iss.'

Davey watched until the platform was clear of uniformed men.

That saved a few day's pay.

Davey purchased a ticket and caught the next local train to Winchester, arriving at his starting point at just after eight o'clock on a dark, cold evening.

He set off for the long walk to camp on an empty stomach, with the threat of punishment fresh in his mind.

A military lorry pulled up a few yards ahead shortly after Davey left the city behind him.

40

The driver leant out of the open-sided cab. 'I saw you in my lights. Where're you off to, soldier?'

'Bordon,' replied Davey.

'I'm heading for Bramshott Camp. I'll drop you at the gate.'

'Thanks very much,' said Davey, climbing into the cab.

There's no sneaking in at the back then.

Conversation was brief and limited due to the noise of the truck and Davey's reluctance to disclose any details about why he was off base.

Ah think he's on tae iss.

'Good luck, soldier,' said the driver. 'We're here.'

Davey got down from the cab, gave the driver a wave and presented himself at the gatehouse.

'Pass,' demanded the armed soldier.

'Ah dinnae have yin,' replied Davey.

'What? Why not?'

'Ah've been off base without yin.'

The guard waved his rifle. 'Wait in there.'

He cranked the telephone then spoke to someone while frowning at Davey over his shoulder. 'An MP will be along shortly.'

'How long you been off base?'

'Since Wednesday night.'

'Three days then, private.'

'Whit'll they dae?'

'Not for me to say. Go with him.'

'You'll be locked up for the rest of the night, private,' said the MP. 'First thing in the morning, you'll report to Major Franks. Understand?'

'Yes, sir.'

'There's a bucket in there. You'll be collected first thing. Be ready.'

Davey spent an uncomfortable few hours trying to sleep on a wooden bunk. As soon as he heard sounds in the corridor, he smartened himself the best he could and waited.

'Bring the bucket and empty it in the lav at the end of the passage,' ordered a sergeant. 'Then come back here.'

Davey emptied the bucket, washed his hands and splashed water on his face and hair.

Well Davey Muir, time tae face it.

'Follow me,' ordered the sergeant.

Davey followed the sergeant out of the building and into the next. The sergeant knocked on the first door on the right.

'Come,' called a voice, loud with authority.

The sergeant opened the door, motioning Davey to enter.

'This is Private Muir, sir.'

'Thank you, sergeant.'

Davey heard the door close.

Major Franks didn't look up as Davey stood to attention before his desk. 'I've recorded seventy-two hours off base without permission on your army record,' he said, putting his pen down. 'What do you think you were playing at, Private Muir?'

'Ma wife is expecting again, sir. Ah wanted tae see her.'

'We all want to see our wives, Muir. Why is yours so special?'

'She isnae, sir. Ah mean she is tae me.'

'You would have got leave before you go over.'

'Ah know, sir. Ah couldnae wait.'

'It's bloody miles to Scotland. Determined sod, aren't you?'

Davey didn't answer.

'Look, Muir. You're a few years older than most of the new recruits. I would rather you set an example to the youngsters. Leaving base without permission is a very serious offence. I have to issue a severe punishment.'

'Yes, sir.'

'You'll be fined a week's pay and leave's cancelled.'

'That's a bit harsh, sir.'

'I beg your pardon. I'll be the judge of that.'

'Ah apologise, sir.'

'I should think so. You don't need to go home, you've already been.'

'Yes, sir.'

'We need people like you. Enterprising. More mature, at least I assumed you were.'

'Ah'm very sorry, sir. It willnae happen again.'

'I've received good reports about your training. Keep it up, private. I understand how you feel. I'm a father too. But discipline comes first. Don't give me cause to add anything to this. You can dismiss.'

Davey saluted, make a smart about turn and left the major's office.

Sorry Kate. At least ah got tae see ee for a wee while.

'Well, whit happened?' Hamish asked Davey when he entered their hut.

'They fined iss a week's wages.'

'Whit did ah tell ee?'

'And cancelled ma leave.'

'Ye daft bugger.'

'Ah took a risk. Ah wis only hame for a day onyway. When's yer leave?'

'Hogmanay. And ah thought we'd garn hame together.'

Mobilisation

The 7th KOSB left Bordon at the end of February 1915. A march of just over twenty miles would take the battalion to Cross, a camp near Winchester.

Sergeant Gibson took charge of the march.

'Ah, Private Muir. You've decided to join us today. Did you have a nice holiday? Front rank. MOVE!'

Davey replaced one of the men in the front rank, avoiding eye contact with Sergeant Gibson.

Uh, oh. Gibson's haeing some fun.

Sergeant Gibson took every opportunity to chide Davey for not setting a fast enough pace, shouting at him loud enough for his company to hear or marching next to him berating him menacingly.

Davey responded by obeying the sergeant's commands calmly and impassively.

Dinnae give him ony cause.

The end of the march signalled release from Sergeant Gibson's attempts to provoke Davey.

He'll nae doubt hae another go another day.

Davey and Hamish collected their personal belongings from where they had been unloaded from the lorry that left Bordon earlier that morning and waited to be allocated to a hut. Agony showed on the faces of Davey's company as they waited.

'Sorry, fellas,' he said. 'Gibson shouldnae be taking it oot on ee.'

'He's trying tae turn us against ee,' suggested Cameron.

'Aye, well ah'm really sorry. Ah had nae alternative but tae set the pace.'

'Well, ee did a daft thing garn off base,' said Angus.

'Aye, ah ken. But it's me he can fettle. He has nae right tae mak it hard fi a'bdy else.'

'Follow me,' said a corporal.

It would have been a shorter walk fri here.

'Another march, another hut,' moaned Hamish. 'And still nae bits. Ah'm not daein any mair in these shoes.'

Hamish sat on his bunk, took off his battered shoes and flung them across the hut.

Wull ee no stop moaning.

Davey turned his boots over in his hands.

Damn. A hole in both.

Packs, tunics, breeches and belts were issued later that day, replacing temporary kit.

'Thank God they measured iss fa bits, at last,' said Hamish as he dumped his pack and new kit on his bunk. 'There's a' sorts of things in here,' he said, emptying the contents of his pack. 'Whit's this? Look, a wee sewing kit. Shaving things. A' sorts.'

'Socks and a balaclava,' said Davey. 'Fork, spoon, and, whit's this, a can fi eating food?'

'Everything ee need fi a holiday,' quipped Hamish. He repacked his pack. 'There's nae much room for onything else.'

'Such as?' said Davey.

'Woolie. Overcoat.'

'Ah dinnae think we'll be carryin' a woolie,' said Davey.

'Ah still can't see how tae put these on,' said Hamish, struggling with puttees. 'That corporal demonstrating wis a bit quick fir iss. Hey, look how lang they are.'

'Several feet, fi a guess,' said Davey. 'Let's hae a go.'

'Whit're they fi, onyway?' asked Hamish.

'They're supposed tae gie yer legs support,' replied Davey. 'Ah think he did it this way.'

Davey started with his left leg, winding and overlapping the thick khaki cloth until he reached his knee. 'That's why the breeches are shorter than trews.'

'Well, yours aren't,' observed Hamish. 'Tak it off and show iss again.'

'No too tight,' Davey instructed himself, as he wrapped his left leg again, this time tying and tucking the excess ties into the top.

Davey walked a few paces up and down the hut, joining other men practising their puttee technique.

He put on the other puttee and his battered boots and strolled up and down the hut.

'Noo yersel,' he said to Hamish.

Hamish unrolled the end of one of his puttees and began to wind it around his left leg.

'Na, too loose. Start ower.'

Hamish persevered until he felt comfortable with them on. 'Jesus, whit a performance.'

'Aye, but ee keep 'em on a' day,' said Davey.

Both men practised putting on their puttees and taking them off again for the next hour.

∗

The familiar pattern of vigorous basic training continued at Cross for the next month. Sergeant Gibson took no part in parade ground drill, denying him the opportunity to badger Davey.

The absence of Davey's apparent enemy came to an end when the battalion transferred from Winchester to Parkhouse Camp on Salisbury Plain on 18th April.

A chorus of groans accompanied the order for Davey to move to the front rank of his company.

'QUIET IN THE RANKS!' bellowed Sergeant Gibson.

Davey looked across to the two men to his right. 'Let's try and tak it easy,' he whispered.

Brief nods sealed their collaboration.

The march of twenty-five miles in new boots was more agonising than marching in their shoes. The men were strong and fit, but their new boots were as hard as rock.

Sergeant Gibson chivvied the front rank from time to time.

'This is oor first march in new bits, sarge,' said Davey. 'Can't ee give iss a chance?'

'No, Muir. There's no time like the present,' he replied, dropping back. 'STEP UP AT THE FRONT, MUIR.'

Davey quickened the pace slightly, looked back to see that Sergeant Gibson had dropped back.

'Slow it down,' he whispered. 'Gibson has disappeared.'

Fi noo.

*

'We had nae time tae break 'em in,' said Hamish as he lay on his bunk in the tented camp.

'Some of the others say ee should pee in 'em tae help soften 'em,' said Davey.

Hamish sat up on his elbows. 'Ah'm nae aboot tae wee in mine. There must be a better way.'

Davey rubbed his tired feet.

Nae blisters. These are tae big though.

Mark III Lee-Enfield rifles were issued after parade the following morning. The battalion was divided into its five companies and marched to different parts of the camp. Davey's E Company sat on the grass while Captain Baird addressed them.

'A period of thorough weapons training starts this afternoon,' he said. 'It's your responsibility to look after your weapon. Do not let anyone handle your rifle. Keep it with you at all times. All yours, sergeant.'

Oh no, Gibson.

Sergeant Gibson showed the men how to fix a bayonet.

'Your bayonet hangs in its holder on your left hip here,' he explained. 'When you hear the order to "fix bayonets", you pull it out, engage it and twist like this.'

Sergeant Gibson untwisted his bayonet, stowed it and fixed it once more. He repeated the demonstration several times.

He pulled Murray out of the front row of seated men. 'Now you,' he said.

Tak yer time.

Murray dropped his bayonet.

'And now you're dead,' mocked the sergeant.

Murray bent to pick up his bayonet.

'Not like that. You'll cut your damn fingers off.'

Get it right this time.

'Try again.'

'Good. But too slow. You can sit down.'

Murray took his place to sympathetic pats on the shoulder.

'Private Muir, let me see you do it.'

Davey tried to engage his bayonet with his right hand.

This doesn't feel right.

'Useless, Muir.'

'Ah'm left-handed, sarge.'

'Swap hands then.'

Davey engaged his bayonet with his left hand.

'By the time you've messed about, you'll have been skewered, Muir.'

'It feels more natural with ma left,' said Davey.

'You'll have to carry yours on your right hip, private,' advised Sergeant Gibson. 'You do everything in reverse. That's fine as long as you can fix it quickly. You've got even more reason to get quicker. Alright, sit down.'

Davey disengaged his bayonet, replaced it in its holder and sat down.

'Looks easy doesn't it, men. Spread out and practise. I'll come round.'

Murray and Davey paired up and practised, facing one another.

'Still picking on ee,' said Murray.

'Aye, as long as it's just iss.'

E Company practised until their hands ached.

'Over to the sacks, men,' said the sergeant. 'You're getting quicker. Practise on your own from now on.'

Lines of men waited their turn to use their bayonets on practice targets.

Sergeant Gibson demonstrated how to run and thrust a bayonet into a sandbag hanging from a wooden beam.

'You don't just run into it. You make a final lunge, like this.'

He ran quicker, bringing his right arm back and forcing the blade deep into the target.

'See where I held the rifle.'

'The real ones move, sarge,' said Hamish.

'You get them first, private,' replied Sergeant Gibson. 'Right, first row. GO.'

Davey watched Hamish, Murray, and Angus make their first charge.

They all got their blades into the sacks of sawdust.

'Again. Faster and noisier this time.'

Angus screamed at the top of his voice, lunging enthusiastically into what was left of his sack. Hamish yelled, but Murray's effort clipped the side of his sack.

'Put some effort into it, private. Again, on your own.'

C'mon, pal.

Murray's next charge didn't convince Sergeant Gibson.

'What's the matter with you? Imagine it's the Boche this time.'

Murray charged again.

'I can hardly hear you.'

Murray lined up with the others once more, shaking his head in dismay.

'Noo he's picking on ee, pal?' said Davey.

'I heard that, Private Muir.'

'Sorry, sarge.'

'That's *sergeant*, Muir.'

'Sorry, sergeant.'

'Let's see if you can do any better. Charge.'

Let's see if he leaves Murray alane.

Davey sprinted the few yards from the line towards the sack, stopped, drew back his rifle on his left side and drove it into the sack.

'Useless, private. You're not supposed to stop. And for heaven's sake make a noise. You wouldn't frighten a child. Can't you do it the other way around?'

'Ah'm left-handed, sergeant.'

'Oh bloody hell, of course. Alright, again. And make an effort this time.'

Sergeant Gibson made Davey repeat the exercise several times in front of the others until he appeared to be satisfied.

On his final charge, Davey slashed his blade rapidly from left to right. Sawdust showered onto his boots, leaving the sack hanging limply.

'Thank you, Private Muir. I think that will do. There's a pile of replacements over there. Go and get one and while you're at it, replenish the lot.'

Bayonet training continued with sacks placed in the bottom of a shallow trench. Davey's platoon were instructed how to run towards the trench, leap in and skewer the nearest sack.

As the afternoon wore on, Davey and his pals became proficient enough for Sergeant Gibson to offer grudging praise to everyone apart from Davey, whom he merely glared at.

'Ah wasnae trying tae show ee up, pal,' said Davey on their way back to their tents. 'Ah just wanted him off yer back.'

'Aye, thanks, Davey,' said Murray. 'We a' ken that. Disnae give up, daes he?'

51

*

After three weeks of weapons training, the 7th transferred from Parkhouse camp. A long march of twenty-five miles took the men to Chiseldon, a tented camp near Swindon. Sergeant Gibson did not accompany the battalion.

Ah hope that's the last o' him.

'Yet another camp. How mony mair transfers?' complained Hamish, as he flopped onto a bunk. 'There must be hunnerds of tents. Can't be just the 7th.'

'Some sort of build up,' suggested Angus.

'At least the weather's warming up. As long as it disnae rain,' said Hamish. 'Ah hate camping.'

'How're ee feet efter that yin?' asked Davey.

'Fine,' said Angus.

'Aye, me tae,' said Hamish. 'Yersel?'

'Aye, grand. Sorry tae leave ma auld bits behind though.'

'D'ye think we'll ever see our auld claes again?' asked Hamish.

'Ah havenae thought about it that much,' replied Angus. 'Is it worth it? Ma jacket and trews were no worth having ony mair.'

The battalion received orders for mobilisation while stationed at Chiseldon.

'Where tae noo?' muttered Hamish as the 7th formed ranks for the short march to Salisbury Plain.

The King inspected the 15th Scottish Division, which included the 7th KOSB, on Salisbury Plain. He saw a well-trained, fully equipped army, a great change since his previous inspection, an army ready for the Western Front.

'It's him again,' said Hamish. 'Hope he's impressed this time. Why is he in uniform?'

'Hush,' whispered Davey.

As he stood to attention during the inspection, the act of volunteering for Kitchener's Army struck home fully. Without moving his head, Davey could see hundreds of soldiers, silent sentinels in their serried ranks, ready for war.

Ah'm part o' this.

He had been taught how to dig a trench, fire a rifle, and bayonet the enemy in the guise of a straw-filled sack. Now the training was at an end. Rifle fire would be returned; practice dummies would turn into German soldiers with bayonets – they would fight back.

Davey almost failed to hear the command to stand at ease. He reacted just in time: no one noticed his slight delay. The march back to camp finally took his mind off what he would be expected to do.

Dae ma duty. Look efter Hamish and get back tae Kate when it's ower.

To the Front

The regimental transport left for Southampton on the 8th July. The battalion marched to Chiseldon railway station for trains to Folkstone, where it embarked on the evening of the 10th July on the cross-channel steamer Invictus, escorted by a single destroyer.

Space was cramped on what was essentially a cross-channel ferry. Davey remained on deck, avoiding the noisy crowds of soldiers in the salons.

After a while he lost sight of the coast of England from his vantage point near the stern. Sea surrounded him, separating him from home with every lurch of the ship. The ache in his stomach wasn't seasickness.

The foam generated by the movement of the vessel mesmerised Davey as he gazed at the sea below the rails until he began to feel drowsy. He found a bench under a low canopy and let sleep overcome him.

'Penny for 'em, pal.' Hamish's voice sounded far away, mingled with the rhythm of the ship. 'Sorry, Davey. Didn't realise ee'd dozed off.'

There's nae peace.

Davey opened his eyes. 'Only fi a few minutes.'

'It's hot and noisy doon there. Ah've been looking for ee.'

'Just wanted some quiet from a' this living on top of one another,' said Davey. 'Ah dinnae ken how much peace and quiet we'll get fri noo on.'

Hamish leant on the rail and stared at the wake trailing behind the ferry.

'Ah'm scared, Davey,' he said suddenly.

'We all are, pal,' replied Davey. 'We'll look oot fi one another, whitever happens.'

'Whitever that'll be.'

'Listen, Hamish. They say it'll be all ower in a few months. We dae oor duty, follow orders and get back tae Scotland.'

'Whit happens next?' Hamish asked. 'They havenae told iss much aboot where we're garn. Well, tae the Front obviously, but nae details on whit happens when we get there.'

'The Front's a way inland,' said Davey. 'Ah expect we'll get detailed orders when we get there. It's getting dark. Let's garn up tae the prow and see whit we can see.'

The two friends joined a large group of soldiers at the prow. A thread of twinkling lights marked the end of their sea crossing. No one spoke. Anxious faces focussed on a foreign country where they were destined to enter a war they knew little about.

Davey watched the thin ribbon of lights draw him nearer to war, wrenching him away from home towards the place where he was duty bound.

Dae ma duty and survive … survive fi Kate.

The ferry slowed and slid into dock at Boulogne. The 7th KOSB arrived in France at midnight on the 10th July 1915 to join the British Expeditionary Force.

Davey joined a long line of men snaking its way down one of the gangplanks. At the foot of each stood a docker, offering a helping hand to any soldier who felt unsteady after the crossing.

Never heard French before. Sounds musical.

The silent streets of the town echoed to the synchronised clatter of boots as the battalion marched up the hill to the large rest camp of huts at Ostrohove on the outskirts of Boulogne. The novelty of the arrival of soldiers at night had faded. No one witnessed their short march to the camp; the reassuring sound of the arrival of fresh troops was heard from behind closed doors.

The 7th KOSB paraded through Boulogne on the afternoon of the next day to a very different reception. Crowds lined the streets of the town centre, cheering and waving French flags and the Union Flag. The good wishes of the citizens of the town raised the men's spirits after arriving to a deserted town the previous evening.

The battalion returned to camp at Ostrohove for a night's rest before the next stage of its journey from the coast of France to the battlefront.

Early on the 12th July, the 7th marched the ten miles to the railway station at Pont-de-Briques for a train to Audruicq, some 35 miles to the north-west on the Calais to Saint-Omer railway line, where it was billeted at Zutkerque just south of the station at Audruicq. The billeting officer allocated Davey and a few others to the school hall. The 7th remained there until the 15th July.

The tedium of hot and dusty marches continued for the next three days. New boots played havoc with tired feet as the 7th drew nearer the Front. On the third day, as they approached Allouagne about fifteen miles from the Front, distant rolls of thunder accompanied the measured thud of boots.

Davey and Hamish were marching next to one another near the rear of the battalion. Davey could see the fear in his friend's eyes as they exchanged nervous glances.

'Whit's that?' whispered Hamish.

'Dinnae worry. It'll be the French guns,' murmured Davey.

Hamish didn't look convinced. He adjusted his pack, hitched his rifle strap further across his shoulder and marched on, muttering to himself.

The thud of artillery continued to echo in a cloudless sky.

Pipers and drums accompanied the 7th as it marched the few miles from Allouagne to Houchin where the battalion bivouacked. The following day, the battalion marched the short distance to what was to be its base near the village of Mazingarbe.

'At least we'll be in one place, won't we?' asked Hamish, as they stood at ease. 'Nae mair marching, ah mean.'

'We've arrived somewhere, seemingly,' said Davey. 'Just look at that lot.'

Mazingarbe was only four miles from the mining village of Loos-en-Gohelle. Loos-en-Gohelle lay behind enemy lines.

At the Western Front

The first thing that struck Davey was the vast quantity of supplies piled everywhere. Wooden boxes stacked as high as a two-storey house along one edge of a rough field added to the profusion of racks of shells and rolls of barbed wire lining the supply dump.

The constant movement of soldiers carrying sand bags and steel boxes of ammunition amplified the frenzy of activity. Everyone seemed to know what they were doing, despite the apparent chaos.

The new arrivals of the 7th looked on in astonishment as they formed ranks and awaited instructions.

'Awe shite, tents again. Ah hate tents,' mumbled Hamish.

The men didn't have long to wait before they discovered what they would be expected to do behind enemy lines.

'More labouring,' complained Hamish. 'Ah could be at hame dain this.'

Davey and Hamish's work platoon spent the afternoon stacking sand bags unloaded from horse-drawn carts.

'Jeez, these things get heavier when ee've lifted a few,' said Hamish. 'There's a hell o' a lot o' 'em.'

Angus picked up sand bags as easily as if they were pillows stuffed with feathers.

Look at the strength o' the maun.

Shells proved harder to unload and stack.

'Roll 'em carefully,' explained an RE[2] sergeant, 'and stand 'em up over there.'

Christ, this feels dangerous.

Angus treated shells like pieces of drainpipe, rolling them quickly along the wooden pallet.

'For Christ's sake, don't bang 'em, private. You'll have the whole place up.'

Angus grinned and slowed down.

After the usual breakfast of mugs of tea and bread and jam, Davey turned to Angus, who was sitting next to him on the bench.

'We've had a week o' this labouring. When are we garn up tae the Front?'

'Ah'd sooner be here. From whit ah've heard, it's pretty grim up there. We'll fin oot soon enough.'

They found out immediately after breakfast.

Davey, Hamish, and Angus formed up together near the rear of E Company. Cameron, Murray, and Fraser were a few ranks ahead. Hamish hadn't spoken since they waited for the order to march.

'A'reet?' asked Davey.

'Ah'm reet enough.'

'Aye, let's get on wi' it.'

E Company were the last to move out of base behind A to D companies of the 7th.

Tightness in his chest and dizziness got worse as Davey struggled to stay in step. He could feel his heart pounding in his throat.

---

[2] Royal Engineer.

Got tae fin oot sooner or later.

As the men marched out of Mazingarbe on their way to the communications trenches, they passed troops coming the other way. Some of them marched with their heads down, weariness weighing on their shoulders; others looked vacantly ahead, fatigue etched on dirty faces. Their muddy uniforms a forewarning of what lay ahead.

Shouts of 'Whit's it like, pal?' met with discouraging replies. 'Bloody awful, mate' hung in the air as the last of the front-line troops to be relieved receded towards Mazingarbe.

God, they looked awfy.

The area between base and the Front line was a coal-mining district of destroyed miners' cottages, slag heaps and abandoned winding gear. Davey had expected a rural area. The devastated industrial landscape was a surprise, but not entirely unfamiliar. The discarded pit gear reminded him of his time as a coal miner in the north of England.

This place must've taken a hell of a battering.

Davey's company halted when they reached the end of Quality Street,[3] a stretch of road that led from the mining hamlet of Philosophe towards Loos.

'Single file, men. Stay near the cottages,' ordered the NCO accompanying E Company.

'Why?' Hamish asked Davey quietly.

'Snipers, fi a guess.'

'Christ! Why are we garn along here?'

'It's probably the only useable road.'

---

[3] Quality Street (QS) was named by soldiers because there was a board at the end of it showing the quality of the coal in that district.

The men moved in single file, away from the centre of the road where they would be easier targets. Davey made sure that Hamish was in front of him as they inched their way along the road.

Nothing prepared Davey for what he saw at the end of Quality Street. The relative normality of the base at Mazingarbe gave way to a shattered landscape, where trenches snaked their irregular passage across a labyrinth of water-filled shell holes and stubs of splintered trees. The devastation created by countless shells had obliterated what should have been farmland between the hamlets and slag heaps.

Ma God, whit a sight.

'Welcome to the Front, private,' quipped a corporal. 'Pick up a sandbag and a shovel. Follow that trench.'

Davey hoisted a sandbag onto his shoulder from the stack at the side of the road and grabbed a shovel. Rolls of barbed wire, duckboards, and other equipment lay around.

Carrying this lot isnae garn tae be easy.

Davey looked around for the others. Hamish was already in the communications trench, followed by Angus. He saw Cameron, Murray, and Fraser near the start of a parallel trench.

Davey adjusted the heavy load on his shoulder and entered the trench behind Angus.

'Surely nothing can be worse than this,' said Angus, turning to face Davey. 'Ah've never seen onything like it. There's nothing left.'

'Aye. Best get on, Angus. Ah'll follow ee.'

The trench was shallow near the stores, deepening suddenly as it struck out across the devastated landscape.

Davey plodded forwards. His left arm ached and his neck throbbed. He resisted the urge to shift the sand bag to the other side.

Dinnae slow doon.

Head bent beneath the weight, Davey kept up with his pal. Angus squelched along the muddy floor of the trench; mud soon covered Davey's puttees and flecked his breeches.

That's whit they're fi then.

After a few hundred yards, the communications trench met the reserve trench before it continued towards the front line. Sand bags piled on either side protected the junction of trenches.

Ah hope we can dump 'em here.

'Ah, our replacements,' said a sergeant. 'You three, put yer bags with the others.'

Davey, Hamish, and Angus relieved themselves of their burden and awaited orders.

God, it must've taken ages tae dig this lot.

'You three seem to know each other.'

'Aye, sergeant.'

'You can work together then. See where it's collapsed. I want that dug out and the top reinforced with earth, front and back,' said the sergeant. 'Stack the bags two deep at the front. A bullet can get through one bag but not two. You new men need to look and learn.'

Posh accent. Edinburgh likely.

Davey, Hamish, and Angus got to work on the pile of earth from the damaged wall of the reserve trench, shovelling it out of the trench and piling it on top on both sides.

'Oh, and keep yer heads down,' said the sergeant. 'I'm Sergeant MacKay. You work for me when you're up here.'

He kens we're new. Must be something in oor faces.

The three pals soon cleared the pile of soft earth from the foot of the trench and piled sand bags either side along the top.

'Good job, men. Get yourselves back to QS and bring up as many sand bags as you can carry. After that, we need duckboards all along here.'

Davey, Hamish, and Angus spent the remainder of the day digging, fetching and carrying sand bags and duckboards.

'We're just glorified labourers,' complained Hamish on one of their trips back to the store at the end of Quality Street.

'Someone has tae dig trenches,' said Angus.

'And repair 'em,' added Davey.

'And ah thought we'd come here tae fight,' said Hamish.

After spending most of the day working in the reserve trench, Davey's first view of the front line trench came as a shock. Empty tins and pieces of wood littered the floor, trodden into the mud or strewn either side of the duckboards. Soldiers dozed awkwardly in boltholes or on the fire step, their day's work done. Others occupied sentry positions.

Christ, a dead rat!

'Disnae onyone get rid o' the rats, sergeant?' asked Davey.

'Too many of 'em, private. We toss 'em out of the trench from time to time, but they're soon back. Not the same ones mind. This yer first night?'

'Aye, sergeant.'

'It's two hours on, four off. Listen and watch. When you're off, get some rest where you can.'

Davey looked for Hamish and Angus.

Must be further along. Can't see round the dog-legs.

It rained heavily during the night. Davey pulled on his waterproof cape, stood on the fire step and rested the periscope on the wall of sand bags.

Won't see much oot o' this the night.

Davey watched as tracers occasionally lit the sky in both directions, streaks of yellow against the darkness looping harmlessly over his head. Sporadic thuds of artillery shells sounded in the distance, momentarily disturbing the snores and heavy breathing of sleeping soldiers.

Well, Kate. Here ah am, trying tae stay awake.

'Get some kip, Muir,' said Sergeant MacKay.

Davey found a vacant spot on the fire step and tried to sleep in a sitting position. He brought his feet up under him in an attempt to avoid them dangling in the layer of off-white mud that had formed in the bottom of the trench.

Davey returned to sentry duty after four hours of fragmented sleep.

It began to get light towards the end of his second stint. Davey peered through the periscope to get a view of no-man's-land.

Whilst the landscape he had walked through to reach the front line was desolate, the ground beyond the barbed wire was completely churned up and bleak beyond his imagination. The edges of a myriad of water-filled shell holes obscured any notion of a route from his position to the German front line.

How are we supposed to cross that?

Davey lowered the periscope, his duty over.

It had been a quiet night, but as daylight limped across no-man's-land, the Germans opened up with a brief barrage. Several shells landed harmlessly short, but one exploded near the parapet.

Davey hurled himself towards the rear of the trench, covering his head with his hands as the shell detonated with a deafening boom. Earth rained into the trench, covering Davey and those nearby with earth.

'Christ, that wis close,' said Angus.

'How come it landed short?' said Davey.

'Dinnae ken, pal. Just as well it did.'

Bloody hell, that could have been it.

'We'll have tae start again,' said Davey.

The short barrage, helped by the rain, undid most of the work that Davey's platoon had started on the previous day.

'Havenae we got any spare wid?' Davey asked Sergeant MacKay. 'We could support the sides.'

'Take Private Gilmore, go to QS and see whit there is. And keep yer heids doon.'

Davey and Angus slogged their way along one of the communications trenches to the dump at the end of QS. They sought out an RE sergeant.

'We need some o' those slatted sections. We've just had a direct hit,' explained Angus.

'Anyone hurt?' asked the sergeant.

'Nah, but the trench needs repairing again.'

'I can't let you have many. We're waiting for more to come up. The two of you can't carry many anyway.'

'We'll carry whit we can,' said Angus.

'Over there,' said the sergeant.

'Some are wider than others,' said Davey.

Davey and Angus found that they could put three of the narrow sections together; they were light enough to hold under each arm.

'Quick, back tae the comms trench,' said Angus.

They heard a shout, 'Hey, where are you two going?'

'Orders of Sergeant MacKay,' replied Angus as he headed for the communications trench behind Davey.

'Bloody hell, that's a dozen,' said MacKay when Davey and Angus returned.

Davey flexed both arms, trying to rid them of a burning ache.

That wis a mistake, garn in front o' Angus.

'Let's get 'em up,' said Angus, who looked as if the effort was nothing.

Davey's platoon spent the remainder of the day improving the parapet of the front-line trench. The ground was soft and chalky and easy to dig when it was dry. When wet, it was almost impossible to work.

'Good work, men' said MacKay.

Davey collapsed with exhaustion on the fire step, his uniform covered in a film of dried chalk.

After two days working on strengthening trenches, the squalor of life at the front rapidly tightened its grip on Davey.

Washing was out of the question and the ordeal of shaving didn't get any easier. Davey either left his mess tin in the rain or saved some drinking water.

Latrines were dug to the rear of the reserve trench and comprised a thick wooden pole suspended over a deep pit. Davey always choose a quiet time to use the latrine. If too many men sat on the pole at once it snapped and hurled the sitters into the pit, a deeply unpleasant prospect that Davey wished to avoid at all costs.

Meals sent up to the front from mobile kitchens behind the lines were lukewarm and unpredictable in their arrival. The water sent up the line in four-gallon petrol cans tasted of fuel.

The wretchedness of the trenches, made worse by rain and the rats, dampened what was left of Davey's spirits. Even Angus gave up whacking visiting rodents with his trenching shovel.

It rained heavily again during Davey's fourth night, making it impossible to sleep during off-duty spells. To make matters worse, there was intermittent sniping during the night.

Bullets thudded into the wall of sand bags or whizzed over the trench while Davey took another stint of sentry duty.

His stomach tightened every time a bullet struck the parapet where he stooped on the fire step.

Glad we stacked 'em high and deep.

Sergeant MacKay passed by, making a downward motion with his arms.

'Sit on the step until they give up,' he murmured.

The reality of being shot at didn't fully dawn on Davey until he relieved Cameron just after dawn.

'Wake up, Muir,' said Sergeant MacKay. 'They've stopped fi noo, but keep extra low.'

Davey stretched and walked half-bent around the dog-leg to find Sergeant MacKay shaking Cameron.

Oh no, trouble. Cameron's dropped off.

'Wake up, MacBain, you're —'

Cameron's body tumbled onto the muddy floor of the trench: half of his face had been shot away.

'Help me move him,' barked the sergeant.

Davey couldn't move, unable to take his eyes off what was left of Cameron's face.

'Muir! Move.'

Sergeant MacKay lifted Cameron by the shoulders and Davey held his legs. Between them they sloshed through the mud, looking for a dry place to put the body.

After a struggle along the trench, passing several men whose faces displayed silent shock as they were woken from shallow sleep, Cameron's bearers found a dry shelf at the rear of the trench and heaved his dead weight onto it. Sergeant MacKay covered Cameron with his own rain cape.

'Yer first?'

'Yes, sergeant.'

'Get used tae it. It won't be yer last.'

'How'd he get shot, sergeant? How come naebdy heard onything?'

'By a damn good sniper. Must've found a tiny gap in the bags, or he moved up high for some reason,' said the sergeant as he pulled the cape higher to cover Cameron's ruined face. 'You wouldn't necessarily hear onything.'

'Ah wis there a few oors afore.'

'You're a lucky man, Private Muir. Get back to yer platoon. And thanks.'

The rest of the pals fell silent as Davey slumped on the fire step.

'Cameron's gaen,' said Davey. 'Gaen.'

Everyone looked at Davey.

'Ah can't believe it. Gaen,' he said again.

'Aye, he's away the Crow Road,' said Murray.

'C'mon, Davey,' said Angus, putting a hand on Davey's shoulder. 'Let's get on wi' it. It's oor last day fi noo.'

Hamish sat on the fire step, staring at his boots.

Later that morning, Davey, Angus and Hamish were assigned to improving communications trenches away from the front line. Several sections needed to be deepened and their sides strengthened. Most shells fell short during the short daily barrage, but some had exploded between the front and second lines, damaging the communications trenches.

Davey and his pals worked mostly in silence, listening out for the sound of incoming shells. None landed anywhere near where they were working for the remainder of the day.

Angus vented his anger by hurling chalky soil out of the trench with greater vigour than ever.

'Y'eel get nae mair o' us,' he muttered as he flung another shovelful of earth skywards.

Hamish worked steadily, keeping up with the others. He didn't speak to anyone for the rest of the day.

'Best leave him be,' said Angus to Davey.

E Company was sent back to base at Mazingarbe at the end of that afternoon. It was their turn to look haggard as they passed another company on its way to relieve them.

No banter was exchanged as the troops passed; the company on its way up to the line had been there before.

Davey lay on his palliasse, exhausted after his first few days at the Front. The shock of Cameron's death lingered long into the night, pushing aside hunger and a desperate need for a long sleep.

Hamish hadn't spoken a word all day.

The following morning Davey had his first wash for days, standing at one of the tanks of water set out on the edge of the field of tents. He also cleaned his kit as best he could on one of the tables provided for the purpose.

'How'd they expect iss tae smarten up after whit we've been through?' said Hamish, as he stood next to Davey. 'There's no enough brushes.'

'Here, use this one,' said Davey.

At least he's talking.

Davey's company spent a few days at Mazingarbe before being sent to the Front for its second stint of duty. Davey dreaded living with the threat of sniper and shellfire, trying to sleep scrunched up on the fire step, and feeling wet, hungry and wretched. At least he knew what to expect this time.

Davey's platoon spent every day of the next six working on more improvements to communications trenches. The tedium of lugging sand bags and duckboards and digging to make the trenches deeper kept them from the front line for most of the time, particularly when they were working near the QS end of the system of communications trenches.

'Ah cannae stand much mair o' this digging,' said Hamish at the start of their third day.

'These trenches are just as important as the ones up front,' said Angus.

'That's why they've got so many of iss working back here,' said Davey.

'Ah weel, it's better than being shot at,' said Hamish. 'Or shelled.'

We'd a' drink tae that.

'At least you can hear 'em,' said Angus.

No sooner had he spoken, a shell exploded several yards clear of the trench.

'A harder target,' suggested Angus. 'Easier to hit a side to side trench.'

This is getting dangerous.

The moment Hamish thrust his shovel into the floor of the trench, shrapnel from a well-directed shell tore into the platoon working a few yards ahead.

Screams followed the explosion.

Then silence.

'That's Murray's lot,' shouted Angus, throwing down his shovel. He pushed past the men in front of him and ran towards Murray's platoon.

'Stay doon,' yelled Davey.

Davey heard another anguished wail.

Christ, whee's been hit?

'Hamish, stay doon,' shouted Davey as he ran to join Angus.

Bodies lay against the sides of the trench: bloodstained and motionless.

'Run tae QS and get stretcher-bearers,' commanded Angus. 'Ah'll see whit ah can dae.'

Davey ran along the trench, shoving men out of the way in his urgency, ignoring their shouts of disapproval until he reached QS.

He ran up to the first NCO he saw.

'There's been a hit in the comms trench, about two hundred yards up.'

Davey dropped to the ground, out of breath.

Stretcher-bearers ran past him. He struggled to his feet and followed.

'Hey, stop and rest, soldier,' cried a voice behind him.

'Ah need tae fin oot,' shouted Davey as he ran to catch them up.

Davey and Angus watched as Murray and Fraser were laid on stretchers and carried along the communications trench.

'They look pretty bad,' said Angus quietly. 'We'd best get back tae Hamish.'

They walked slowly back to find Hamish slumped against the side of the trench, his features rigid with fear.

Angus picked up his shovel.

'Davey, we'd best help 'em repair that lot.'

'Where it fell.'

'Aye.'

'Hamish,' said Angus calmly. 'Hamish …'

Hamish picked up his shovel without a word, followed Angus and Davey and dug furiously, flinging chalky soil over the side of the trench.

Word came up the line later that day: Murray died from his injuries. Fraser survived, badly wounded, and would be sent home.

There's just the three o' iss left.

There were no more casualties during E Company's second stint of duty at the Front.

The pattern of four or five days working at the Front, followed by a similar period billeted at base lasted for several weeks until the 7th KOSB was granted a week's rest at Mazingarbe in mid-September.

Early in the rest week, Captain Baird gathered his company in a corner of the field of tents that housed the 7th, 8th and other battalions of mainly Scottish divisions based at Mazingarbe.

The men of Company E sat on the grass while the captain stood on a wooden box and addressed them.

'As you know, we've been granted a week's rest along with the 8th KOSB.'

A few sardonic cheers broke out amongst the weary, seated soldiers.

'You have all worked hard, both here and up the line. I thank you for that. You'll be assigned to light work duties and PE for the rest of the week because we want you in tip top condition for what is about to happen. So, clean your kit and your rifle and take the opportunity to prepare yourselves.

'The purpose of gathering you together this afternoon is to do what all company officers are doing today – briefing you as to what is planned for this week. Starting tomorrow, there will be a four-day barrage of the German positions. This will break up their wire. On Friday evening, we will move into the assembly trenches in readiness for a dawn attack on Saturday.'

Captain Baird paused to let the enormity of his announcement sink in. He scanned the faces of the men in his charge.

'I will lead you out of the front line trench. We will go in waves, company by company. A first, then B, C and D. We will go last.'

He paused again and glanced at his notes.

'I realise that you've been in France for only a few weeks, but this attack is crucial. We, the 7th, are more or less at the centre of the attack. The German front line is about half a mile from ours and their second line is a couple of miles further back. The village of Loos is between the two and our target, referred to as Hill 70, is just beyond the village. Our task is to occupy Hill 70 after we've cleared their first line. Is that clear? Any questions?'

'How big is this hill? Is it easy tae spot?' asked the solider sitting next to Davey.

'It's more of a ridge, beyond the village,' replied the captain. 'It should be easy to see. We've received reports of snipers occupying some of the deserted miners' cottages, so we need to be thorough when we clear the village.

'Next, gas. It is very likely that the Boche will use gas. You'll be trained how to use a gas mask later. We will also use gas.' [4]

Captain Baird paused again, glancing up from his notes.

'Some of you will have handled the canisters. Later this week, these will be transported to the front line and placed at intervals along it. Men in C Company

---

[4] The battle of Loos was the first time that gas was used by the British Expeditionary Force in the war.

have been trained to use it. Gas will be released, weather permitting, along with smoke before we leave the trench. The artillery bombardment and the gas will cause as much damage as possible before we reach their front line.'

Captain Baird folded his notes and replaced them in the top pocket of his tunic.

'I'm immensely proud of what you've achieved in the short time that you've been here. Now it's time to put your training into practice. Rifle ranges and sandbags are one thing: this is now time for the real thing. You know what will be expected of you. God willing, we will succeed.

'Thank you, men. We parade on Friday afternoon. Good luck. I'll hand you over to Sergeant Patterson, who will show you how to put on your gas masks.'

Sergeant Patterson led the men to a covered store and handed each man a gas mask container. The company was divided into groups assigned to an NCO, who demonstrated how to unfold the mask and carefully refold and store it in its bag.

'The bag is worn on yer chest,' explained Corporal Telfer to Davey's group. 'We go over the top without packs. The only kit we'll wear is this and yer ammo pouches. The next bit is very important, so watch carefully. I'll show you how to put on yer gas mask. You grip this piece in yer mouth when it's on.'

Corporal Telfer demonstrated how to put a mask on: chin in first, then its hem tucked into the shirt collar and secured by doing up the top shirt button.

'The eyepieces are made of a special material. Not glass. Keep them clean for obvious reasons. Now, let's see you all practise. You need to be able to get it out of its bag and on in just a few seconds. Don't rush to start with. Take yer time and learn how to do it properly but quickly. Don't sit down, any of you. You'll be putting it on in a crowded trench.'

Davey's group spent the next hour practising and helping each other out. Ribbing each other over how ridiculous they looked and sounded with their masks on took the edge off the seriousness of the procedure.

After larking around for a while, the men set to practising in earnest when Captain Baird approached Davey's group.

'How're they getting on, corporal?'

'I think they've got it, sir. They just need to get quicker.'

'Look after your masks, men. It and your rifle are your weapons. We will all be wearing gas masks, so look out for my hand signal to climb out. Carry on, corporal.'

Davey was satisfied that he could don his mask to the count of five. He stowed it and wandered off to find a quiet corner in the field. Hamish followed him.

Cannae ee leave iss alane just for a minute.

'Dae ee want tae be on yer ane?' Hamish asked.

'Nah. It's a'reet. Just haen a quiet sit. The guns start in the moran. We'll no get much peace efter that.'

'Ah can hardly breath with this thing on. How're we supposed tae fight wearing it? Ah can hardly see oot.'

Davey shrugged. 'We'll just have tae get on wi' it. Ye heard the captain: we might be attacking through the gas, so we've got tae keep 'em on.'

Davey could see that Hamish was troubled; his right leg was shaking.

'So, this is it, Davey. We garn on the attack soon. Ah'm scared.'

Davey turned to face his friend. 'We all are, pal. Most dinnae show it, but they are. They lark about in camp. Perhaps that helps 'em. Anyone who says they're nae scared is fibbing.'

'Ah'm nae scared of dying,' said Hamish. 'Ah'm scared o' losing a leg or something. Ah'd sooner get killed than be blown up and end up living as half a maun. A cripple. We have tae face facts, Davey. Some of us willnae see next week.' Hamish sighed deeply, stared at the ground and gripped his right leg, suddenly aware of the involuntary movement in his outstretched limb.

'Hamish, listen. Easy for me tae say. Try not tae think aboot whit might happen. If we stick together and get 'em before they get iss, we'll come through this. We'll be surrounded by hunnerds o' oor side. The high-ups will have planned this attack down tae the last detail. We look oot fi each other. Stay close tae me when we leave oor trench and move across tae theirs. Stay close.'

'Ee cannae tell who's who in these things. We a' look the same.'

'Ah'm no sure how we can tell when it's safe tae take 'em off,' said Davey.

'Me neither. Wait for orders or watch whit the others are daen?'

Both men set to cleaning their rifles and checking their gas masks for the next hour or so. They chatted about home while they worked on looking after their kit, talking about anything to take their minds off thoughts about climbing out of the trench.

It didn't last. As Davey was fixing and unfixing his bayonet, Hamish stopped what he was doing and said, 'How dae ee think it feels sticking that intae a maun's flesh?'

'Different from a sandbag,' replied Davey. 'Hamish, when it comes tae it – and it must – remember whit we've been trained fi. Get 'em before they get ee. Dinnae think, just dae it.'

Hamish grinned weakly. 'Stick him before he sticks me,' he muttered. 'Ah'll see ee later. Ah'm away tae get a cuppa.'

Davey carried on cleaning and checking his rifle. He held its bayonet in his right hand, turning it over carefully before fixing it once more. He had tried to sound calm and practical, encouraging Hamish to be plucky and confident.

He stared at his rifle and its deadly extension and wondered how it would feel to plunge it into the flesh of a man. Images of Kate and the children drifted across his mind, shutting out thoughts of death and duty, and dismissing the possibility that he might not survive the attack.

Ah wull survive. Ah wull get hame.

Davey stowed his bayonet in its sheath, gathered up his rifle and gas mask and went in search of Hamish. He'd been sitting and fretting on his own for too long.

The Battle of Loos[5]

The artillery bombardment began in earnest on Tuesday 21st September and continued for four days and nights.

The noise deafened the men waiting in their tented billets at Mazingarbe. Davey tried stuffing pieces of rag into his ears at night, but very little sleep accompanied the thunderous roar of the guns aimed at the German positions in and around the village of Loos.

Ah wonder whit it's like under that lot.

The men of the 7th rested as best they could amidst the clamour of the artillery offensive. Davey and his pals cleaned, checked and rechecked their rifles and gas masks in readiness for the impending attack. They tried to keep busy. Taking their minds away from the possibility of death or injury was fundamental to morale – officers and NCOs knew this and organised boxing bouts and tug-o-war contests.

Davey excelled in the boxing ring. He knocked down several opponents from B Company, in spite of his short stature. After several bouts, he was banned from the makeshift boxing ring: no one would take him on.

---

[5] Pronounced 'Loss'.

'Bloody hell, Davey. Where'd ee learn tae box?' Hamish asked him after he had defeated another challenger.

'After ee left the schuil, ah had tae defend mysel. Ma Uncle James taught iss. He wis an amateur boxer in the navy.'

'And ye're a southpaw. Nae one's got the hang of ee yet.'

While Davey was putting his shirt back on, a sergeant from the 8th approached.

'Oor man versus your man,' he suggested to Hamish.

Their man turned out to be a soldier a foot taller than Davey.

'He's garn tae be much slower than ee,' whispered Hamish, as Davey ducked under the rope.

Davey and his new opponent eyed one another from their respective corners. A large crowd had gathered. Friendly rivalry between the 7th and 8th would be well worth the spectacle of watching two men of differing heights and build slug it out.

Egged on by the spectators from the 8th, their man made several clumsy lunges at Davey, who skipped and danced out of the way of ill-targeted swings and haymakers.

Hamish's reet. He's tae slow.

Cries of 'C'mon, Muir', 'Wallop him, Davey' and 'Belt him, laddy', rang out from the general hubbub of the watching crowd.

Tak yer time.

Davey stepped aside from another poorly aimed punch and let fly with a straight right to his opponent's solar plexus, followed by a left jab to his flabby stomach.

Davey's next few punches had his man doubled-up on the ropes, moaning and clutching his saggy body. He slipped down the ropes and sat on the floor of the ring to the cheers of the 7th.

Davey hauled his defeated opponent to his feet. The two men touched gloves and murmured friendly and respectful thanks to one another.

'Give the Boche hell,' shouted someone amongst the spectators.

Davey stepped out of the ring and went to the oil drum to wash himself again.

'Bully beef stew's up soon, Davey,' said Hamish. 'We could win the war if ee took on the Boche's best maun.'

Davey grinned. 'C'mon, the fun's ower. We garn up the line the moran's night.'

The 7th and the 8th battalions paraded at Mazingarbe on Friday 24th September in the late afternoon. Captain Baird of E Company took his men aside and gave them their final orders.

'We go in companies fifty yards apart. When we climb out the firing trench, keep walking forward. Don't stop to help anyone; you must keep walking. Our first objective is their first line, then Hill 70, which is between their first two lines. Gas will be released, so you will be given the order to put on your masks before we climb out.

'Good luck, men. Apart from me, there's Lieutenant Carruthers and Second Lieutenant Linwood. Watch for our signal. Follow us. God willing, we'll meet victory tomorrow. Get some rest.'

Towards the end of their last meal before the attack, the ribbing and wisecracks that usually accompanied meals taken outside at the long tables died down. Davey, Hamish, and Angus exchanged nervous glances: looks that said what the voice kept at bay.

Some of iss willnae come back. Ah bet we're a' thinking the same thing.

At 10 p.m. all assault brigades marched along QS to enter the communications trenches, which were badly flooded from recent heavy rain.

Davey entered the trench immediately behind Hamish.

Must keep an eye on him.

He squelched along, each step squirting mud over his boots and puttees and those of Angus following behind.

The reserve trenches were in better condition, but were still under water apart from some stretches where duckboards had been laid.

At least we got these down.

Once in position, the men were under orders to maintain strict silence while waiting to move forward out of the reserve trenches.

Seems a bit pointless: the guns are still making a hell of a racket.

By the early hours of Saturday, the 7th moved to the front line. The 8th and other battalions were distributed to the left and right, leaving the 7th in a central position in the wide front of the assault.

Hamish leant on the parados[6] next to Davey, asleep on his feet. Davey couldn't sleep. He propped himself up against the wall of the trench and let his mind wander.

The Boche must ken we're garn tae attack. They'll be ready for iss.

Davey closed his eyes and tried to shut out the din of the bombardment. Daydreams overtook his fear of going on the attack. He conjured images of Kate and the children, of Ecclefechan High Street, and the fields and glens he longed to return to.

Whit a lang wait.

The contrast could not be more acute. A few months earlier, Davey had left the gentle countryside of home as a volunteer for the unknown. The initial rush of enthusiasm to enlist and do his duty had been transformed into an ugly truth: in a few hours time, he would be expected to kill – *this* was his duty.

Ah volunteered and here ah am, waiting and waiting.

At 4 a.m. the shellfire increased to a tumultuous, ear-splitting crescendo, shaking the air and vibrating in the chests of the waiting men. The next hour was the most agonising and threatening of Davey's life. Merciless fear drove all thoughts of family and home out of his mind.

Calm down, laddy.

Davey looked to his left and right. Hamish stared ahead, mouth half open. Angus managed a manic grin.

---

[6] The elevated rear of a trench, opposite its parapet.

Captain Baird moved along the trench, quietly addressing each of his men.

He's a guid maun.

By 5 a.m. the captain had got all of his company in position below the parapet; ladders were in place. He gave the order to fix bayonets.

Hamish's hand was shaking as he tried to engage his bayonet.

Davey laid a hand on Hamish's shoulder, 'Ee'll be a'reet.'

Hamish eventually got his weapon ready.

The Captain gave the order to put on gas masks.

Captain Baird moved along the trench again, making sure that everyone was ready.

Davey gripped a rung of the ladder immediately in front of him, Captain Baird to his left and Hamish to his right. Angus stood immediately behind the Captain.

Davey looked up and down the line of hooded heads.

We a' look the same noo.

Davey adjusted Hamish's gas hood to make it more securely tucked into his collar.

Davey closed his mouth over the mouthpiece of his mask, then he used the cleanest corner of his grubby handkerchief to wipe the eyepieces of both of their gas masks. Hamish answered with thumbs up.

The artillery assault ceased abruptly at 4.45 a.m. The immediate silence, eerie and chilling, revealing the stillness of a pale dawn.

Whit'll the Boche be thinking noo?

The hiss of gas and smoke broke the silence. Forty minutes of alternate gas and smoke emissions commenced at 4.50 a.m. precisely.

The length of the gas and smoke attack was even more unbearable than the long wait in the front trench. Davey tried to banish all feelings of fear with an urgency that he had never felt before; he wanted to get this over. He tried to breath as slowly as he could, testing his mask, putting his trust in the awkward device that covered his head and face.

The wind's wrong.

From his position at the foot of the ladder, Davey saw clouds of smoke drifting into the trench to his right. Men were clutching at their masks, yanking them upwards.

NO! Keep 'em on.

The noise of the cylinders ceased. A dread silence settled on the trench. Officers looked at their wrists.

Davey stiffened as Captain Baird raised his arm, oblivious as to what was happening further along the trench: he was still looking at his watch. The silence seemed to elongate and suspend in the stillness until 5.30 a.m.

Zero Hour.

Davey looked to his right. Men climbed out of the trench and vanished into the rolling cloud.

Captain Baird waited until Company's A, B, C and D had gone over before he thrust his arm forwards and climbed the ladder.

Davey scrambled out of the trench.

The ground immediately ahead was slippery.

He pitched forward, breathing heavily, cursing into his mask. 'C'mon ee daft bastard. Get tae yer feet.'

He made for the nearest cut in the wire, picked his way through the narrow corridor made for the attack.

Davey could barely see more than a few feet in front of him.

He lost sight of Captain Baird almost immediately. The smoke and gas cloud had hung back and the men had no choice but walk into it.

Jesus, where's Hamish ... where is he?

Davey heard the faint skirl of bagpipes[7] behind him.

Whit the ... ?

He kept walking into the dense fog, struggling to get a firm footing on the wet, uneven ground.

Ghostly figures of men swam in and out of his vision. Several of them tore at their gas masks, others dropped to the ground.

'KEEP IT ON!' Davey yelled into his mask.

Ferocious machine gun enfilades met them as the waves of the 7th emerged from the thickest part of the cloud. Bullets whizzed past Davey's head. He could hear them thudding into the bodies of men to his right.

They can see iss noo.

Davey drifted left and continued to walk forwards. The machine gun fire kept up its relentless sweeping volley to bring down more men to his left and right, their ghostly outlines dropping to the ground in the haze of gas and smoke.

There were bodies in front of him; bodies piled on bodies. Davey stepped over them; going round increased the risk of falling into a water-filled shell hole. He pushed on.

Heads smashed.

Limbs severed from bodies.

---

[7] Piper Daniel Laidlaw was awarded the Victoria Cross for his valour. He took off his gas mask and marched toward the German front line playing his bagpipes until he was wounded.

Faces shot away.

Bloodied extremities where men had been reduced to parts of men.

Bodies and limbs scattered on the sides of shell holes, partly submerged in muddy water.

An officer still held his pistol. Most of his head had been shot away, what remained reduced to a bloody pulp.

Is that Baird?

Davey paused, dazed and horrified by what confronted him; the eyepieces of his gas mask revealing their restricted view of the havoc before him.

Nah. Cannae dae onything.

He pressed on, following vague shapes in the thinning fog that rolled across no-man's-land.

Davey became aware of where he was as he emerged from the last of the gas and smoke release. The remnants of the attack had reached the German front line a few yards ahead.

The deep wire defences had been only partially cut by the artillery bombardment. Worse still, it had almost obliterated the corridors cut into the wire in readiness for the Germans to attack.

So much fi days o' shelling.

Davey picked his way through the nearest narrow corridor, passing several bodies suspended from the tangle of wire, some with their faces staring open-mouthed at the sky, their tunics already stained dark. Others appeared to lean on the wire where they had fallen forwards still clutching their rifles.

Davey stood for a moment, mesmerised by the carnage.

Rifles discharged at close range just ahead shook him out of his inertia.

The machine gunners must've been killed.

Davey jumped into the trench behind two other men. They ran left; Davey went the other way, rounded a dog-leg in the trench to be confronted by a German soldier pulling back the bolt of his rifle.

Davey fired one round without raising his weapon to shoulder height.

The soldier crumpled sideways against the front of the trench, his chest shattered and bloodied.

Bile rose in Davey's throat.

His hands shook.

His rifle became heavy.

His head throbbed.

Jesus, ah've killed a maun.

'Are there any more?' yelled a voice behind him, shaking Davey out of his trance.

Davey shook his head.

German casualties lay on top of one another further around the angle in the trench, blood seeping from their inert bodies. Two men joined Davey; both had taken off their gas masks.

Davey's hands continued to quiver as he tried to stow his gas mask.

'Is it safe tae take 'em off?' he asked pointlessly.

'Reckon so,' came the reply.

'Where tae?' asked Davey.

'The village first,' came the suggestion.

Their trenches are better built than oors.

Dozens of men made their way out of the rear of the trench in the direction of the village of Loos, not a single officer amongst them. Davey didn't recognise any of the men.

Must be fri other companies.

The remnants of the 7th came under rifle fire as they reached the edge of the village.

'Spread out and clear 'em out,' ordered a sergeant. Davey didn't recognise him either.

The stragglers from the attack stormed into the main street of Loos, their boots hammering on the cobblestones as they swept past ruined houses.

Davey ran past two bodies, each with their bayonet sticking into the other.

Davey stopped and turned. He couldn't drag his eyes away from this horrific distraction to the frenzy around him.

A shout above the crack of rifles turned his head.

A German soldier ran out of a doorway, screaming and lunging.

Davey skipped to one side and countered with his bayonet.

It entered the man's side easily.

He withdrew it just in time to see another German skewer a soldier while he lay on the ground crying out.

Davey ran across the road, anger erupting in an angry yell.

'NO!'

His fierce bayonet thrust knocked the German off his feet.

Davey pulled his weapon from the German's stomach. The wounded soldier lay still.

'Sorry, pal. They'll come for ee,' he said before he ran along the street towards the other end of the village. A group of Germans at the far end of the street laid down their rifles and raised their hands.

Three of them were shot on the spot.

'No!' yelled Davey. 'They should be taken back tae oor lines.'

Davey hurried past the incident and attached himself to a large group of stragglers from the 7th. Men from the 8th and other Scottish divisions joined them at the end of the street.

'The village is clear,' announced a sergeant from the 8th. 'We've lost a lot of men and most of our officers. How about you?' he asked Davey.

'Ah havenae seen ony officers. Dinnae ken aboot losses. There's no many of the 7th here right noo.'

Hamish. Where's Hamish?

'Our objective was the village. What was yours,' asked the sergeant.

'Hill 70,' came several replies.

Exhausted and excited by their apparent successful attack on the village, the remnants of the 7th and 8th mingled and drifted towards the huge landmark of Tower Bridge.[8]

A sergeant pointed. 'Hill 70 should be that way. Spread out and make for the top of the ridge.'

The men were glad to be given a sense of purpose and followed the instructions of the NCO.

Long lines of men made their way unopposed up the slope of Hill 70, over the crest of the ridge, and began to descend its eastern slope.

A fierce sweeping volley of machine gun fire halted their progress.

Jesus, their second line.

Men were falling ahead of Davey and to his left and right. It was all over in seconds.

---

[8] Tower Bridge was a massive double pithead lift that reminded men of Tower Bridge in London. It formed a landmark near the village of Loos.

Davey felt searing pain in his right leg. His legs gave way and he fell face first in the soft earth.

His leg felt hot.

The pain grew to a crescendo of utter agony.

Davey lost consciousness.

His mouth was full of soil when he came to. He rolled onto his left side coughing and gasping. His trouser leg was soaked and sticky.

He could hear the moans and cries of men.

Wull they come and collect iss?

Davey saw soldiers coming up the slope; German soldiers distinct in their grey uniforms moved amongst the wounded, ignoring their pleas for help.

Davey raised his left arm as they swept past.

'Help ... help me.'

One of the Germans casually lifted his rifle to waist height and fired –

Wracking, searing pain ripped through his body.

Davey wanted to scream. No sound left his throat.

Play deid ... they might be back.

Davey closed his eyes against the weak mid-morning sun, his mind drifting into a fractured stillness, fused in a moment of pure time and heightened existence where the cries of the wounded could no longer be heard.

Stay alive fi Kate. Kate ...

Kate's Story

Ecclefechan

'Whit daes it mean?' said Kate.

Chrissie stood by the fire, reading the official-looking letter. She read it for a second time before answering her sister.

'It means he's missing.'

'Missing. Nothing else?'

'No. Just missing.'

Chrissie handed the paper back to Kate.

Kate held the letter in her lap, where it made a gentle fluttering noise. Chrissie crouched on the floor and calmed her sister's shaking hands. She reached up and wiped a tear from Kate's pale face.

'He's only been gaen for a few months and noo he's gaen for ever.'

'We dinnae ken that, Kate. We dinnae ken.'

The two women held each other awkwardly; Kate sitting, Chrissie squatting. The loud ticking of the clock on Chrissie's mantelpiece marked the intensity of Kate's sobs and moans until her sister's whispers soothed and eased her into quiet submission. When Kate's tears stopped, she took a deep breath and disengaged herself from her sister's embrace.

'Ah should see tae the bairns.'

'At least they're too wee tae understand,' said Chrissie. 'Yee never know, there might be mair news soon.'

As the days turned into weeks and months, no news came. Gradually, Kate resigned herself to widowhood. She had two young children to look after, without their father.

*

Times were hard in the village during the war. Many of the menfolk had volunteered at the beginning of the conflict, and conscription soon took the remaining eligible men. Most families struggled to earn enough to feed themselves.

Kate took in washing for a while, and earned a little money working part-time for a well-off family that lived just outside the village on the Lockerbie Road. The family were kind to Kate, and gave her clothes for her son Davie and her daughter Marion.

Kate and Chrissie lived opposite the Ecclefechan Hotel, next door to one another in the row of single-storey terraced houses in the High Street. Kate spent two mornings a week cleaning the public bar, while Chrissie looked after her children.

A new salesman made an appearance soon after Kate began work at the hotel. Kate wondered why he hadn't been called up. She asked herself whether spirit salesman was a reserved occupation.

Thomas was always polite and touched the peak of his cap when he passed through the bar on Monday mornings with his crates of bottles while Kate was polishing tables. She thought that she detected a slight Irish accent to his 'Good morning,' and 'How are you today?' pleasantries.

Their conversations lengthened gradually, inas-much as this was possible without interrupting Kate's work. Thomas was aware that Kate needed the work badly. He would always blame himself if the landlord saw them chatting.

'Sorry, Michael,' he would say. 'I'm holding the lassie up.'

Thomas's easy manner combined with Irish charm endeared him to Michael, the landlord, and his wife Betty. Neither was his outward appeal lost on Kate.

'He's a charmer, that yin. He's got his eye on ee, Kate,' said Betty one Monday morning after Thomas had finished his delivery.

'He kens ma circumstances,' replied Kate.

'Just dinnae let him tak advantage of ee,' said Betty.

'He's just being kind.'

'Hmm,' muttered Betty as she wiped glasses furiously in readiness for the lunchtime opening.

Davey's Story

Behind Enemy Lines

Rain lashed down mercilessly from a starless sky on the dead and wounded of Hill 70.

Davey closed his eyes against the stinging rain that stabbed his face.

A vice-like grip of pain wracked his body.

How lang've ah been lying here?

The constant hiss of rain was interrupted by the cries of wounded men, cries that Davey had thought were in his dreams.

The plaintive pleas became less frequent as the night took its toll. No one came. Bodies lay still, cries for help faded, unheeded into the cruel darkness.

Davey felt utterly alone.

He tried to sit up, but he couldn't move. He longed to escape the cold and damp that seeped into his back.

It must be bad. Ah cannae move.

The light of a pale dawn crept from the east the next time Davey recovered consciousness. The rain had almost ceased its relentless drenching of the battlefield. He tried once more to raise his head.

Bodies lay scattered across the downward slope of the ridge, all the way to the German second line where figures hung from the uncut wire.

Davey lay back; his neck ached from the effort of trying to sit upright.

Why disnae someone come?

The throbbing pain in his stomach and leg had eased, subsumed by raging thirst and a hunger that gnawed at him.

Why didnae he finish iss?

Hours passed. The weak sun arced higher in the sky, heralding another afternoon.

Davey heard voices below him.

With another supreme effort, he raised his head again and waved frantically.

'DON'T SHOOT! Please don't shoot … please!' he yelled.

Davey rested on both elbows, hoping he had been seen and heard. Soldiers came up the slope towards him.

'Don't shoot. Ah need help.'

One of the soldiers appeared to be in charge. He sent two of his men up the slope beyond Davey and ordered the two that remained to put him on a stretcher.

'*Ach*, Tommy,' one of them said in heavily accented English. 'You good now.'

The two men wore Red Cross armbands. They heaved him up, dropped him on a stretcher and carried him down the slope.

Ma rifle! Where's ma rifle?

Each jolt of the stretcher forced a cry as the pain in his body railed with each lurch of the flimsy framework.

Yin tried tae kill iss. Others carry me.

His bearers kept up a conversation, ignoring Davey's cries. He heard the occasional '*Engländer*' and other names in tones of voices that didn't sound complimentary.

'Ah'm Scottish,' he announced, to the surprise of his bearers. '*Nicht Engländer.*'

The two men stopped talking for a moment, laughed and echoed Davey's denial until they got bored trying to mimic him.

They picked their way through a corridor cut through the barbed wire defence of their second line. Davey raised his head again.

There's masses of the stuff. Completely untouched by oor guns.

'*Ordentlicher Drahtverhau, was?*' said the German behind Davey's head. '*Was*, Tommy!'

'*Ja, gut,*' replied Davey. He'd heard the German word for 'wire' somewhere.

Might help if ah praised their work.

More laughter and banter continued as they carried Davey for several hundred yards through German communications trenches.

'*Guter Graben,*' suggested Davey.

Praise for the standard of their trenches was met with approval. Davey's rescuers carried him rather more gently and slowly than hitherto.

After several turns at junctions, the stretcher party emerged from the end of the network of trenches and put him on the ground near a large tent.

'*Schotte,*' he heard them say to someone. '*Wiedersehen*, Tommy,' said one. '*Viel Glück,*' said the other.

'*Danke,*' replied Davey.

Whit noo?

Struggling to raise his head once more, Davey soon became aware of the constant movement around where he lay. Stretchers were being carried in and out of the tent; others lay on the ground near where he had been left.

A wounded man near Davey's feet was crying out more loudly than anyone else. Davey sat up as best he could and tried to attract someone's attention.

'Hey, this man's in a lot of pain. Hey, someone.'

'*Halt's Maul.*' The response was accompanied with a kick to the leg. Fortunately, Davey's left leg was the target.

'Not me, him. Him!' Davey pointed.

Two orderlies took the injured man inside the tent. *The Boche gets priority. Tae be expected.*

From time to time an orderly emerged, carrying a limb. These were tossed onto a stinking pile of human detritus that was only partly covered by a tattered tarpaulin.

Ma God, look at that!

It was late afternoon when someone who looked like they might be in charge bent down to examine Davey. He gave an order to a passing orderly.

'Your leg looks bad, Tommy,' he announced in perfect English.

'Dinnae chuck it on there,' pleaded Davey.

The orderly returned with a tin cup of water and helped Davey to sip slowly.

'You are at a field hospital. We will take you inside in a moment. We have a great many of our own men to see as well. You understand.'

Davey nodded. 'You speak very good English.'

'They tell me that you are not English,' he said while he carefully cut Davey's right trouser leg.

'Scottish.'

'We have had a lot of Scottish here in the past few days.'

'Are there any left up there?'

'We are still looking.'

'Thank you for picking iss up,' said Davey.

'You're a lucky man, Tommy.'

'Ah'm no a Tommy. Jock wull dae.'

'Right, take him inside.'

Davey was tipped carelessly from his stretcher on to a canvas bed at the end of the large tent crammed with moaning wounded men.

Whit a stench!

The medical officer who had spoken to Davey outside scolded his bearers.

'Sorry, Jock. They are not in the medical corps.'

Davey's doctor called a passing orderly who returned with a large pair of scissors.

'My name is Weber. I'm going to cut away the rest of your uniform.'

'Whit happened tae ma rifle?'

'It will have been confiscated.'

Doctor Weber removed Davey's ammunition pouches and gas mask bag and handed them to the orderly. He was then able to cut away the bloodstained sections of Davey's tunic and what remained of his trouser leg.

'We will clean and dress your wounds and send you to hospital. You might need operations to remove bullets.'

'Wull ah lose ma leg, doctor?'

'One bullet passed through. There might be at least one other. I've seen worse.'

'Ah also got hit here.' Davey pointed to his waist.

'I'm going to turn you over.'

Weber turned Davey onto his left side and cut away more of his tunic, shirt and vest.

'Ah,' he declared. 'It looks like this one came out the other side. We'll get that dressed too.'

Davey kept quiet about how he came to be wounded in the stomach.

This yin is kind; he disnae need tae ken.

'As soon as we can get your wounds dressed, I'll arrange transport. There's not much more we can do for you here.'

Weber dabbed gently at the entry and exit wounds to Davey's leg and abdomen.

'Your wounds have congealed to some extent,' said Doctor Weber. 'This helps to stem the loss of blood. How long have you been lying there?'

'Ah dinnae … I don't know … a day, a night and a day.'

'You Scottish are very tough. There were not many survivors out there.'

'Whit day is it, doc?'

'Wednesday.'

'Wednesday! We went into battle on Saturday.'

Doctor Weber stopped what he was doing for a moment, glanced at Davey, shook his head and applied dressings to his cleaned leg wounds. A large bandage was wrapped around his waist.

'You will be moved first thing in the morning, Jock,' Weber told Davey when he had finished attending to his wounds.

'Thanks, doc.'

'Good luck,' replied Weber as he moved on to another bed.

Davey was given a thin blanket and another drink of water. Hunger gnawed, almost drowning the pain in his stomach. He hadn't passed water since he took the opportunity to do so when the village of Loos had been cleared; he wondered what he should do if the need arose.

That's why it stinks. Wounded men piss themselves.

Davey closed his eyes. Sleep would be impossible. The pain was too great and the stench of urine and stale blood kept him awake. Sporadic shelling added to his discomfort.

Dinnae shell the bloody hospital.

Davey wondered if the groans of the wounded were from fellow Scots or from German soldiers.

We're a' the same in here. Jesus, Ah've been lucky.

At first light, orderlies taped open the flaps that covered the entrance to the field hospital. A chill draught drifted through the opening, freshening the fetid air. The shelling had ceased.

Men who could sit up were given coffee and bread. Davey's hands were shaking with anticipation as he held the warm tin cup and the chunk of rough dark bread: his first food for days felt like a feast.

Davey and two other patients were carried outside on stretchers, where three covered wagons had been hitched together behind a large horse, showing its impatience by stamping as its harness was adjusted.

Davey's sign language to one of the orderlies met with a shrug and a harsh order to one of the others milling about. Davey was given an empty tin and carried to the middle wagon.

Ah'll wait 'til we get garn.

One of the stretcher-bearers removed Davey's blanket as he was tipped roughly on to a layer of hay. His blanket, tossed into the wagon after him, landed out of reach.

Davey called out to the nearest orderly, 'Boots; where are my boots?' He pointed to his bare feet.

'*Nix Shuhe*, Tommy,' came the reply with a dismissive wave of the hand.

'Yes, shoes. Where are my shoes?'

The orderlies walked away, laughing.

Whit dae they think ah'm garn tae dae, walk oot o' here?

'Can anyone hear me?'

'*Ruhe!*' barked one of the orderlies.

Ah'll try again when we're away from these miserable bastards.

When the orderlies were satisfied that the train of wagons was ready, a soldier mounted the front wagon and shook the reins. The ambulance train set off along a rutted track.

Davey couldn't see out; the canvas cover was closed at the end near his feet. He soon began to sweat and breathe heavily in the stuffy enclosure of the field ambulance. The flaps on both sides of the cover of the wagon drew Davey's attention. He lay staring at them. They were taped shut in a fashion that he couldn't work out, a predicament that was amplified by the constant jolt of the wagon, causing him to lose focus on the problem of opening one of the flaps.

Davey closed his eyes for a moment and tried to relax his aching limbs before summoning reserves of strength to manoeuvre out of his supine position. He managed to sit up and lean on the end of the wagon. He shuffled forward, leant on the side of the wagon and tugged at the ties.

The flap turned out to be larger than the hole it was meant to cover. As soon as Davey undid the bottom of the flap, cool air settled on his face. He breathed eagerly, gulping fresh air, and held the flap open as far as he could, letting the draught fill his mobile ambulance.

His body ached from the effort of holding the flap open, forcing Davey to let it go and slump backwards. At least lying down on the straw offered some relief from the constant pain of his wounds, heightened by the sudden need to urinate. He refused to give in to wetting himself; instead he managed to turn onto his left side to use the tin.

Ah'll get rid o' this. Ah'm no garn tae mess ma straw.

Davey found a gap in the boards of the wagon by pushing some of the straw aside. He carefully emptied the tin, replaced the straw and placed the tin within arm's reach.

Noo fi a peek.

Adopting the same position as before, Davey lifted a corner of the flap and looked out cautiously.

There no be onyone tae tell iss not tae.

The ambulance train must have travelled some distance from the German lines. Davey didn't see any evidence of warfare as they passed unblemished trees and ploughed fields on a road that was much smoother than the first part of the journey. The scenery revealed by his letterbox view of eastern France shocked Davey. He was taken aback by the normality of it all. Trench warfare was only a few miles away, a world apart from the ordered rural landscape behind the Front.

A church spire stood tall in the flat countryside.

A village?

The ambulance train rounded a bend, almost pushing the church out of view. Davey let go of the flap the moment he drew close to a row of cottages. He didn't want to be seen peering out.

They might ken which side ah'm on.

But Davey's curiosity got the better of him. It had been weeks since he saw a French village that hadn't been destroyed by war. He lifted the corner of the flap.

Houses receded as the ambulance train crossed a village square, passing a café where civilians and German soldiers were enjoying mid-morning coffee at separate tables.

Is this whit occupation looks like?

The ambulance train attracted no more than fleeting glances from the café's patrons.

Must be a common sight. The injured passing through.

The wagons rattled through several more villages and a large town. Davey scanned the shop fronts for a name, a clue to where he was: Lens.

Must look it up when ah get hame.

Beyond Lens, Davey let go of the flap, shutting out the light. The effort of peering out had made his shoulders ache. He spent the remainder of the journey lying on his back as the train of canvas-covered wagons bumped over rough roads, shaking him from side to side in the gloom.

After hours of discomfort, relief came as the wagons came to a standstill. Davey heard voices; the rear flap opened and the three ambulances were separated.

That head gear. They look like nuns.

Several people stood at the end of Davey's wagon, discussing matters amongst themselves, pointing and looking at him from time to time. They were not speaking in German.

Davey lifted himself onto his elbows so he could get a better look at his reception committee.

'Hello,' he said.

'Ah, hello,' one of them said. 'Welcome to Saint Clotilde. I am Doctor Wigniolle. We will have you out of there in a moment.'

Oor English teacher got iss tae stop Fechan speak for yin lesson a week. Ah need tae make mysel understood.

Doctor Wigniolle gave orders to those around him and approached one of the other wagons.

Davey was carefully lifted, placed on a stretcher and carried inside a low building. A nurse walked alongside; she smiled briefly and said something to him.

'*Tout va bien.*'

French.

Although Davey didn't understand what she said, the nurse's words sounded comforting and kind. After the field hospital, he expected to be treated by Germans. Instead he found himself in one that appeared to be staffed by French nurses and doctors.

Ah'm in guid hands here.

Saint Clotilde

Davey's stretcher-bearers took him along the main corridor of the hospital, entered a large ward and gently transferred him to a bed. A colleague joined the nurse accompanying Davey; between them they drew the curtains around the bed and cut away what little was left of his filthy uniform.

Doctor Wigniolle entered and stood at the end of the bed. 'We usually wash and return uniforms, but yours is beyond saving.'

'Bit of a mess, isn't it?'

'I hope you don't mind if we destroy it.'

'Fine by me,' replied Davey. 'They might make a fuss in the stores when I get back.'

Doctor Wigniolle looked puzzled.

'You speak very good English, by the way,' said Davey.

'I worked in London before the war. Where you are now is purely for French and British prisoners. You are in safe hands here.'

'Thanks, doc. Can I get something from my shirt please, before you take it away? It's in the top pocket.'

Doctor Wigniolle spoke to one of the nurses. She found what Davey was asking for: a photograph of Kate and Marion. She glanced briefly at it, smiled and handed it to Davey.

'Keep it under your pillow. I'll send someone over to take your details for the Red Cross. One of my colleagues will examine your wounds later. The nurses will wash and dress them first.' Doctor Wigniolle nodded towards the nurses and left, drawing the curtain behind him.

Davey felt embarrassed to be stripped naked; he closed his eyes in an attempt to avoid the faces of the nurses while he was given a thorough wash.

God, ah must stink.

He opened his eyes when the nurses lifted him expertly so that they could put a clean sheet under him and dressed him in a kind of all-over gown.

Next, his stomach and leg dressings were removed, his wounds were cleaned with saline solution and re-dressed.

'*C'est fini,*' announced one of the nurses.

'Thank you,' replied Davey.

Fini. Finished. God, ah feel better already.

The curtains were pulled back and he was propped up on pillows. Davey took in his surroundings.

He was at the end of a ward of about two-dozen beds. High windows let in soft light. Nurses, doctors, and orderlies milled about, moving from bed to bed.

French and British, they said.

Davey turned to the man in the bed next to him. His head was almost completely bound with a large bandage. 'Hello. Are ee … are ee a'reet?'

His neighbour turned slowly to face Davey. '*Bonjour,* Tommy,' he replied in a weak voice.

'*Bonjour.* Sorry, I dinnae … don't speak French. My name is Davey.'

His neighbour understood. '*Je m'appelle* Didier.'

'Didier,' replied Davey. '*Bonjour,* Didier.'

'*Bonjour*, Davey.'

Didier's eyes registered the word 'Loos' when Davey tried to explain how he came to be captured.

'Artois,' said Didier. '*Moi aussi*,' he repeated, turning away from Davey, signalling that the conversation was over for the time being.

'Get some rest, said Davey quietly. 'I'd get up and shake the hand of an ally, but I dinnae … don't think I can just yet.'

Looks like a bad heid wound.

Davey caught the eye of Doctor Wigniolle as he approached his end of the ward. 'What day is it, doctor?'

'Thursday 30th September.'

'Thanks, I've lost track. Just checking what they told me at the field hospital.'

'I'd like you to wait until later before you have some food. Are you hungry?'

'Not really,' Davey lied. 'Thirsty though.'

'I'll send someone with some water. I'd like to get you to theatre this evening. Your leg wound is giving me cause for concern. I want to see if there are any bullets lodged in there.'

'I'm all yours, doctor. And thank you. We're all lucky to be here, properly cared for.' Davey lowered his voice, 'Where are the Germans? I don't feel like a prisoner.'

'German wounded are treated in a separate hospital in town. Only French and British captives are here. Although this part of France is under German occupation, I have a free hand. This is my hospital. We aim to give the wounded here the best possible

114

treatment. The German authorities don't interfere with us.'

'That's lucky for us.'

'We'll take you to theatre soon.'

The last thing Davey remembered were his dressings being removed from his right leg as he lay in the operating theatre.

'When you wake up, you might find something in your hand,' said Doctor Wigniolle in a calm voice. 'Don't be alarmed.' Then he put a mask over Davey's face.

Davey woke not knowing where he was at first, until the ceiling of the ward came into focus. His right leg stung ferociously, reminding him where he had been taken to earlier that evening.

Whit had he said?

Davey's left hand was closed over a piece of gauze; there were two bullets in the palm of his hand.

One of Doctor Wigniolle's colleagues approached.

'Ah, you are wake. My English is not so good as Doctor Wigniolle. Your operation did well.'

'Your English sounds good to me. I see you found these.'

'We sure we found everything. Your thighbone is slightly chipped, but you will recover. Your leg wound is not infected, so will heal. We look at your abdomen tomorrow.'

'Thanks, doctor. It stings more than aches. Is it stitched?'

'Yes. It is a large wound. It will heal in time.'

'Doctor, may I know your name? I'll have quite a story to tell when I get home to Scotland.'

'Scotland! We have a few of your countrymen here. This ward is French. British are in a different ward. The only spare bed for you was here.'

'That's grand, doctor.'

'My name is Doctor Fabron.'

'Doctor, where's Didier?'

'Ah, you spoke with him?'

'We managed a few words.'

'I am very sorry to tell you that he passed away this afternoon. His head injury was too great.'

Davey stared at Doctor Fabron. 'Oh no,' he whispered.

'We did everything we could.'

'Of course you did.'

'Rest now. If you need more morphine, just let someone know. We have to use it sparingly.'

'I'm fine, doctor.'

'Try and sleep. Goodnight, Mr Muir.'

He kens ma name?

Davey looked at the empty bed, stripped of the presence of Didier.

Whit a terrible shock for his folks.

Davey lay awake. An image of Kate holding a letter in her lap, red-faced, hands shaking, flickered and faded as he eventually fell asleep.

His dreams were vivid. He stumbled through smoke and gas, unable to see, falling over bodies, sliding into shell holes until he reached the top of Hill 70, only to enter a hail of machine gun bullets that met their mark. He fell, unable to hear his cries for help over the crackle of machine gun fire. He lay on his back, eyes open to a clear night. Silence replaced the thunder of war.

116

The starry blackness turned into the ceiling of the ward.

Christ, ah hope ah didnae cry oot.

The ward was in darkness, save for a candlelit glow at the far end.

The night nurse.

The only sounds were the breathing of men who could sleep and the groans of those who couldn't.

Davey watched the nurse attend to men in distress until she returned to her dimly lit watchfulness before he fell into a dreamless sleep.

Breakfast at Saint Clotilde was basic. Orderlies came round the ward with a wooden trolley bearing a large urn and several long loaves of bread, trailing a tantalising aroma. They started at Davey's end the morning after his leg operation.

Davey watched one of the orderlies cut pieces of bread from one of the lightly crusted loaves, while the other orderly in charge of the urn poured a dark liquid into a tin cup.

That's no tea then.

'*Sucre*?' asked the orderly, hovering over a large bowl of sugar, teaspoon in his hand.

Davey held up one finger.

Coffee and bread were placed on a rectangular tin tray and set on his lap.

'*Merci.*'

The coffee smelt slightly burnt and tasted faintly of chocolate, sensations new and strange to Davey, as was the slightly salty taste of the bread in its crisp, thin crust.

Ah'd love some mair o' that brid.

The trolley came round for a second time in answer to Davey's silent wish.

'*Encore?*' asked the orderly, smiling broadly.

'*Merci*,' said Davey as a second helping of bread and coffee was put before him.

Later in the day, the same team of orderlies came round with a large steel tureen of soup, giving off a familiar odour.

How dae they cook cabbage without smelling the place oot?

Morsels of grated cheese and leftover bread added as portions were ladled into deep, tin bowls transformed the thin broth into a thick, nourishing soup.

There's pieces of ham or something.

The tureen was large enough for second helpings.

The hospital did its best to ensure that the men were well fed. The evening meal consisted of boiled potatoes and carrots with pieces of sausage, and coffee.

This sausage tastes much mair spicy than at hame.

After Davey had made short work of a bowl of soup at lunchtime on his second day, Doctor Fabron came to see him. 'After change your dressing, we take you to theatre to see your other wound.'

'That's grand, doc.'

'You can see your leg, if you like.'

Davey watched the nurse unwind the dressing on his right leg; the stitched wound was several inches long.

'You will have a fine scar to show children,' said Doctor Fabron, a wide grin spreading across his youthful face.

'You've done a grand job, doctor. It hardly hurts now, just a dull ache.'

'That will fade. It will be some time before you put your weight on it. I will see you later.'

The nurse bathed the wound with saline solution before re-dressing it.

Davey returned to his bed empty-handed after his second operation in as many days. He came round to find Doctor Wigniolle standing at the foot of his bed.

'We think that a bullet passed through the flesh near your hip. You were very lucky.'

'Lucky he was such a bad shot.'

Doctor Wigniolle spread his arms and shrugged without a word.

'Thanks again for mending my wounds. I'm very thankful.'

'We do our best.'

Aye, that ee dae.

The Long Road to Captivity

One day in early November, Doctor Wigniolle appeared at the end of Davey's ward, held up his hand and addressed everyone. Davey understood very little of what, evidently, was an important announcement.

Davey knew that the head of the hospital had finished his short speech. He understood *'Merci, messieurs'*, but not the significance of the hubbub that broke out as soon as Doctor Wigniolle had stopped speaking. The ward was filled with an outburst of French, spoken loudly and rapidly.

Ah wonder whit that wis a' aboot?

Doctor Wigniolle walked the length of the ward and stood at the end of Davey's bed. An uncharacteristic frown replaced his usually warm and friendly countenance. He turned to face the ward and said something that calmed the chorus of raised voices to a quieter level. He turned back to face Davey.

'Mr Muir, I have news that distresses me greatly. The German authorities are closing my hospital.'

Doctor Wigniolle's voice faltered. 'All of my patients are to be evacuated to camps in Germany. I am very sorry to have to tell you this. I have made a personal appeal to the highest authority in Douai to no avail.'

Doctor Wigniolle spread his arms wide in one of his now familiar Gallic shrugs; on this occasion there was no smile.

'Please don't blame yourself, doc. You and your staff have taken best care of us,' said Davey.

'*Merci, monsieur.*'

'*Merci* to you,' added Davey.

Doctor Wigniolle nodded and made his way out of the ward to a ripple of gentle applause.

The day before the closure of the hospital on 18th November, Matron provided Davey with a full set of clothes, including an overcoat and boots, khaki army tunic and trousers.

Probably from patients who've died.

Doctor Fabron approached as Davey was trying on the boots while sitting on the edge of his bed.

'Do they fit?' he asked.

'Pretty good. Thanks.'

'The coat and boots were Didier's. He would approve we used them. He was your same height. It is not easy to find small boots.'

A blue coat!

'I'll look after them,' said Davey.

'I don't want you to put your full weight on both legs. I have written a note with instructions to be given to the camp hospital when you arrive. There is more healing to be done. That is why we have given you a walking stick. Do not use it yet. Take it with you. You will need it later.'

Camps have hospitals?

121

Doctor Fabron handed Davey an envelope, which he put under his pillow with the photograph of Kate and Marion.

'This was Didier's pack also. You will find some useful things in it for your journey.'

Doctor Fabron placed a small, pale-coloured pack on the end of Davey's bed.

'You will be taken to the railway station early tomorrow morning by ambulance. I must go, *Monsieur* Muir. We have things to arrange.'

Doctor Fabron moved from bed to bed with matron and teams of nurses. The French patients were also being kitted out for tomorrow's journey.

Davey opened the pack, eager to explore its contents.

Look at this!

Biscuits wrapped in brown paper, underwear, a shirt and three pairs of thick woollen socks lay on his bed.

Ah wonder if these were Didier's?

One of the side pockets contained a small shaving kit and a sewing kit.

Similar tae oor kit bag.

Davey put Doctor Fabron's letter and his treasured photograph in the other side pocket.

After an early breakfast the following morning, the ward began to empty. The walking wounded shuffled outside, waving at their bed-ridden comrades.

'*Bonne chance*, Jock,' called the Frenchman who had occupied the bed opposite Davey.

'*Merci*,' replied Davey.

Stretcher-bearers ferried the remaining patients to a fleet of motorised ambulances that were parked outside the main entrance. Davey recalled the day almost two months ago when he had arrived bloodied, filthy and in a great deal of pain. Now he was on his way to an unknown destination, somewhere he hoped he could complete his recovery.

As he was being made ready to be transferred to a vacant shelf in one of the ambulances, Doctor Wigniolle and Doctor Fabron approached and shook Davey by the hand.

'You are a very strong man, *Monsieur* Muir, said Doctor Wigniolle. 'You will mend.'

'Thanks to you two and your staff,' said Davey. 'I can't thank you enough.'

Matron sat Davey up and got him into his overcoat.

'It is cold today. Wear your coat until your arrive. I do not want anyone taking it,' explained Doctor Fabron.

When the doctors and nurses were satisfied that Davey and the other three occupants were ready, they lined up near the rear of the ambulance. Davey could see one of the nurses crying.

He felt his chest and throat tighten.

Dinnae scold her, Matron.

'*Prêt?*' Doctor Wigniolle said to someone.

Cries of '*Au revoir*' from the assembled hospital staff preceded the closing of the rear doors of the ambulance, calls that could still be heard as the small fleet of vehicles drew away from Saint Clotilde on its way across Douai to the railway station on the east side of the town.

A chaotic scene greeted Davey's ambulance upon arrival. Groups of walking wounded stood around or were sitting on the rough ground outside the entrance to the station. German soldiers shouted orders and pushed men around with the butts of their rifles.

Davey was manhandled out of his ambulance and dumped at the end of a line of stretchers against a wall.

He sat up, leaning on his elbows. He soon realised that there was a large group of wounded German soldiers separated from the French and British by a line of rifle-carrying Germans facing away from their wounded comrades.

Cries of 'Hello, Tommy,' and 'Hello, Fritz,' flew over the heads of the nervous-looking German soldiers.

'Would you Adam and Eve it?' said the occupant of the stretcher next to Davey. 'If this is a hospital train, then it carries both sides.'

'If we're garn tae a camp, where are the Germans garn?' said Davey.

'Beats me, mate.'

Signs of movement came after a long wait lying where Davey had been left with the other stretchers. The German wounded shuffled into the station, followed by their stretcher cases. The ribaldry between groups of wounded combatants continued, to the annoyance of the German officers present, until all of the wounded Germans had gone and the last cries of 'Good luck, Tommy,' faded.

A German officer stood on a wooden box and held up his hand until it was quiet enough for him to address the prisoners waiting outside.

'Gentlemen,' he began, 'you are about to board a hospital train. As you saw, we loaded our troops first. They are destined for various hospitals in Germany. As for all of you from Saint Clotilde and elsewhere, you are prisoners of war. You have a long journey of more than eight hundred kilometres to your camp at Ingolstadt. German Red Cross personnel at stations along the route will attend to you. Please co-operate with my men. They will put you aboard. We leave in an hour.'

The officer stepped from his temporary dais, gave some instructions to soldiers standing to his rear and marched into the station.

'That answers your question,' observed Davey's neighbour. 'Polite, wasn't he?'

'Aye. And Good English,' rejoined Davey.

'The officers are educated. You can tell. Less so the frontline troops.'

'Same as iss, ah reckon,' said Davey. 'The lads that hae just gaen in there are nae different fri iss. They're probably wondering whit the hell they're daen in France.'

'Well at least we know what's in store for us.'

Davey watched as the walking wounded were organised into an orderly group and escorted into the station.

At length, only the stretcher cases remained. Pairs of German soldiers carried them into the station. Davey was the last to be moved. His stretcher-bearers set him down on the platform beyond the entrance hall next to a small group of British soldiers.

Davey raised himself on his elbows again. The carriages of the long train didn't appear to be as well looked after as the ones further along the platform.

The Germans must be alang there.

Davey and three of the men standing nearby were ordered into a vacant compartment in the end carriage. Two of them were commanded to carry Davey. There was just enough room for him to be laid on one of the wooden benches; his companions occupied the bench opposite.

A German soldier entered the compartment from the platform and retrieved Davey's stretcher. He tried to take Davey's walking stick.

A large Scotsman stood in front of the soldier. '*Nein.*'

The German pulled at the stick again.

'I said *NEIN*!'

The German dropped the stick and fled in fright.

'Yours, ah believe,' said the Scot.

'Thanks, pal. Ah hope he disnae complain tae an officer.'

'Ah dinnae care if he daes. Ah'm Ross.'

'Ah'm Davey. Thanks for whit ee did.'

'Cheeky fucker,' muttered Ross.

Everyone burst out laughing.

'I'm Stan.'

'I'm Will.'

'Were ee a' at Loos?' asked Davey.

'Aye, in the attack on the 25th,' said Ross.

'Me too,' said the other two together.

'We lost oor officers,' said Ross. 'Didnae ken where we were garn and ran intae machine gun fire near the redoubt. Ah got hit in the airm. Lucky really. Men aroon me were shot tae bits.'

'We were all mixed up after their first line. Sixth and Seventh,' said Will. 'He was with me,' he said pointing at Stan.

126

No just Scots in the KOSB then.

'We tried to go forward, but the fire was too great. We were both in a shell hole when a bunch of the Boche appeared. We had no choice but to surrender.'

'How'd ee get wounded?' asked Davey.

'One went clean through my shoulder,' said Stan. 'It's a bit stiff now, but those nurses at Saint Clotilde!'

'Upper arm, me,' said Will. 'Could have been worse. Lucky we were at Saint Clotilde. How about you, Davey?'

'We were meant tae take Hill 70. Cut tae bits on the other side. Ah lay for days before they picked iss up.'

'Days!' said Ross. 'How lang?'

'Saturday to Wednesday.'

'Bloody hell,' said Ross. 'Ye should be deid.'

'Thanks, pal.'

Ross and the other two stared at Davey for a moment.

'What's this Ingol place, then?' said Will.

'A holiday camp where they'll be welcoming iss wi open arms,' quipped Ross.

'A warm bed.'

'A warm nurse.'

'Hot food and whisky,' suggested Ross.

The banter continued for several minutes.

'Anyone got the time?' asked Will.

'They pinched ma watch at the field hospital,' said Ross. 'Bastards. Ma faither gave iss that before ah came oot.'

A sudden jolt of the carriage partly answered the question as the train shuddered into life and lurched forward. Everyone looked out of the window as signs for Gare de Douai receded, leaving the town behind.

'The vor is over for you, Tommy and Jock,' announced Ross in very passable German-accented English.

The compartment fell silent. Will and Stan dozed, encouraged by the rhythmic rattle of the train.

Ross left his place on the bench and sat on the floor under the window so that he could chat to Davey.

'We were dammed lucky, whit wi the staff being French,' said Ross.

'How lang will yer airm be in a sling?'

'Ah dinnae really need it,' replied Ross. 'It's pretty much healed. Better than getting it in the leg like ee did.'

'Ma stitches are oot. Ah just need tae get the strength in ma leg back. Ah cannae put weight on it yet. Ah got yin in the stomach tae.'

'Oh, ye didnae say earlier.'

Ross looked fixedly at Davey, shaking his head. 'Ah speak a little German. Ah'll try tae fin oot if we're garn tae another hospital in – whit was it called? – in the town or a camp hospital or whit.'

'How long've we been going?' asked Stan, evidently awake. 'I'm dying for a piss.'

'I don't know what the arrangements are for that,' replied Will.

'P'raps were aboot tae fin oot,' suggested Ross as the train began to slow down.

'Lille,' announced Stan. 'We're still in France.'

The train drew alongside a low platform a short distance away from the main station and shook as it came to an abrupt halt.

A German soldier flung the compartment's door open, waving his rifle from side to side.

'*Raus*,' he shouted.

'That means "oot",' explained Ross. '*Und was ist him?*' He said, pointing at Davey.

Sign language and impatient gestures were clear enough: the soldier demanded that the compartment must be emptied. Ross supported Davey's weight with an arm around his chest and held his stick in his free hand. Stan and Will lent a hand to get Davey onto the platform.

'Whit noo?' muttered Ross.

Several armed German soldiers were standing near the end of the train, guarding the British wounded. One of the soldiers motioned to Davey, Ross and the others to follow him.

'Ah've got ee, pal,' whispered Ross.

'Gie iss ma stick. It'll tak some o' ma weight.'

'Jesus, ee're nae weight at a',' said Ross.

'Garns wi ma lack o' height,' replied Davey.

The occupants of the rear coaches of the train were escorted to the rear of a building where a large pissoir stood at the head of a long queue of soldiers.

'The German wounded wull be elsewhere,' observed Ross. 'This could tak ages. How mony cubicles dae these things hae?'

Some of the men couldn't wait and were using the wall of the building to relieve themselves. None of the German soldiers stopped them. Davey managed to seek relief while leaning on Ross.

Davey and his fellow passengers were escorted back to their compartment, along with the other occupants of the end carriage. Friendly banter was exchanged as the men milled about, reluctant to get aboard, until the shouts of their guards began to clear their end of the platform.

Ross was the last to emerge from the crowd and climbed aboard. 'Ah've had a word with some of the others. We're less crowded than the other compartments, so p'raps we're lucky.' He flopped heavily onto his place by the window opposite Davey's head. 'The really annoying thing is that the German Red Cross are up the other end of the platform. The German wounded are getting food and drink.'

'Maybe they'll get to us last,' suggested Will.

The jolt of the train almost propelled Ross into Davey's lap. 'There's yer answer, pal.'

Hunger and thirst pushed idle chatter into the background as the train trundled out of Lille. Davey stared at the nicotine-stained ceiling of the compartment, which swayed gently from side to side with a motion that induced sleepiness in his fellow prisoners. Only Ross remained alert. He was grinning at Davey, his finger to his lips. Davey closed his eyes and let his thoughts take him home.

The sudden slowing of the train heralded a juddering standstill.

'The outskirts of another town,' observed Will.

Progress resumed after a long wait.

'Is this Newcastle?' enquired Stan, stretching from another doze.

'Bruxelles, or something' replied Will. 'It's a huge station.'

'It's pronounced "Brussels", like yer sprouts,' said Ross. 'We grow 'em on oor farm.'

'Capital of Belgium,' ventured Davey. 'We crossed the border somewhere. Germany's next.'

'Could be where they're taking the German wounded before shipping iss off tae a camp,' suggested Ross.

The violent flinging open of the door of their compartment revealed a medical orderly; he motioned everyone to get out. Ross pointed at Davey.

'*Nicht er,*' said the orderly, pointing along the platform where a crowd of walking wounded were standing. '*Los, Dahin,*' he said, pointing again.

'He wants iss along there,' said Ross. 'See ee later, Davey.'

Davey felt alone and abandoned. A hubbub further along the platform filtered through the open door of his empty compartment; the orderly was out of sight.

Whit noo?

Davey sat up and swung his legs gingerly off the wooden bench, bracing himself to stand. Just as he was on the point of pushing himself upright, the orderly returned, gesturing vigorously when he saw what Davey was doing.

'*Hinlegen,*' he commanded, waving both hands from side to side, '*bitte.*'

Davey resumed his original position.

That seems tae have satisfied him.

The orderly disappeared again, to be replaced by two stretcher-bearers who took great care lifting Davey. They put his stick and his pack, which he had used as a headrest, on the stretcher and carried him along the platform where he was set down at the end of a long row of stretchers. Another orderly covered him with a thin blanket.

Ross emerged from a group of men standing nearby.

'Whit's garn on?' asked Davey.

'The guid news is that we're garn tae be on another train. There's a proper carriage for stretcher cases. Ah dinnae ken where the rest of iss wull be.'

Ross bent close to Davey's ear. 'Ah'm garn tae mak a run fi it, before we cross intae Germany.'

'Ee must be mad. There's too many Germans around.'

'It's really chaotic here. Ah've got a chance tae slip away.'

'Ee could get shot trying,' whispered Davey.

Ross adjusted Davey's blanket. 'Ah'll tak a chance.'

'Good luck, pal,' whispered Davey.

Davey watched as Ross rejoined the group.

Crazy chancer.

The cold from the stone platform seeped into Davey's back. More stretchers had joined him since Ross took advantage of Davey's end position to reveal his foolhardy plan.

The soldier to Davey's left wore a wide dressing on his head; his left foot was also heavily bandaged.

'Where've ee just come fri?' Davey asked him.

'Hospital in Lens. You?'

'Douai. Ye look cold.'

Davey beckoned to a passing orderly, picked up a corner of his neighbour's blanket and attempted to indicate 'one more'. The orderly brought another blanket and spread it out.

Davey pointed at his neighbour's exposed foot. The orderly was again quick to understand Davey's gestures and carefully covered the man's right foot with the blanket; he left the wounded foot on display.

'Thanks. I hope they see that one so they'll know my injuries.'

The stretcher cases were dealt with before the walking wounded. Davey waited as the men in the line next to him were loaded onto the train on the opposite platform. Stretcher after stretcher passed through the double doors of a carriage near the rear of the train until his turn came.

Davey searched the crowd of men standing on the platform for a familiar face: there were none to be seen as he was carried towards the train.

He heard shots and shouting.

Jesus, Ross!

Davey's bearers stopped for a moment, waited for the clamour to die down before he was passed into the confines of the train.

The hospital carriage was equipped with two rows of bunks, one above the other on both sides of a passage that ran along its length. Davey was lifted from his stretcher onto one of the lower bunks near the front of the carriage. An orderly walked up and down, pointing and counting. Davey could see the door; no more stretchers were passed into his carriage.

'Hey, pal.' The voice came from the occupant of the bunk across the passage. 'Where're ye from?'

'Ecclefechan,' replied Davey.

'Where the hell's that?' The owner of the voice leant on one elbow so that he could make eye contact. 'I'm Gavin.'

Davey sat up. 'Near Dumfries. I'm Davey. Yersel?'

'Inverness.'

'Did ee come off the train opposite?'

'No. We've been here for hours.'

'This is better than the train ah came in on,' said Davey. 'This is luxury compared tae that yin.'

'This is a military hospital train,' said Gavin. 'The Germans are in separate carriages further up.'

'Ah hope we get something on this yin. Ah'm starving,' said Davey.

'Cold or hungry?'

'Both,' replied Davey. 'We were ignored on the way here.' He lowered his voice to a whisper. 'The German wounded were fed. We wusnae.'

'Only tae be expected.'

'Aye, ah suppose,' said Davey.

'It stinks in here,' said Gavin.

'Perhaps that's why they've got flowers at the end where the orderly sits,' said a voice from the bunk above Davey.

'They'll need more than a few flowers tae compete with us,' replied Gavin.

The hospital train remained stationary all night. The orderly turned off all of the gas lamps apart from one near to where he sat. There came the occasional moans of pain during the night, audible over the sound of men sleeping.

Morning light filtered through the slatted window just above Davey's head. It took him a few moments to register where he was when he woke up with a raging thirst.

The carriage doors opened; Davey could see movement on the platform. Two orderlies entered, carrying trays of enamel mugs and plates. Davey sat up, ready when his turn came.

He was given a mug of lukewarm dark liquid and a plate with a large slice of bread on it – the first he had eaten since leaving Saint Clotilde. It gave off an aroma that filled the carriage.

'Thank you,' muttered Davey between mouthfuls of the sweet-tasting bread.

'Hells bells, this must have been made this morning,' said Gavin.

'Whit's the drink? It tastes of nuts or something,' said Davey.

'Probably some kind of coffee substitute,' replied Gavin.

Red Cross nurses helped the men who couldn't help themselves and mugs and plates were refilled for those who could.

Gavin spoke to one of the orderlies as he passed his bunk.

His German sounds good.

'What's happening, Gavin?' said a disembodied voice from one of the upper bunks.

'Cologne is the next stop. There's a military hospital there. My guess is that the German wounded will be going there. We could be at Cologne for a while. By the way, if anyone needs the latrine, ye've tae ask the male orderly.'

'How far is Cologne?' someone from the far end of the carriage asked.

'Well over a hundred miles,' replied Gavin.

This could tak a' day.

The men were given a mug of weak soup upon arrival at the city's large, noisy station, after a journey of several hours.

Davey could see stretcher-bearers passing to and fro with empty stretchers under their arms in one direction, laden with wounded Germans in the other.

'We're off,' announced Gavin after a few hours of unloading the wounded German troops. His announcement was short-lived. Their train was shunted into a side dead-end platform, followed by several juddering lurches of their carriage.

'Relax, they're taking off the Boche carriages,' said Gavin.

'Leaving us to go where?' came a voice from further along the row of bunks.

After more jolting and banging, followed by a final violent thud, their train creaked with relief and lay silent.

Whit the hell's happened tae Ross?

The train drew out of Cologne in darkness.

Davey slept fitfully as the train continued its painfully slow journey deeper into Germany. Several lengthy stops in sidings allowed trains to pass.

The hospital train arrived at a large station later that morning. Davey could make out the name 'Frankfurt' by peering through the slats of his window.

The men were given a mug of a bitter, tepid liquid at Frankfurt, but no food was provided.

Whit the heck was that supposed tae be?

The cheery chatter across the aisle of Davey's carriage dwindled as the interminably slow journey east continued. There were the familiar lengthy waits at sidings and at stations. Sometimes the wounded men were given a drink of water or a bowl of weak soup. On other occasions, they were ignored.

At Nürnberg, two medics came aboard and made a perfunctory examination of each of the wounded. One man was carried out with his face covered.

Christ, they let him die!

Davey stared at the roof of the carriage. He'd known hunger when he was a younger man, away from home working in the quarries. He felt it again on this hellish train journey and, perhaps, he would feel it again where he was going.

As the journey neared its end, Davey noticed a distinct change in the demeanour of the staff accompanying them. The further they were from the Front, the more hostile their replacement medical staff became. Any semblance of medical care that was evident at the start of the journey had been replaced with antagonism as the train neared its destination.

The ambulance train pulled into Ingolstadt station on the second morning since it left Cologne. Its occupants were hungry, thirsty, and unwashed.

'Are we at Waverley?' quipped the man above Davey. 'I cannae see Edinburgh Castle.'

His attempt at cheering everyone up met with groans of derision.

The double doors of the carriage opened. Orderlies holding stretchers carried the wounded men onto the platform and laid them out in a row.

Here we garn again.

Ingolstadt Prisoner of War Camp

A German officer stood next to the line of stretchers. He explained, through an interpreter, that the less urgent cases would be transferred to a camp on the outskirts of town and taken to its hospital.

At the end of the officer's short address, he gave orders to a group of soldiers. Davey and the others were loaded into trucks and driven through Ingolstadt.

The convoy of makeshift ambulances drove slowly through the town centre, to the jeers of bystanders.

How dae they ken we're prisoners?

Soon after the last of the jeering faded, the trucks came to a halt.

This must be it.

The tailgate of Davey's truck was lowered and two men dragged out its occupants.

'Alright, mate?' said one of Davey's bearers.

'Welcome to the Ritz,' said the other.

Inmates unloaded the trucks and ferried the wounded to the hospital.

'It's aye grand tae hear a friendly voice,' said Davey.

'It's not much of a hospital, mate,' replied one of the men. 'You're in good hands though. We have a British doctor. Here we are.'

Davey was carried into a hut with a large red cross painted on its door, one of several wooden huts arranged around the four sides of what looked to Davey like a large rectangular parade ground.

Looks like an airmy barracks.

'Where d'you want this one, doc?'

A tall man in a shabby white tunic pointed to an empty wooden cot. Davey's bearers carefully laid him on its thin mattress; he was still clutching his stick and pack. The doctor said something to the bearers, made a note on his clipboard and continued filling beds.

'That's the lot, doc,' was the parting comment from one of the stretcher-bearers.

Davey was easily able to sit up and take in his new surroundings. What he had been led to believe was the camp's hospital turned out to be an ordinary wooden barracks hut whose occupants happened to be recovering from their wounds. He counted thirty beds, most of them occupied. Davey reckoned that about half held new arrivals from the ambulance train.

The conditions were nothing like Saint Clotilde. The camp hospital smelt of unwashed clothes and bodies and unidentifiable stains discoloured the concrete floor.

The hospital's only apparent doctor appeared to be assisted by a few men in blue uniforms with Red Cross armbands.

'I see you're curious,' said the doctor when he approached Davey's bed, 'I'm permitted to choose assistants from the prisoners here. Makes it easier for the German authorities. I'm Doctor Watkins. Your name please.'

Doctor Watkins found Davey's name on his list.

'How come you're here?' asked Davey.

'I'm a captured RAMC.[9] Long story. We do our best with what we've got here.'

Davey's pack, boots, and overcoat were stowed under his bed along with his stick.

'This is for you,' said Davey. 'From my previous hospital.'

Doctor Watkins read the note quickly. 'I see, thanks. I'll return later to examine you. Interesting coat, Private Muir.'

Over the next few hours, the new arrivals were stripped, shaved, washed, and fumigated with a white powder that stung Davey's skin. He was washed for a second time and returned to his bed where his dressings were changed for the first time in days.

'They've healed nicely,' observed Doctor Watkins as he supervised the removal of Davey's stinking bandages. 'Someone's done a good job.'

'Ah wis in a French hospital,' explained Davey.

'I thought so. Their letter is very detailed. You're a lucky man. How well can you walk with your stick?'

'Ah've no had much chance tae try since we left Douai. Stuck on trains fi days.'

'I'd like you to exercise every day. Strengthen your leg muscles gradually.'

Davey was glad to have the use of Didier's overcoat and boots as he increased the frequency and length of his daily walks around the perimeter of the camp from hut to hut.

---

[9] Royal Army Medical Corps.

The chill November air didn't deter the inmates. Prisoners stood around in groups or strolled casually XE

The chill November wind didn't deter the inmates. Prisoners stood around in groups or strolled casually across the open area in the centre of the camp.

A group of prisoners approached Davey during one of his walks.

'*Anglais?*' asked one.

Remember - proper English.

'Scottish.'

'Ah, *Écossais*. You are wearing one of our coats,' said one of the others, a man with a long scar across his forehead.

Ah wonder how he got that scar.

'A Frenchman died in the bed next tae me. They gave me some of his things.'

Murmurs of approval rippled around the group.

'This is Luc, Maurice and Max. I'm Jean,' announced the man with the scar.

'David. People call me Davey.'

Later that day, Davey repeated his route. Jean saw him approach and invited him into their hut.

It was similar to the hospital hut, with its row of closely spaced wooden cots set against each wall. A thin mattress filled with wood shavings covered the wooden-slatted base of each cot. A wood burning stove stood near one end of a long table.

The Frenchmen's hut smelt of coffee. Davey accepted the offer of a tin mug.

'That's the best coffee ah've had in days.'

'That, *mon ami*, is real coffee. Sent to us from home,' said Jean. 'You only get the ersatz stuff in here.'

141

'Ersatz?'

'A substitute, using nuts, chicory and the like.'

That explains a lot.

Davey's visit to the French hut became a regular feature of his daily walks. He learnt that there were several thousand prisoners at Ingolstadt, mostly French and British, along with a large group of Russians in an adjacent compound fenced off from the main area of French and British huts.

'You are getting stronger, David,' observed Jean on one occasion.

'Doctor's orders, Jean,' replied Davey.

'You soon might not need the stick.'

'This too came from Saint Clotilde. Ah almost had it taken from me, more than once.'

'Who tried to take it?' asked Jean.

'The Boche guards here and there.'

'Bastards,' muttered Luc, from his position lying on his bunk.

'*Connard*,' added Max.

Davey didn't need a translation; he got the picture quickly.

'What're the guards like here? We dinnae … don't have any contact with them in the hospital.'

'If you keep your head down, they are no problem to us,' said Jean. 'They are a bit ready with their rifle butts if they don't approve of something. Most of the guards are too old to fight at the Front, with the result that they hate the job of guarding us.'

'I've been told that you have to work for the Boche if you're fit enough,' said Davey.

'You will be excused, David,' replied Jean. 'Just keep up the limp and you will be fine. Prisoners of war are not supposed to do war work. They have work details in factories. Most of us in this hut work around the camp, in the kitchens and the like.'

'The food is terrible … sorry, I didn't mean to —'

'That's all right, David. We're not given much to work with.'

'Sorry, sorry. You do your best.'

'Don't you get parcels from home or from the Red Cross?'

'Not yet. Early days, perhaps,' replied Davey.

Davey also made himself known to the inmates in the hut next to his French pals. He first met them on a Sunday, a day off from enforced labour. Their hut was deserted on every other day of the week.

'Always walking,' said a tall soldier who was sitting outside on a chair below the window.

'Aye, doctor's orders. Ah got hit in the leg.'

'I'm Harry.'

Davey extended his hand.

'Davey.'

'Where d'ye fellas work?' he asked.

'At a timber yard,' said Harry.

'Can ye refuse tae work for the Boche?' asked Davey.

'I don't know. Besides, it relieves the boredom and you often get bits of extra food.'

Harry offered Davey his chair.

'I'm fine. Got tae get used tae supporting ma weight.'

'How'd you get wounded?'

Davey explained.

'Bloody hell, all that time! You Scots are sturdy buggers.'

'How'd ee get captured?' asked Davey.

'I was sent on a scouting recce, at night. We walked into a trap. Had to surrender. Would have been mad not to.'

Harry sat down; he seemed disconsolate.

Perhaps he feels guilty having tae surrender?

'Do you know where you'll go when you're discharged?' asked Harry.

'Ah assume ah'll be here,' said Davey. 'In some ways ah dinnae want tae leave the hospital. In other ways ah'll be glad tae be given the a' clear.'

*

Christmas 1915 passed almost unnoticed by the inmates of Ingolstadt camp. The prison authorities gave all prisoners Christmas Day off, despite it falling on a Saturday, a workday.

Davey volunteered to work in the camp kitchens. He could easily support himself on his injured leg and could help dish out the soup at mid-day. His French comrades managed to make the soup on Christmas Day more nourishing than the usual fare of poor quality cabbage and gristle.

'The Germans gave us some carrots and potatoes,' said Max. 'Slice them as thin as you can, David. See how far they go.'

When the queue of hungry prisoners dwindled, word came back from the men who were eating their soup outside, rather than in their huts: the day's soup was a success.

After the clearing up in the kitchen was done, Davey called in on Harry's hut. Their hut was warm and welcoming. Davey was chilled to the bone after serving soup in the open. He kept his overcoat on even when he was offered a chair near the stove.

Everyone had pooled their Red Cross parcels. One of the English prisoners, Bert, had been sent a fruit cake from home.

'We get extra soup rations in the hospital,' explained Davey. 'Ah dinnae ken how Doctor Watkins manages it.'

'You're not getting parcels yet?' asked Harry.

'No yet. Thanks for this.' Davey ate his sliver of cake slowly, relishing every morsel.

A beefy inmate they called Slim passed around a box of shortbread.

'Have ee Scottish relatives?' asked Davey.

'Not that I know of. We always get shortbread at Christmas. My mum sent these.'

'Mind if ah tak a couple tae the French fellas next door?' asked Davey.

'The old alliance between France and Scotland holds true, even in here,' observed Harry.

'You've got a coat like the fellas next door. Where the hell did you get it?' asked Slim.

'It belonged tae a Frenchman who was in the bed next to me.'

'A short arse, like you, then,' said Bert.

Everyone burst out laughing.

'That's why ah didnae get shot in the heid. They aimed high and kept missing,' rejoined Davey when the laughter had died down, only for it to break out again as Davey made to leave.

'See ee later, fellas.'

Davey met Jean and some of the other French prisoners as they were leaving their hut.

'We're going to the Russian camp with some food.'

Davey limped across the main compound to the wire fence that separated the Russians from the rest of the camp. This was the first time that Davey had been anywhere near the Russian compound.

The Russian prisoners looked a sorry sight to Davey, noticeably thinner and shabbier than the French and British inmates as they scrabbled for the small gifts of food on offer.

The guards in the nearby watchtower took a keen interest in the apparent fraternisation across the wire divide, but gave no sign of intervening.

Davey soon ran out of shortbread biscuits. He pushed the last one through a gap in the fence towards a pitiful-looking man of his own height. His meagre gift was received by a grubby hand, which was partly covered by a tattered green mitten.

The two men made eye contact. There were tears in the eyes of the Russian soldier, as he kept saying what sounded like '*spasiba*' over and over again.

'That's a'reet,' replied Davey. 'Ah wish ah had mair.'

It took only a few minutes to share the small amount of food. Davey walked back to the French hut on the way to the hospital. His French friends walked in silence, shocked by the sight of the wretched Russian prisoners.

'They don't receive parcels,' explained Jean at the door of their hut.

'Ah can't imagine being more hungry than we are,' said Davey.

'This is a well-run camp. The NCOs in charge have come to an agreement with the Germans. This makes life easier for them and for us. We're not fraternising with the enemy, just co-operating. Things between the Germans and the Russians are not the same.' Jean gestured with his usual Gallic shrug. '*Joyeux Noël, mon ami.*'

'*Et vous,*' replied Davey.

'There is a football match tomorrow. France versus England. Who will you support?'

'Now you've put me on the spot,' replied Davey. 'I'll ask Doctor Watkins if it's a'reet for me to watch. He might not want me standing still for that length of time.'

'See you tomorrow afternoon, perhaps. *Au revoir.*'
'*Au revoir.*'

Jean's hut provided Davey with a chair, which meant that he watched the match sitting at the front of a large group of noisy French supporters.

Most of the prisoners played in vests and cut-off army breeches, battered army boots or regular shoes. The French side were identified by blue armbands and looked smarter than the opposition.

Ah wonder whit they tore up.

Luc played in goal for France. The only other player that Davey knew was Harry from the hut of English prisoners next door to Luc's hut.

Harry turned out to be England's secret weapon: he was an amateur footballer before the war.

The English side spent most of the first half giving the ball to Harry as often as possible, resulting in several one-to-one finishes between Harry and Luc.

'*Magnifique,*' cried Jean, as Luc pulled off another spectacular save from Harry, denying him a hat-trick.

England were two-nil up by half-time.

'It's only two down,' said Davey. 'They've only got Harry. The rest are nae much yiss.'

Harry was targeted by the French defence the first time he received the ball at the start of the second half.

'REFEREE!' shouted the English supporters standing on the opposite touchline when Harry was brought down by a brutal tackle.

The Scottish referee spoke severely to the French captain, pointing and gesticulating, threatening a sending off.

'Free kick in their half,' commented Davey.

'*Allez*, Yves,' yelled Jean, '*allez*,' as a tall Frenchman jinked around the English full back and looped the ball over the goalkeeper seconds after England lost possession after the free kick.

'*Effronté, encore, encore*,' echoed the French supporters as Yves strolled back to the centre spot.

Two one tae them.

It was the turn of the French to dominate during the remainder of the second half. Yves scored twice more.

'*Allez la France*,' chorused the crowd surrounding Davey.

Over and over the cry '*allez, allez*,' drowned out the English supporters.

After the second re-start, the French defence lost the ball.

Harry pounced.

Luc got his fingertips to it.

Hands covered faces.

'There wasnae much he could dae about that yin,' said Davey.

'*Oui, malchance,*' echoed Jean and his hut mates. '*Malchance. Jusqu'à la prochaine fois.*'

Luc wandered over. '*Merde … merde.*'

Harry followed. The two men shook hands. 'Well played,' said Harry.

'*Et vous,*' replied Luc.

'We'll have a return match sometime.'

'*Oui, bonne idée,*' said Luc.

Davey always returned to his hospital bed following his twice-daily walk around the camp. Doctor Wigniolle at Saint Clotilde had told him it could take up to six months for Davey's leg muscles to gain strength. His leg and abdomen wounds healed slowly during the first weeks and months of 1916 until he was able to walk without the aid of his stick.

'The limp will be with you for some time,' said Doctor Watkins. 'Thanks for leaving your stick behind. I'm sure that we can make use of it. When do you leave?'

'Ah wish ah could stay,' replied Davey. 'Well, ah wish ah could garn hame obviously. Ye ken whit ah mean. Ah wish ah wasnae being transferred.'

'I can't justify not discharging you. The Germans have ordered me to release as many patients as possible. They say that the camp is overfull so you'll have to be moved to another camp. I need the beds anyway.'

'Of course ee dae, doc. Ah understand that. Thanks fi everything.'

At roll call in the hospital the next morning, the camp Kommandant, Hauptmann Huber, told the ward, through his interpreter, that prisoners who were well enough to be discharged should be ready to leave the following day.

After the usual breakfast of ersatz coffee and black bread, Davey left the ward with the intention of saying farewell to the friends he had made at Ingolstadt camp.

He made for the French hut first. His last full day was a Sunday, a day off from work parties. Despite a chill in the air, the clear blue sky gave a hint of the promise of spring.

Groups of prisoners were strolling across the main compound or sitting outside their huts. A game of football was in progress – the return match between England and France.

Davey made his way along the line of supporters until he came across Jean and the others, just as half-time approached. He explained that he was being transferred.

'We heard about the transfer,' said Jean. 'The camp has been overcrowded for a long time. One of our NCOs is on the camp committee. The Germans have selected prisoners for transfer, including some of you from the hospital.'

Handshakes all round told of the warmth that had grown between Davey and his French pals. The final farewell fell to Jean. '*Bon chance, mon ami. Courage.*'

'*Courage,*' echoed the others.

'*Merci, au revoir et courage à vous,*' he responded. 'Hope you beat them this time.'

Davey turned away with a heavy heart and left them to the second half.

He spent the remainder of the morning saying goodbye to the other prisoners he had befriended. It turned out that none of them had been selected for transfer.

'You'll probably have to march to the station,' said Doctor Watkins after soup was served that evening. 'Are you alright with that?'

'Ah feel strong enough,' replied Davey. 'Thanks a lot for looking after iss. Ah've been so lucky. A French doctor then an English yin. Ah'm very thankful.'

'I reckon you'll be alright. What worries me is what work they will order you to do in your next camp. Be careful.'

'Aye, ah wull,' replied Davey.

The patients who were being discharged assembled outside the hospital hut the next morning. Davey wore Didier's greatcoat on Doctor Watkins's advice: 'The best way to stop it being pinched.'

Davey had packed the few belongings he had into Didier's backpack: the clothes given to him at Saint Clotilde; a scarf donated by the French hut; and a few biscuits given to him by one of his English pals.

Doctor Watkins went from man to man with a few words of encouragement and a handshake for each of his ex-patients. The German guards watched these formalities with boredom until one of them waved his rifle in the direction of the main gate.

Five months had elapsed since Davey had entered the camp on a stretcher. Now he was leaving as a much stronger man, his wounds well on their way to healing. He joined the ranks of men that had formed up just inside the gate – at last, no longer an invalid; he felt equal to his fellow prisoners.

Kommandant Huber was in conversation with several of his underlings as the group of prisoners shuffled around impatiently. Anyone who stepped out of line was met with shouts of '*Zurück in die Reihe*', accompanied by the prod of a rifle butt.

At last, Hauptmann Huber addressed the men through his interpreter. He was brief and to the point, but he gave no reason behind the men's transfer to Nürnberg, about one hundred kilometres to the north: he merely stated that this was their destination. With that, Huber gave a flourish with his black leather clad hand and the gate was opened.

Nürnberg he said. Back tae there then.

The ranks of men shuffled forwards to shouts of '*Raus!*' and '*Schneller!*' from the German soldiers positioned at intervals on either side of the group of prisoners. Davey was near the rear; he took a last look at Ingolstadt camp and fixed his eyes on the tunic of the man in front of him.

'Dinnae make eye contact wi 'em,' Davey advised the man to his right who was grumbling at every shout of their impatient guards. 'It annoys 'em.'

'Thanks, man,' came the reply in a Geordie accent.

Shouts of '*Ruhe!*' joined the chorus of commands as the men filed out of the camp gate and settled into a brisk march.

'Ah think they want iss tae march in silence,' whispered Davey.

With the camp behind them, all that could be heard was the sound of dozens of men's boots and shoes thudding on the dusty road towards the centre of Ingolstadt. As they approached the outskirts, townsfolk jeered and hurled insults at the prisoners. Several women followed up their screamed abuse by spitting either on the road or, by stepping as near as they dared, hawking in the faces of the men as they filed past homes and shops. The soldiers did nothing to discourage the evident wrath of the citizens, apart from gesturing at angry-looking women if they got too close to take aim.

The extreme animosity of the townspeople came as a shock to Davey.

God, how they hate iss!

The demoralised troop of prisoners tramped on.

'Hold up yer heads, boys,' yelled a voice ahead of Davey. 'Show 'em some dignity.'

This dissenting voice was met with a clamour of '*Ruhe, Ruhe!*' from the guards. The owner of the plea got a rifle butt in his back for his defiant cry.

The response from the front ranks of the prisoners was a silent agreement to march in step. This rippled through the lines of men until arms and legs were co-ordinated and the sound of marching in time almost drowned out the jeers of passers-by.

Every step shot pain through his right leg as he slogged forwards, but Davey gritted his teeth and matched those around him making as much noise as they could with their stamping march.

Kate's Story

Widowhood

Christmas 1916 was a muted affair in Ecclefechan. News of the death of loved ones who were away in France struck at the heart of several families. Grief cast a long shadow and seeped into the life of the village.

Despite the cloud of the distant war that hung over the village, Kate and Chrissie celebrated Hogmanay in traditional style by visiting friends and relatives up and down the High Street, giving gifts of homemade shortbread. Kate carried Davie while his sister Marion trotted at her side from house to house until Kate decided that Marion was probably feeling cold and tired.

It was well before midnight when Kate announced that she would take the children home to bed. She spared a few coals to warm the front room and heat the kettle. She put Marion in her cot and Davie in his sleeping basket.

Kate sat at the table with her back to the front door, trying to shut out the raised voices coming from the street and the hotel. She stared at the fire until the coals almost lost their glow.

Kate shivered, pushed back her chair and took down the photograph of Davey from its place on the mantelpiece. Kind eyes looked back at her. She held the photograph until the ache in her chest shortened her breath.

Ah didnae think ah'd be a widow.

The sound of knocking lifted her out of her thoughts. She replaced the photograph and answered the door.

'I'm a bit early for first-footing,' announced Thomas, as he touched the peak of his cap. 'Oh, I can see this isn't a good time.'

'No, come away in.'

Thomas stood inside the front door, took off his cap and waited for Kate to say something.

'Wull ee no sit doon. Ah'll mak up the fire fi the kettle.'

Thomas drew a small bottle of whiskey from his coat pocket. 'Do you have any glasses?'

Davey's Story

Nürnberg Prisoner of War Camp

The prisoners assembled on a low platform adjacent to a siding away from the main part of the town's railway station. Some were standing, others sitting in groups. Orders of '*Hinsetxzen*' signalled the prospect of a long wait.

Davey sat dutifully on the platform, the cold from the concrete seeping through his greatcoat.

There's more here. Where're they from?

Bloody hell!

Ross!

Davey got to his feet. 'ROSS, ROSS.'

Ross looked across from where he towered over the men standing nearby, a huge grin of recognition lighting up his features.

He made to walk over to Davey, prompting a German soldier to motion vigorously to him not to move.

Ross said something to the soldier, ignoring his order to stay where he was. He received a violent prod in the stomach from the soldier's rifle, a response that moved Ross almost to the point of retaliating, saved by those around him pulling him back into the centre of the group.

Davey looked on anxiously as the incident played out. A German officer approached the nervous-looking soldier. A brief conversation ensued, followed by the officer speaking to Ross's group. Davey saw Ross grin broadly. A dangerous situation had been defused.

'Ah'll see ee later,' Ross called out.

Where the hell has he been?

The sight of an approaching train diverted everyone's attention.

No fi iss. It's a goods train.

A long train of cattle wagons reversed slowly and noisily into the siding and stopped a few feet from the buffers. There was little talk amongst the prisoners as they stood, waiting to be told what to do.

It is fi iss.

Davey was alarmed at the sight of the wagons.

'Bloody cattle wagons again,' muttered a prisoner standing next to Davey. 'I came here in one of these.'

'Ah came in a hospital train,' said Davey.

The prisoner didn't reply.

Armed German soldiers moved along the platform, sliding open the doors. A strong, musty aroma drifted out of the wagons, a mixture of straw and manure.

Whee wis last in here? Men or cattle?

German officers, assisted by guards, organised the loading of the train starting with the rear wagon. Davey tried to keep count as prisoners climbed into wagons under shouted orders from rifle-waving soldiers.

That's another forty!

The crowd of prisoners to Davey's left dwindled until it was his turn to clamber into the next available wagon. He immediately went into a corner, then thought better of it and returned to the open door to give a hand up to the waiting men.

One of the German officers appeared to be satisfied that no more men could be squeezed in and moved his team of soldiers to the next wagon. Davey stood near the open door, opposite a tall soldier who had remained at the other end of the opening, offering a second helping hand.

'That's your lot, then,' he concluded.

Posh English accent.

There wasn't room for everyone to sit.

'They've bloody packed us in,' observed a voice from the opposite side of the wagon.

'Anyone know how long we'll be in this thing?' came another voice.

'It's about sixty miles to Nürnberg,' replied the Englishman. He thrust out his hand, 'I'm Frank.'

Davey responded with a handshake, 'Ah'm Davey, Davey Muir. Ah came through there on the way here. Cannae remember how long it took though.'

'Could take all day, if my previous train journeys are anything to go by.' Frank looked up and down the platform. 'Shit, they're closing the doors.'

No si posh then.

A guard passed two large buckets up to Davey. '*Zum Reinpinkeln.*'

'Pretty obvious whit these are,' said Davey.

The guard plunged the wagon into semi-darkness, oblivious to the groans of its occupants as the door rapidly slid with a scraping sound followed by a clang.

Davey attempted to ease the door open to let in some light, but it would not budge.

'The noise we heard must've have been some sort of bolt to seal us in,' said Frank.

Bastards.

'Best get as comfortable as we can,' suggested Frank to everyone.

'There ought to be some air slots or something for the cattle,' suggested a voice from the rear of the wagon.

'See what you can find,' replied Frank.

Seems to be a natural leader. NCO?

'D'ye hae a rank?' asked Davey, still holding the buckets.

'Sergeant.'

'Aye, sergeant,' replied Davey. 'Can ah suggest that we rig up a screen aroon the buckets and pit it in a corner on this side. There's a few gaps in the wooden slats just there. Might let in a bit o' fresh air.'

'Good idea. I've got a blanket in my pack,' said Frank. There's some hooks on the back wall. Something to do with transporting livestock, for a guess.'

Frank turned away from Davey. 'Can someone see if they can lever out a couple.'

They're treating iss nae better than animals.

The wood was rotten in places and yielded easily to a few firm tugs. Two hooks were passed to Davey.

'Wait until we're on the move before you bash them in near the corner. If we do it now, we might attract attention from the Boche,' ordered Frank.

Shafts of light suddenly spilled into the darkness, dragging fresh air in their wake, accompanied by a loud cheer from the prisoners.

'Shh,' implored Frank. 'Keep it down. Don't pull any more wood out until we move.'

The wagon pitched forward, almost knocking Davey off his feet. He hung on to the inside door handle while the train jerked into life and crept slowly forwards.

At last.

The train settled into a steady but slow speed.

'It'll be hours at this rate,' observed Frank. 'Get the screen rigged up, private.'

Davey used the heel of his boot to knock the hooks into place and hung the blanket to screen the rudimentary toilet area. There was a pile of straw in the corner of the wagon; Davey spread some of it on the floor around the buckets.

'It'll cost ee a penny,' announced Davey.

'Bollocks,' came several replies. 'There's no paper.'

Good point.

'Onyone get onything we can yis?' asked Davey.

No one came forward with anything.

'I've had no food, so I'm unlikely to need a crap,' someone commented.

This statement was met with general agreement and some laughter.

'Anyway, let's make the best of it,' suggested Frank. 'Private Muir's bog looks pretty good to me.'

Some of the men leant on the sides of the wagon; others sat where they could. Davey and Frank leant against the door. There was little talk. Several of the seated men were sent to sleep by the rhythm of the train, bobbing heads resting on their knees. Those not asleep seemed lost in thought, longing for the dark foul-smelling journey to be over.

After a few hours, the train came to a stop, reversed and drew to a juddering halt.

'Here we go,' said Frank. 'Letting others pass.'

Just as Davey was wondering if they would be let out, the clatter of the bolt preceded the sliding open of the door.

'*Raus, raus!*' came the now familiar command from German guards.

Cattle wagons were emptied of men up and down the railway siding. Groans answered the shrill urging of '*Schneller! Schneller!*' if stiff bodies did not respond quickly enough.

A guard pointed at Davey. '*Mistkübel.*'

Davey looked blank.

'Toilet,' he said with a gesture that Davey understood.

Davey carried both buckets and emptied them into a ditch than ran alongside the siding, holding his breath as he did so.

Dinnae suppose the fairmer'll appreciate this.

A long line of men formed near the front of the train. A mobile urn had appeared from somewhere. Davey put the buckets back in the wagon, wiped his hands on his trousers and joined the queue.

Ah could dae wi weshing ma hands efter that lot.

The line of men moved quickly as each prisoner was given a drink from a shared tin cup. Davey watched as dispirited men passed him without speaking on their way back to the wagons, their faces etched with defeat, their silence spoke of hope lost.

Whit've we got?

Davey sipped his water ration slowly, without making eye contact with the guard operating the tap on the urn. The liquid tasted of metal.

That's familiar.

He caught up with Frank on the way back to their wagon. The team of guards was urging the prisoners to get on board.

There's the Boche gaird whi wus bothering Ross.

'At least it's aired,' said Frank.

'Bloody miserable ration,' said Davey.

Frank set about organising swapping the seated and standing men for the next part of the journey.

'Take a turn sitting, private,' suggested Frank.

'Nah, ah'm fine leaning on the door. Ah wonder whit the guards have got in their carriage. Did ee see it? It's just behind the engine?'

'Don't think about food. It'll drive you nuts.'

Davey and Frank resumed their places, leaning on the closed door of their wagon.

'How did you come by a French greatcoat?'

'Hmm, sad story,' said Frank after Davey explained.

'They gave iss his pack tae. Ah, almost forgot … biscuits!'

Davey searched his pack.

'If ah break these intae four, they should garn roon.' It was only a mouthful, but it was met with quiet murmurs.

A team of guards met the train at Nürnberg. Doors were flung aside and harsh commands and rifle waving emptied the cattle wagons of their human cargo. The prisoners were dirty, hungry, thirsty and stiff from several hours of sitting or standing in stuffy, stinking confined spaces.

At last, some air.

The guards that met the train were older than most of the German soldiers Davey had encountered since his capture.

More Boche who hate being in charge of prisoners.

When the officers in charge were satisfied that all was ready, the men marched out of Nürnberg station by a side exit.

Where's Ross?

The rhythmic tramp of the feet of the prisoners turned heads and drew the usual jeers, mostly from women passers-by; men merely stared at the ranks of dishevelled prisoners, unwanted in their town.

'Heads up, lads,' urged Frank. 'Show 'em we're still soldiers.'

Someone at the head of the column took up the challenge as before and called out the commands to march in time. The guards appeared to be slightly amused by the men's attempts to act like soldiers, and chose not to do anything to discourage them.

We're soldiers just fi a wee while.

After just over an hour of brisk marching, the city centre behind them, open countryside greeted the men as they approached their new camp. The command *'Halt!'* rang out as the men reached the main gate.

From his place near the rear, Davey could see a high double-fence and watchtowers.

Just like Ingolstadt.

The prisoners marched into the camp.

'Halt' brought the ranks to a stop in the centre of a large open area.

'Rechtskurve,' came another order.

Davey followed suit and turned to his right, just as he heard the scrape of the gates close.

Another camp; another commandant.

Two German soldiers carried a large wooden dais and placed it in front of the assembly of new prisoners. The Kommandant, resplendent in his grey uniform complete with breeches, strode out of a side building, mounted the platform and addressed the prisoners in English.

'You are now subject to German military law. You are expected to obey anyone in a German uniform, irrespective of their rank, and salute officers. It is an offence to speak to a sentry. Punishment will result if you disobey these orders. Anyone attempting to escape will be shot on sight.'

The Kommandant stepped from his platform, spoke to a subordinate and strode back inside.

Tae the point. This place seems harsh.

Officers with clipboards organised the new prisoners into groups and marched them under guard to huts arranged along the sides of the rectangular central space of the camp. Other huts were arranged in rows on the side of a gentle slope that led away from the compound. Davey was marched partway up the slope to Hut 12 in a group of about thirty men.

An NCO met Davey's group. He stood at the end of one of the long tables that was placed along the centre of the hut. An iron stove stood between the tables, its chimney exiting the roof.

'I'm Sergeant Williams, one of the camp committee. We try to run things, but we're pretty limited with what we can do, as you might imagine. We're all prisoners. We don't get any privileges, if that's what you're thinking. I'm in Hut 6 at the bottom of the hill. If there are any problems, come to us first. Don't take matters into your own hands.'

'Will we be expected to work for the Boche?' came a voice.

'Chances are you will be. This is a working camp.'

'But the Hague Convention —'

'I know what the Hague Convention says. Work isn't usually war-related, not directly anyway. I don't recommend refusal. Besides, it relieves the tedium of life in this place.'

Sergeant Williams went on to inform the occupants of the hut about routine matters: when and where to get meals …

Meals!

… and the like.

'Any questions?'

'Whit's a' this aboot obeying orders?' Davey asked. 'Dinnae we only tak orders from oor ain officers?'

'There are no officers imprisoned here, private.'

'Well, from yous then?'

'We don't issue orders. You heard the Kommandant. It's their law you obey now.'

'Why?' Davey asked.

'Look, private. You've a lot to learn. I'm not going to argue with you. We're their prisoners.'

'Ah ken that, obviously,' Davey continued. 'Ah just don't see why we should salute … '

'Enough!'

'Sorry, sarge.'

'Any more questions?'

'Why were we sent here from Ingolstadt?' someone asked.

'I've no idea, soldier,' replied Williams. 'This is a large camp. The town's garrison used to occupy the barracks around the flat area. Their training ground was where you came in. The camp has since been

170

expanded up the slope here. These huts haven't been occupied until now. By the way, looking after the hut is your responsibility, all of you. It's bloody cold in the winter. The wood ration is barely enough to get by. Enjoy the weather while it lasts. You know where to find me.'

Sergeant Williams left the hut, casting a look of disapproval in Davey's direction on his way out.

The men sitting on beds stayed where they were, others claimed the empty ones. Davey ended up with the first bed on the left inside the door to the hut.

'We can always move around to give everyone a fair crack,' suggested the soldier next to Davey. 'I'm Davies, Phil Davies.'

'Ah'm Davey. Ah'm a'reet here.'

'What were you getting at just now?' asked Phil.

'Oh, ah dinnae ken really. The sergeant just seems tae have given in tae them,' replied Davey.

'Perhaps that's what happens if you've been banged up for a long time.'

He's right. We could be here fi a lang time.

The remainder of the evening was spent making introductions and taking stock of their new surroundings.

Davey had been inside similar huts at Ingolstadt camp; living in one was going to be very different from the relative ease from hardship of its hospital hut.

Hut 12 looked well constructed. The roof appeared to be rainproof and the wooden walls were sturdy enough to suggest they would keep draughts at bay.

Davey's bed had a thin mattress stuffed with paper, resting on a chicken wire base. Each bed was provided with two threadbare blankets.

The first night he couldn't sleep. Tiredness fought with hunger and his injured leg ached from the hours of marching and standing.

Loudspeakers roused the camp into life the next morning shortly after a clear chill dawn. Roll call was organised by huts on the parade ground at the foot of the slope. Camp guards took their time checking names on clipboard lists.

The twice-daily drudgery of the roll calls soon became part of Davey's routine. Ersatz coffee and a piece of black bread followed the morning roll call; a thin soup followed the evening assembly. A similar watery soup with unidentifiable slivers of barely edible vegetable matter and black bread comprised midday rations served outside on long tables.

The soup's worse than at Ingolstadt.

It took only a few days for Davey to resign himself to the routine in his second camp, its daily pattern accompanied by constant, nagging hunger.

A week after his arrival, Davey was walking up the slope towards his hut with a few of his fellow inmates when he saw a familiar figure striding down towards him.

'Ross! Whit're ee daein here?'

'Daft question, pal. Same as yesel.'

'Come tae oor hut. Ah want tae hear whit happened.'

Everyone crowded around Ross.

'Ross, this is Phil Davies, Dusty Miller, Chris Baker. This is Ross. We wis on the train oot o' France.'

'Ah didnae get far in Brussels. Worth a try though. A policeman spotted iss. At least ah think it was the polis. Dinnae think he was a Belgian. Otherwise he might have been sympathetic. Some sort of Boche polis, ah think. There wis a lot of shouting when ah ran. Soon stopped when they started shooting at iss.'

'Ah heard shots,' said Davey. 'Ah thought the worst.'

'Ah was afraid a civilian might get hurt, so ah gave up.'

'Thank God ee didnae get shot,' said Davey.

'Anyway, they grabbed iss and brought iss back tae the station.'

'Ah didnae see ee there.'

'Ah got sent tae Ingolstadt.'

'Ah didn't see ee there either. It's a big camp, but ah thought ah might have spotted ee.'

'No the camp – the Fort. A castle affair in the toon. Mostly officers there. Ah got sent there because ah tried tae escape. Then ah was sent here.'

'Ah didnae see ee get off the train.'

'They kept iss under gaird away from yous.'

'Well it's grand to see ee.'

Davey couldn't decide if his hut mates were in awe of the big man or regarded his escape attempt as foolhardy.

'There's not much chance of getting out of here,' suggested Phil.

'Ah only tried it because we hadn't reached Germany. We're deep in Germany here, so ah dinnae ken if ah'll try again.'

'There might be a chance from a work detail,' chipped in Dusty.

'Possible,' replied Ross. 'Some o' the officers at the Fort tried mair than once. That's why they were there. Ah heard about men being shot attempting tae escape. Not from work details though. Officers don't work.'

'Best not to think about escape,' concluded Chris. 'Something else to drive you nuts.'

'Listen, fellas,' said Ross. 'Would ee save yer spent matches for iss. Ah'm up the hill. Hut 20. Ah use 'em tae make models.'

A murmur of approval followed Ross as he left the hut with Davey.

'By the way, ah saw that gaird who was pushing ee aboot at the station. He wis on the train.'

'Oh, him,' said Ross. 'He wis at the Fort. Must've been transferred here.'

Davey re-entered the hut.

'Crazy bastard,' said Chris. 'He could have got himself killed.'

'Or someone else,' said Phil.

'He's a guid pal though,' said Davey. 'He looked after iss on a lang train journey, whit wi ma leg wounds. Stood up tae the gairds. Ah think they wis scared o' him.'

'Not surprising,' said Dusry. 'He's just about the biggest bloke I ever saw.'

*

As April turned into May, camp life took on a well-worn pattern of roll calls, meagre meals of soup twice a day, ersatz coffee and black bread.

Hunger was the constant companion to routine and boredom. Irregular distribution of Red Cross food parcels was a lifeline to hungry prisoners. A few men in Davey's hut received them and shared their contents. It was a joy to taste bully beef and drink a cup of tea. The occasional treat from a food parcel almost sufficient to stave off the relentless pangs of hunger.

A furious row broke out in Davey's hut following a rare Red Cross parcel distribution towards the end of May.

'This isn't the first time my parcel's gone missing,' shouted Dusty, banging the table with his fist.

'Well it isn't me,' protested Phil.

'Me neither,' added Chris.

'Mister fucking nobody, then,' roared Dusty, waving his arms about, taking in the whole hut.

Everyone avoided eye contact with Dusty.

'It must be somebody,' he added in a quieter voice as he sat down.

Davey heard the commotion from where he stood in the doorway.

'It could be a gaird,' he said in a calm voice.

All heads turned towards Davey.

'What?' said Dusty.

'It could be a gaird,' repeated Davey.

'Go on,' said Phil.

'Some of the French told iss aboot the blockade. Germany's short o' food. When parcels arrive, it looks like we've got mair food than them. Some guairds might be tempted tae pinch food from iss. They probably steal 'em onyway, but some of 'em might steal from huts as well.'

'Alright then, we've got to prove it,' said Phil.

'Ah've got an idea,' said Davey.

Everyone sat either on the end of their beds or around the table, eager to hear Davey out.

Cries of 'Let's hear it,' greeted him.

'Ah'm the shortest man here.'

'Short arse!' chorused most of the hut.

'Let's hear him,' pleaded Phil above the din.

'Part of the roof space is covered at the far end. There's some spare planks under the hut. Ah spotted 'em when ah was looking fi a hiding place for ma greatcoat. Yin o' the gairds has been eyeing it recently.'

'And … ' said Phil.

'We pit some planks across the beams and increase the roof space enough for iss tae hide up there. Pit some chocolate on the table. Ah'll hide and see whit happens. If it's one o' iss, then nothing wull happen. If it's a gaird, ah'll see.'

'Gotta be worth a try,' said Phil.

'Do we tell the camp committee what we're doing?' asked Chris.

'No,' came the reply, in unison.

On his third day in hiding after morning roll call, the hut was empty again. Everyone not assigned to work details had agreed to be out of the hut for the day, either walking around the camp or visiting other huts.

Davey stretched and tried to rub the stiffness out of his legs as he lay on the planks.

The door of the hut opened slightly as if to allow someone a glimpse inside. A head appeared, followed by the body of guard Baumann, nicknamed Droopy by Davey's hut due to his downturned mouth.

Droopy wandered aimlessly from bed to bed, idly picking items up and dropping them. He turned his attention to the long table where the trap had been laid. The lure of chocolate was too much for him to ignore; Droopy pocketed the unopened bar of chocolate and left quickly.

Gotcha. Ee chanty wrastler.

Davey waited until he imagined that Droopy was out of sight before he dropped to the floor and left the hut in search of his hut mates. He found Chris, Phil and Dusty strolling around the perimeter of the parade ground.

'Saw him lift it,' said Davey, breathless with excitement.

'Who?' said Phil. 'Lift what?'

'Droopy. He took it.'

'Well done,' said Dusty.

'Got the bastard,' said Phil.

'What now?' asked Dusty. 'He's not likely to be punished for pinching food from prisoners. I bet they all do it.'

They continued walking.

'No, but we've got a bargaining chip,' said Phil.

'How d'you mean?' asked Dusty.

'Who speaks German in our hut?' replied Phil.

'What about Wilkins? He told me he's been on a course in Blighty,' replied Dusty. 'Why d'you ask?'

'Maybe Droopy is getting more than his mates by nicking our food. Maybe he keeps it a secret,' suggested Phil.

'Ah've got an idea,' chimed in Davey.

'Uh oh, another one from our ideas man,' said Chris.

'Why don't we offer to give him things in exchange —'

'For what?' asked Chris.

'Whit ah mean is we – that is Wilkins – has a chat wi Droopy. We offer him things such as chocolate or ciggies. Tell him that he disnae have tae steal from iss. We'll leave stuff for him in exchange for things we need – fruit, vegetables, eggs, and the like. We could risk making a deal with old Droopy.'

'Great idea,' said Phil. 'What if he's not interested though. He might think that he's entitled to nick our food parcels. There's no sanction against what he's been doing.'

'Let's try it onyway,' said Davey. 'If he disnae dae a deal, ye could threaten tae report him tae the Kommandant. See how he reacts.'

Phil outlined the plan to the hut prior to lockup for the night.

Davey felt pleased with his part in snaring Droopy.

Onything tae alleviate the hunger. Ah'm wasting away. We're a' thinner.

Droopy accepted the arrangement. The hut was blessed with pieces of fruit, the occasional egg, and fresh vegetables from time to time. Potatoes and vegetables were cut up and boiled in a biscuit tin on the top of the hut's stove, lit for the purpose despite the onset of warm weather.

If anyone brought their mess tin of soup into the hut, pieces of vegetables were added, courtesy of Droopy.

The hut endeavoured to keep their arrangement secret, in the knowledge that similar deals had been struck elsewhere in the camp.

*

Days spent in idleness came to an abrupt end later in May when the German authorities increased the number of prisoners allocated to work outdoors.

At six o'clock every morning, with the exception of Sundays, a group of about fifty men, including Davey and several others from his hut, marched for over an hour to work on building a road through a nearby forest.

The work was hard for a fit man, arduous for weak, half-starved prisoners. A truck brought a dixie of coffee and soup to the site, affirming the men's disappointment that there were no extra rations for labouring for the Germans.

The prod of a rifle butt would greet any man who was slacking in the eyes of the guards.

There's the gaird who argued wi Ross.

Davey kept his head down and did what was necessary to avoid drawing attention.

At the end of the first week one of the civilian engineers tossed a piece of fresh bread in Davey's direction during the midday soup break. Davey caught the man's eye and put the bread in a pocket of his worn-out tunic that was lying on the bank next to where he was spooning soup out of his mess tin. None of the guards saw what happened.

No a' civvies hate iss then.

Davey shared the bread that evening.

The talk turned to working for the enemy, as it had every evening of their first week laying the road.

'It's not war work, though. Not directly,' said Wilkins.

An argument ensued. Everyone agreed that working drove out the boredom of camp life and everyone also agreed that they were regarded as slave labour.

'Apparently, Ross's hut refused tae march when they assembled by the gate last Monday,' said Davey.

'What happened?' asked Dusty.

'There wis a lot o' shouting – threats o' shooting onyone who didnae march. Efter a few minutes they gave in.'

'They had no choice,' said Wilkins. 'I heard about it too. Your pal Ross'd better be careful. They've got him marked out as a troublemaker.'

'Ah'll have a wee word wi' him,' said Davey. 'Remind him that he's pitting others in danger.'

At six o'clock on the following Monday, Ross joined Davey's work detail.

'Whit're ee daen here?' asked Davey.

'Ah've been transferred tae your lot.'

'Why?'

'Dinnae ken. Ah reckon they've decided Kurtz will keep an eye on iss.'

'Who's Kurtz.'

'That stocky fella on the back of the truck.'

Ross turned away.

'Dinnae look ower,' he said.

'*He's* Kurtz!' said Davey. 'He's following ee aboot.'

'Aye, it all started at Ingolstadt camp didnae it. Ah'm stuck wi him on ma back a' day noo.'

'Listen, Ross. Promise iss ee'll behave yersel.'

'Aye, ah wull. Ah need ee tae keep an eye on iss as well. Ee just watch whit Kurtz gets up tae. Right, we're away.'

Davey kept an eye on his wayward pal and tried to keep Kurtz in view as soon as work began.

Kurtz took an early opportunity to goad Ross, even though he was working at the same rate as those around him. Kurtz ignored the civilian engineers who were organising the prisoners.

'*Schneller! Schneller!*' he shouted, prodding the big man with his rifle butt. '*Los, schneller!*'

Ross rubbed his back, smiled sweetly at Kurtz and carried on shovelling gravel until his wheelbarrow was empty.

Davey watched in alarm as Kurtz jabbed his rifle butt into the back of the bent figure of Ross for a second time.

Ross spun round, raising his shovel high.

'ROSS!'

Ross lowered his shovel the instant he heard Davey's shout.

Davey didn't understand what was said between the engineer in charge and Kurtz, but the tone and accompanying gestures defused the situation.

Ah reckon he's saying that he's in charge, no the gairds.

Davey worked as near to Ross as he could for the remainder of the day. His pal hovered on a knife-edge.

Must be their plan. Provoke him until he reacts.

Davey did what he could to reassure Ross that evening before returning to his own hut.

'Ah'll work next tae ee,' said Davey. 'Ah'll try and distract him. Gie him someone else tae pick on.'

'Thanks for stopping iss. He wants iss tae retaliate,' said Ross.

'Dinnae give him the satisfaction, pal. See ee in the moran.'

'Aye. Be careful Davey.'

'What an idiot,' muttered Dusty when Davey came in. 'That Kurtz bloke is pushing his luck. Picking on someone twice his size. What's his game?'

This cannae garn on.

Hostility between Ross and Kurtz continued for several more days, until Kurtz appeared to largely concede defeat in the face of Ross's refusal to retaliate. The evidence for this apparent change of tactic consisted of aggravating Ross marginally less whilst attempting to divert attention from his actions by picking on other prisoners.

On one occasion, Davey received a violent prod in the back from a rifle butt as he bent down to fill his shovel with gravel.

'Hey, mind ma wound,' said Davey with a wince.

Davey stood, turned quickly to find himself eye to eye with Kurtz.

'That was near ma wound. Ye ought tae be mair careful.'

Everyone stopped working; the engineers looked on in alarm.

Kurtz merely sneered.

'*Suas mise,*' said Davey calmly.

'*WAS?*' barked Kurtz.

'Ah just swore at ee in Gaelic,' added Davey, equally calmly.

The two men glared fiercely at one another.

'*WAS?*'

'Ah asked ye tae garn away and leave iss alane,' continued Davey.

'*Komm, lass ihn,*' pleaded one of Kurtz's comrades.

Kurtz mumbled something indistinct and wandered off.

'See whit ah mean,' said Ross as the men lined up ready to march back to camp at the end of the shift. 'The fella is a total bassa.'

'No just a bassa,' added Davey. 'He's a dangerous bassa.'

∗

The spring of 1916 turned into a hot summer as the road made progress. Working in the shade of the dense forest gave some relief from the heat of the day, but the ever present sawdust from felled trees brought its own hazard – a constant thirst.

The engineers continued to pass morsels to the prisoners when the guards were not looking. They were particularly wary of the whereabouts of Kurtz.

Davey and other members of the hut working on the road got into the habit of emptying their pockets onto the table at the end of the day in an attempt to create equal shares.

'Bloody hell, Davey,' exclaimed Wilkins one evening. 'That's the first piece of cheese I've seen for ages.'

The work on the road took its toll on Davey's clothes. He noticed several prisoners wearing distinctive dark blue uniforms instead of regular army khaki as they strolled around the camp.

He enquired at the NCO's committee hut. Clothes were sent from Blighty in separate parcels and, yes, they had accumulated spare tunics and trousers. It took one of the corporals a while to find something that didn't look too large on Davey's small frame.

'Have some socks too, private. You'll have to find something to hold up yer trousers.'

Davey stowed his new kit with his precious greatcoat in its hiding place under the hut. He decided to use the clothes given to him at Saint Clotilde as working clothes for as long as they held together while he was shovelling gravel for Germany's road.

Ah might come back efter the war and fin the bit o' road ah helped build.

Work continued into late autumn, by which time it took the men longer to march to work due to their progress in lengthening the road. Its completion was signalled on a bitterly cold day at the end of November when the road emerged from the forest. Finishing touches were applied to joining the new road with an existing one.

The prisoners formed up into ranks ready to be escorted back to camp on their last day. Many of the civilian workers exchanged handshakes and words of encouragement with the men in the ranks.

'*Viel Glück,*' chorused the engineers.

Sounds friendly.

The guards looked on, unwilling to intervene. Even Kurtz held back, apparently disinterested.

The engineer who singled out Davey for gifts of food approached, hand outstretched. Both men exchanged knowing glances. Davey felt something touch his palm during a long, firm handshake. He dropped the coin into his trouser pocket and waited for the command to march.

'*Fàg mi a bhith,*' whispered Ross.

184

'Dinnae count on it,' said Davey. 'He's still a gaird.'

'Ah dinnae think ah can stand another winter as a prisoner,' murmured Ross.

'Try tae hang on, Ross. The war'll be ower eventually.'

Ross sighed, muttering in Gaelic as they started the long march back to camp.

Davey patted his tunic pocket. Carrying Kate's photograph had helped him through another day.

Kate's Story

The Image is the Bond

'Aye, ah can see that ee are showing a wee bit,' said Chrissie. 'Whit'll ee dae?'

Kate sighed and shook her head, unable to meet the disapproval of her sister.

'Oh, Kate … Kate.' Chrissie topped up the teapot and sat opposite her sister. 'We'd best think aboot practical things. Whi kens?'

'You, Ma and Pa, and Thomas.'

'How'd he react?'

'He's asked fi a transfer back tae Glasgow. He wants isss tae live there.'

'Whit dae ee want to dae?'

'Ah'll garn. We cannae stay here. Ah dinnae want the whole village tae ken.'

'Whit aboot your two?'

'Ah'll send fi them when we're settled. Ah'm garn tae ask Ma tae look efter them, just until ah get things sorted. Will ee help her?'

Chrissie sighed. 'Aye, of course ah wull. Whit's happened has happened. Ee'll hae three bairns tae feed.'

'Thomas has a guid wage. He's in a reserved job. There'll be mair coming in for iss a'.'

'Ah wish this hadnae happened, Kate. Ye leaving the village. Ah'll miss ee. We've never been apart.'

'Dinnae be cross with iss. Ah'll mak the best o' it.'

'We ought tae keep the hoose on,' said Chrissie. 'The Muirs are a growing family. Ah'll look intae it. Talk tae Ma.'

'Whit'll ee say tae folks when ah'm away?'

'Ah'll think o' something.'

'Ah'll be lost without ee.'

'So it seems ... so it seems,' sighed Chrissie. 'C'mon, ah'll help ee pack.'

The day of Kate's departure dawned cold and grey. Thomas helped Chrissie put Kate's belongings into the back of his company van and stood discreetly aside while the sisters hugged in silence.

Chrissie watched until the van turned onto the Lockerbie Road at the top of the hill out of the village and was lost from view. She went back inside the empty house, sat at the table and rested her head on her arms.

The dampness of the sleeve of her smock made Chrissie sit up and look for her handkerchief; she tried to focus through swollen eyes. There were no sounds of children, only their echoes and a shadow of her sister remained. Chrissie's gaze was drawn to the mantelpiece: Kate had left Davey's photograph behind.

Davey's Story

Kurtz's Last Stand

Davey was assigned to labouring work in camp after completion of the road. He took turns in the kitchens and washrooms during the winter of 1916, preferring tasks that helped his fellow prisoners rather than the country that enslaved them.

Christmas Day found Davey and his hut mates striving to improve the day's soup ration with the help of deliveries from Droopy.

The hut was bitterly cold during the winter months. Icicles hung like inverted candles, dripping their cold silver wax onto the frozen ground outside. Wood rations were barely enough to keep the stove burning for an hour to two during the dark evenings.

Some of the occupants of Davey's hut were assigned to a work detail in a woodyard on the edge of the forest, near the beginning of the new road. Slivers of wood brought back from the yard at great risk to their bearers found their way into the stove. The hut came through its first winter without anyone being caught filching small pieces of wood from the yard.

The spring of 1917 marked Davey's first year at Nürnberg camp. Resignation to the privations and mundanity of camp routine represented a kind of life, a petty existence in the hands of his captors, the body barely surviving with the mind in shadow. Davey turned to his inner life to find refuge from the unrelenting existence as a prisoner of war, letting images of Kate and the children push the uncertainty about how the long the war would continue out of his mind.

Some inmates didn't adapt as readily as Davey. He had experienced hard labour and poor food before joining the army. A number of his fellow prisoners died of malnutrition during Davey's first year at Nürnberg.

Most prisoners stayed in their huts if they were not attached to a work detail. Davey continued his long walks, just as he had done at Ingolstadt. His injuries had almost healed, but his leg ached if he stayed still in the hut. Walking gave him a chance to exercise his wounded leg more than labouring work did, so Davey used his daily walking routine to call in on Ross and cement friendships with soldiers in the French section of the camp.

Davey had never smoked, unlike most of the prisoners who smoked incessantly. He picked up spent matches during his walks from hut to hut and gave them to Ross, whose Viking longboat was almost complete after months of intricate work. Made almost entirely out of matches, the model was a thing of beauty, standing proudly at one end of his hut's central table.

Where'd get the glue?

Davey was pondering this for the umpteenth time as he approached Ross's hut one Sunday morning in June, hearing raised voices long before he entered.

Three men restrained Ross, pinning him to a chair while he raved and shouted, curses in Gaelic filling the air.

194

'*Ith mo chac, bassa,*' he roared over and over again.

Davey saw the cause of Ross's wrath as soon as he entered the hut: the longboat was in pieces.

Davey stared at the heaps of matches, some still glued together in sheets of various sizes, others had returned to their individual state.

Ross calmed down when he saw Davey staring at the debris. 'Ah'll fuckin' kill him, ah wull,' he murmured slowly.

'No, ee willnae,' said Davey. 'Whit the hell's been garn on?'

The culprit was identified as Kurtz.

'He was seen going in and coming out when the hut was empty,' said Armitage, one of Ross's hut mates.

'Why wid he dae this?' asked Davey.

'Ah didnae move quickly enough fi him yesterday. We were packing oor tools away. Ah got a rifle butt in ma groin.'

'Whit? He's back on yer work detail,' said Davey.

'Aye.'

'Ah thought we'd done with a' this efter the road.'

'Well, he's at it again.'

'Disnae give up, daes he?' said Davey.

'Crazy little fucker's trying it on again,' groaned Ross. 'He kens he can get away wi' it.'

'Ye sure he did it?' Davey addressed the men restraining Ross.

General agreement followed.

'Daes oor man Kurtz like chocolate?' Davey asked.

'How the fuck should ah ken,' replied Ross with a note of irritation.

Ross recovered enough self-control for his minders to let loose their grip on the big man. 'Whit's that got tae dae with onything?'

'Have ee had Red Cross food pinched?' Davey asked.

'Aye, we have. Never caught Kurtz or onyone else red-handed though.'

'Let's assume he's a glutton fi chocolate. We get more than they dae. Lay a trap.'

'How's tempting him with chocolate going tae help?'

'Ah've got a plan,' said Davey.

The occupants of the hut gathered round Ross's chair and began to pay full attention to the conversation between the two Scottish friends.

'Ah ken where there's some buckthorn,' continued Davey.

'Yer no making ony sense, pal.'

'It can be used as a purgative.'

'A what?'

'It gives ee the shits.'

'And how the hell —'

'Melt some chocolate, mix in some juice fri the berries and let it garn solid.'

All eyes were on Davey.

'How much of this stuff do we need and will he eat it?' said Armitage. 'Won't he detect it?'

'Ah dinnae ken how much juice it'll need for it tae take effect. We'll just have tae try it oot.'

'How the hell d'yee know a' this?' asked Ross.

'There's an auld biddy lives near oor village in a bothy away up beyond the glen. She kens a' sorts o' things. Whit're poison, whit're good tae rub on yersel. She taught me things when ah wis wee.'

Everyone continued to pay attention to Davey.

'Dae ee want tae give it a go? Ye deserve revenge for this,' said Davey.

'Let's get the bastard. Ah cannae think of ony other way just noo, apart from beating the jobbies oot o' him,' said Ross calmly.

'The bush is behind the kitchens, at the end o' Jerry's vegetable patch. Ah was looking for extra things tae put in the soup. The fruit should be ripe enough.'

'Bring whit ee need this evening and show us whit tae dae,' said Ross.

The straggly bush close to the trip wire next to the perimeter fence was partially out of sight of the nearest watchtower. Davey slipped out of the kitchen and pocketed some of the ripest berries. He laid them on the table in Ross's hut after the evening soup.

'Is everything else ready?' Davey asked. 'Melt the chocolate very slowly.'

Dennis Armitage kept a close eye on the tin of chocolate on the edge of the stove.

'Guid. It wullnae be si hot there,' said Davey.

He watched the tin, advising Armitage to lift it from the heat from time to time.

When Davey was satisfied, the tin was transferred to the table onto a piece of wood. 'We dinnae want tae burn the table,' he said.

Davey worked quickly, carefully pressing the juice of the berries into the liquid chocolate.

'That should dae the trick,' he announced after stirring the mixture slowly. 'Whit have we got tae set it in?'

Fraser produced an empty biscuit tin, a flat one with a hinged lid. When it had set, Davey removed the flat block of chocolate and laid it on a clean handkerchief. A knife that Davey had smuggled out of the kitchen finished the job.

The block of adulterated chocolate was skilfully cut into bite-sized chunks and arranged in the biscuit tin. Everyone stood back from the table, admiring Davey's handiwork.

'Ah'm no about tae test it,' announced Ross.

'Ah just hope that the sweetness of the chocolate masks the taste o' the juice. It might be too bitter,' said Davey.

'Muir the alchemist,' pronounced Ross.

'Leave the rest tae us,' said Ross. 'We'll set the trap and let ee know whit happens. Ee've done yer bit.'

Ross sought out Davey two days later after his shift working on the market garden next to the camp's kitchens. The grin on Ross's face could not have been wider as he strode into Davey's hut.

'It worked, pal.'

'Whit happened?'

'We were oot on a work detail; Kurtz wis yin o' oor gairds. He had tae keep disappearing intae the forest. He must have gone half a dizzen times during the moran. His pals were getting really annoyed. Efter the midday break, he disappeared altogether. Must've garn back tae camp.'

'Well done, Ross.'

'Thanks t'ye, we fixed him. We havenae had him as a gaird today. Dinnae ken where he is. Dinnae fuckin' care.'

'Hae some tatties,' said Davey, emptying one of his pockets. 'This is part of today's haul fri the garden.'

198

'Keep some for yersel,' insisted Ross.

'It's a'reet, we've got a store under the hut.'

'You're taking a risk, pal,' said Ross. 'Thanks. Be careful.'

∗

Davey's expertise in the camp's small market garden resulted in him being assigned to a farm work detail. The farm he was to be attached to supplied potatoes and other vegetables to the camp, for use by the kitchen that fed the Germans and the larger kitchens that fed the prisoners.

On the first day of his new work detail, Davey and a dozen prisoners were ordered to climb into the back of an open truck to be driven out of camp shortly after dawn on a cool September morning. Davey was the first to be dropped off after a drive of a few miles.

The guard accompanying the prisoners in the back of the truck got out first. He gestured for Davey to get down.

'*Warten Sie hier*,' he ordered, pointing at a place at the side of the road.

Davey looked puzzled. He had assumed that they would all be working on the same farm.

'*Hiergeblieben*,' said the guard, making a threatening gesture with his rifle. '*Warten*,' he repeated.

The guard climbed aboard, banged his rifle butt on the floor of the truck signalling for it to drive on. No one said anything or called out to the diminishing figure, their silence reflecting their disbelief in the apparent trust that the work detail appeared to promise. A few hands went up, thumbs in the air.

Davey raised a thumb in response and watched the truck until it turned a bend towards a line of tall trees.

Is this a trick?

Davey was left waiting at the end of a long farm track. There were no signs of anyone working in the ploughed fields on either side. A small herd of cows inhabited a scrubby field on the other side of the road.

Despite his unnerving solitude and the sudden silence, Davey felt thankful to be outside the confines of the camp once more. He tried to ignore the slight chill of the morning and the normal agony of hunger, letting his apparent freedom embrace his senses, unlocking the almost forgotten pleasure he always felt in the countryside. Treasured memories of working on a farm near the Fechan pushed the reality of captivity to one side.

Ah wonder whit the work'll be?

The mounting feeling, verging on joy, which almost overwhelmed him was interrupted when he heard a shout: a man was striding along the track. Davey hesitated for a moment, reluctant to disobey the guard's order.

'*Komm hier*,' was all too easy to understand.

The Farming Year

The man waited for Davey, giving him an opportunity to take in the appearance of the person he assumed would be his employer.

Dressed in heavy-duty brown trousers held up by braces, he was jacketless despite the early morning chill, and his collarless shirt was open at the neck. To Davey's surprise, the man extended his hand. Davey returned the firm handshake, disbelieving the civility afforded to him.

Ah dinnae understand this. Whit's garn on?

'My name is Christoph Hoffmann. Welcome to my farm, Mister Muir.'

'You ken ... you know my name.'

Remember yer schuil English.

'Of course. Please come with me.'

The two men walked side-by-side along the track.

'You speak very good English,' said Davey.

So mony of 'em dae.

'I worked in East Anglia before the war.'

'I'm puzzled by all this,' said Davey as they drew near a group of buildings. 'Am I tae ... to work here on my own? Where are the guards?'

'We had a Russian prisoner, but we need another pair of hands for the potato harvest. You will be working here for a while. There are no guards.'

'Nae guards?'

English … English.

'No guards. I have given an undertaking that you will not attempt to escape while you are in my charge. Do you agree to that?'

'Aye. Yes. Of course.'

'You can wash your hands over there. Please to leave your boots by the door before you come into the house.'

Davey washed his hands under the tap in the yard. His socks were threadbare and full of holes.

Ah cannae garn in there in these. Why dae ah need tae garn inside onyway?

Davey dried himself as best he could on the piece of sacking hanging on a nail next to the tap before he knocked on the door of the house.

The farmer opened the door.

'I can't come in in these socks. Can you give me my work out here?'

'I will find you some socks later. Please come in.'

A short passage led into a large kitchen.

His family?

Davey stood nervously in the open doorway while everyone took a good look at him.

The farmer said something to those gathered in the kitchen before introducing each one in turn to Davey.

'My wife Agnes.'

Agnes, a youthful-looking woman with blond hair tied back, smiled briefly and returned Davey's handshake.

'*Guten Tag*, Agnes.'

'My daughter Anna.'

Anna returned Davey's handshake with unexpected firmness, fixing him with a fleeting inquisitive gaze.

'*Guten Tag*, Anna.'

'And my son Heiner.'

Heiner, a gangling youth a little taller than Davey, returned his handshake hurriedly.

'*Guten Tag*, Heiner.'

Heiner beamed from ear to ear.

'This is my family. We have some labourers, women from Poland mostly. They are already at work. Please sit down.'

Davey hesitated before taking the place that had been set for him. 'Please excuse my appearance, Mister Hoffmann, it's —'

Christoph held up a hand. 'No need to apologise; I know what it is like in the camp. You are welcome here as you are.'

Anna served Davey with the best coffee and bread he had tasted for a very long time. The bread was covered with a thin layer of butter. Davey gazed at the bread and cheese on the plate that Anna had set before him. He looked from face to face looking at him expectantly.

Davey could barely speak, choked with emotion, on the verge of tears.

'You cannot work on an empty stomach,' said Christoph. 'Eat slowly. You aren't used to proper food.'

Davey wanted to devour what was on his plate many times over. It took a great deal of restraint to eat slowly. Conversations broke out amongst the family members. To his relief, they stopped watching him eat.

After the family meal, which Davey took to be breakfast, probably taken after work had already started on the farm, Davey put his boots back on and waited for Christoph to emerge from the house.

'Give me your worn out socks. Agnes has found these old ones of Heiner's. He's only a little more than you in height.'

'Thank you very much, Mister Hoffmann.'

'Please call me Christoph.'

'I apologise if I appeared to be a bit ... it's just that I didn't expect such treatment.'

'You are still a prisoner, but you will be well-treated if you work hard.'

'I've done farm work. Show me what's to be done.'

'My son isn't able to be in the army. He is rather slow, if you understand my meaning.'

Ah thought there wis something.

'There are just three men including you, well two men and my boy, as well as my women immigrants who work here and a few part-timers, local men who are too old to be in the army.'

'Won't they object to my presence?'

'No. I've spoken to them about why you are here. My son will show you what to do. Any problems, he'll report to me.'

Heiner caught up with Davey and Christoph.

'Our first job is finish the potato harvest. We are one of the suppliers to the nearby camp. Have you done potato harvesting before?'

'Many times.'

'I'll leave you with Heiner.'

The boy took Davey by the arm and led him to a nearby field. The tops of the potatoes had been cut sufficiently for the workers to see where to dig with a wooden implement. Heiner pointed to a pile of sacks and showed Davey where to start.

They set off along adjacent rows, Davey watching how Heiner located the crop and when to stop and fill a sack.

It wasn't long before Davey's back ached. In spite of his agony, he almost kept pace with Heiner working in the next row.

Heiner looked across to see where Davey had got to, waiting for him to catch up at first, then racing ahead, leaving Davey lagging behind in their private race.

Heiner's sign language and broad grin endeared him to Davey as they raced one another. He giggled and chattered in his slurred German, between casting toothy grins in Davey's direction.

Halfway along the row, Davey got ahead for the first time only for Heiner to catch up with him. The lead changed hands several times until Heiner and Davey finished their rows together.

The potato pickers left their filled sacks at intervals along the rows. Heiner motioned to Davey that they should be carried to the end of the field. He obliged until the rows were clear of bulging sacks.

After a morning's back-breaking work, all of the workers drifted towards the end of the field where the sacks were piled. Agnes arrived, carrying an enamel jug of milk; Anna carried a tray of tin mugs and a large cloth bag over her shoulder.

Davey accepted a mug of fresh milk. It tasted warm and slightly sour, nectar to his damaged palate used to camp soup twice a day. In one morning on the farm, he had tasted more real food than he'd had in months.

The women and elderly men workers drew cloth bundles from canvas bags or jacket pockets and sat on empty sacks to eat their lunch. Anna handed Davey and Heiner a cloth bundle from her shoulder bag.

Ah'm surrounded by women.

Anna glanced at Davey over her shoulder as she walked away, eyes radiant, a smile playing around her mouth.

My, she kens she's pretty.

Davey followed the example of the others and sat on an empty sack. He placed his bundle in his lap and untied the corners: bread, a different kind of cheese from breakfast, and an apple revealed themselves.

Hells bells, an apple!

He held the shiny sphere close to his face. A lost aroma met his senses.

They'll never believe this in the hut.

After the break for lunch, Christoph brought a horse and cart along the track that led to the potato fields.

'The army let me keep one of my horses for deliveries,' he said. 'We need to take a load of sacks to the station at Erlangen. It'll take us most of the afternoon to get there and back.'

Davey helped load the cart and climbed up alongside Christoph.

'There's a jacket and a cap for you. It might be better than going about in your camp uniform. Less explaining for me to do if people ask who you are.'

Davey and Christoph unloaded the heavy sacks of potatoes in the goods yard next to the station in the town.

Erlangen looked smaller than Nürnberg to Davey, but its centre was just as busy. No one paid him any heed on the way into the town or on the way out.

Ah must look like a fairm labourer.

On their return to the farm, Christoph explained, 'It is almost time for you to be taken back to camp. You will be dropped at the end of the track early tomorrow, just like today. The potato harvest will take another week or two. You have worked hard today.'

'Thank you, Christoph. It's been a grand day. And thank you for the food.'

'Keep that to yourself. Your camp mates will be jealous. Until tomorrow.'

Best not tell 'em.

The two men exchanged a handshake before Davey set off for the end of the track. He didn't have long to wait for the returning truck.

If they dae it in reverse, ah'm last.

Davey exchanged greetings and nods with the others in the back of the truck.

'We didn't get much of a chance this morning. I'm Muir, Davey Muir.'

'Perkins.'

'Marshall.'

'Noakes.'

'Foster.'

'Harris.'

'Were ee a' at fairms?' Davey asked the others.

'Perkins and me were together,' said Marshall.

'The three of us were the last to be dropped off,' said Harris.

'Ah thought we'd be under gaird,' said Davey.

'The truck driver and guard stayed at our farm,' said Harris. 'They kept to themselves all day. Dozed in the truck most of the time.'

'No point in them driving back to camp only to come out again,' said Marshall.

'They wouldn't be able to put a guard at each farm, I suppose,' said Noakes. 'For some reason, we're trusted.'

'Whit wis yer food like?' asked Davey.

'Better than camp soup,' replied Harris.

'Thinking about food all the time could be a thing of the past as long as we get farm work,' said Harris.

'We should keep it tae oorsels,' suggested Davey. 'Oor hut mates will be envious. Agreed?'

They all nodded.

'They're bound tae ask,' said Davey. 'Let's reply with something bland. The usual black bread with some tatties, say. They'll soon give up asking. It disnae tak a genius tae guess that ee might get better food wi fairm work. Tae bad. Let's enjoy it while we can.'

'I don't know about you, but I eat very slowly,' said Perkins.

'Oor insides are no yissed tae it,' said Davey. 'We need tae be careful.'

'It's not so bad in camp if you get a food parcel,' said Foster.

'No everyone daes, though. Ah dinnae,' said Davey. 'Besides, the Germans hold them back. Wouldn't ee just like tae get intae the stores?'

The constant chatter in the back of the truck soon began to irritate their guard.

Silence and depression replaced the temporary sense of joy as the gates of Nürnberg camp swung open, admitting the farm workers to resume their life as prisoners under guard.

*

Davey worked on the potato harvest for the next two weeks. The contrast between work on the farm during the day and sleeping in a crowded, fetid hut disturbed his usual calm demeanour. The change in mood of the men leaving for the farms early each morning and returning to their wired enclosure at dusk was palpable: Davey felt it, they all felt it as the end of the harvest loomed closer, sealing off their privileged outside existence. Even on Sundays, Davey wished he was at the farm. Work was better than lying on his bed for most of the day, immersed in thoughts of home.

At the end of the next working day, following a particularly anguished Sunday, Christoph met Davey in the yard where he was washing himself and making ready to leave.

'The days are getting shorter, David.'

'You won't be wanting me when the crop is all in,' he replied.

'There is still work to be done here. You are my best worker.'

'Thank you. I do what I can.'

'I'll come to the end of the track with you. I've got a letter to send to camp. Your driver can deliver it. If there is a reply, tomorrow's driver will give it to you.'

*

Davey handed Christoph an envelope the next morning before he set off to work with Heiner; there were still potatoes to bag up and carry to the barn. Christoph approached Davey as he sat amongst the workers at the lunch break.

'Don't get up, David.'

Christoph took an empty sack from the pile and sat next to Davey.

'I didn't tell you this before. I went to school with your camp commandant, Herr Fischer.'

'Oh aye,' replied Davey.

'As you know, we are one of the farms that supplies vegetables to the camp.'

Not that we see much o' them.

'I know what you are thinking,' Christoph said. 'I don't have any influence.'

'Your potatoes are very good. We heap them up a little more in Scotland.'

'I might try that next year. Thank you for your advice.'

'Oh no, I'm hardly experienced enough to —'

'The reason I wanted to talk to you today … do you have any personal belongings in camp?'

'Not much. Why do you ask?'

'I've said this before. You are my best worker. Previous prisoners I had to let go. We had a Frenchman and a Russian last year. The Russian was lazy and the Frenchman became very ill. Not from here. Something in camp. He was repatriated eventually.'

'You asked me about my belongings.'

'Oh yes. I've arranged for you to stay here. All this travelling to and fro is inefficient.'

'Stay here! You mean overnight?'

'Yes, of course. Are you willing?'

This cannae be true.

'How can this be? I'm a prisoner of war.'

'You still will be. The difference is that I will be responsible for you.'

'I don't know what to say.'

'Do you want to think about it, David?'

'No, no. I mean, I don't know what to say. It's just that it's a surprise that it's possible.'

'It can be done. There are prisoners billeted here and there, not just at farms. We did it with the other two. There was just about enough room. It's easier for the camp authorities. I'd like you to stay on after the harvest.'

Christoph extended his hand.

Davey took it, replying, 'I'd very much like to carry on working for you and your family. It will be an honour.'

'That's settled then.'

Both men stood.

'I have a particular job for you in mind. The Russian started it, but I had to send him back. I'll tell you about it tomorrow. Bring your belongings in the morning.'

'What if the guard won't let me on the truck with my things?'

'Don't worry. I've seen to that. Until tomorrow.'

The two men shook hands again before Christoph set off in the direction of the yard.

Davey stood at the end of the potato field, his heart thudding, spreading an almost forgotten feeling of happiness throughout his body.

Ah'll show 'em how a Scotsman can work.

*

Didier's army pack and greatcoat had survived their long period of hiding beneath the hut. Davey packed the tunic and trousers given to him at Saint Clotilde, a shirt acquired at Ingolstadt and some underwear.

'Some work clothes to change into,' Davey explained to his hut mates the following morning.

The guard ignored what Davey was carrying on his back while he waited for the truck.

'Nice coat, Davey,' said Foster, as the truck bounced along familiar roads out of town.

'Yissed tae belong tae a Frenchman. He was in the bed next tae me in the hospital. He didnae survive.'

Respectful silence followed Davey's brief explanation. No one even felt the need to ask why he was carrying a pack.

'The harvest's over,' said Perkins after a while. 'What's the betting we'll be stopping this work soon. God, I'll miss the food.'

'Won't we all,' added Harris.

'P'raps next spring they'll want us back,' suggested Perkins.

'Or someone else,' said Davey.

'Besides, we're forgetting,' put in Perkins. 'When will this bloody war be over and we can all go home? There might not be a next year.'

The question posed always lurked in everyone's mind, lingering and festering silently. On this occasion it put an end to further talk for several minutes.

Work taks yer mind off it.

'See you later, Davey,' chorused the men as Davey stepped down from the truck. He raised his arm and

212

watched the truck disappear around the bend in the road.

Ah couldnae tell 'em. Ah wonder whit they'll be thinking the night. Ah couldnae tell ma hut pals either.

Davey started up the track to the yard. The chill of early autumn accompanied his morning walk to work, eagerness quickening his pace.

Christoph met Davey in the yard. 'I'll show you your quarters after breakfast.'

Quarters?

Davey's living quarters turned out to be in one of the barns, a little way from the farmhouse, across the yard.

'The Russian, Dimitri slept here. And the Frenchman, Lucien. Agnes has given it a clean.'

An iron bedstead was positioned against one wall, several grey blankets folded on its ample mattress. A small table, a wooden chair, and a faded cupboard completed the furniture. A coal-fired stove stood in the centre of the barn, its exhaust pipe rising up and out of the roof.

'This used to be the living quarters generations ago, before my grandfather built the larger house. You'll be comfortable here.'

'I'm sure I will,' said Davey, looking round the spacious barn. 'I won't let you down. I'll work hard for my keep. I'm used to that.'

This is overwhelming.

'Being here gets you out of war work, which you are not supposed to do anyway.'

'I'm very grateful for what you're doing for me,' said Davey.

This is whit prisoners think aboot a' the time: a hame, warmth, food.

'You can hang your things there and you can use that old cupboard. I'll show you where coal is kept. There's plenty, despite the naval blockade. That's something that Germany has enough of for now.'

Ah wonder if the blockade's getting worse.

'You are welcome to use the stove during the winter and to heat water for a wash. There's a steel bowl and jug you can use. Otherwise it's the tap in the yard.'

Davey left his pack on the bed and went with Heiner to gather the last of the potato harvest.

Davey lay on his bed in the barn at the end of his first day billeted at the farm. He stared at the rafters, unable to sleep on a comfortable bed, unused to being on his own at night listening to the uneasy silence.

He replayed his first evening meal with the Hoffmann family over and over again: it was the finest meal he had eaten for many, many months. There were potatoes – of course – and root vegetables similar to those grown in his part of Scotland, gravy and a strong-tasting sausage. Davey felt full for the first time since his captivity.

Anna had fixed her unsettling gaze on Davey several times during the meal, turning quickly away when her mother or father noticed.

Blaming the state of his insides on his inability to sleep, Davey turned over onto his uninjured side, Anna's gaze lingering in his mind until he fell asleep.

The cockerel alerted the farm at daybreak, jerking Davey to wake up and wonder where he was, his new surroundings settling into focus, dispelling any doubt that luck was still on his side.

*

It took Davey, Heiner, and the other farm workers a few more days to finish the harvest and store the bulging sacks of potatoes in one of the large barns.

A final trip made to the station at Erlangen left Davey in charge of the horse and cart. He wondered how the camp at Nürnberg was supplied.

Perhaps he disnae want iss tae gam there wi him.

'Take the reins, David. There's something I need to do,' said Christoph when they had unloaded the cart.

Davey sat nervously waiting, hoping that no one would approach him.

'Herr Hoffmann?' asked a roughly dressed man.

'*Dort,*' said Davey, pointing to where Christoph and another man conversed out of earshot.

The three-way conversation continued for several minutes. On one occasion when Davey peeked across warily, he could not help but notice something pass from hand to hand.

Davey got down quickly and adjusted the horse's feedbag.

'You can take that off now, David,' said Christoph. 'We are ready to go home now.'

Christoph entered the barn the following morning while Davey was getting ready for work.

Ah wonder whit's next tae be din.

'Are you comfortable in here?'

'Thank you. Yes I am.'

'Do you miss your fellow soldiers, your fellow inmates at camp?'

'Not any more. I do wonder what my hut mates are doing, but I'd rather be here than working on the roads. I did that for a while. Here, I've been very lucky. You are good people. Seems daft to think that we're at war.'

'The army and politicians are at war, David. But you and me... '

'But I'm in the army.'

'Not any more. Let's talk about this again later.'

'Christoph, can I ask you something? Do you have any books that might help me learn some German? School books, say?'

'Ah, I might have the very thing. I have books that I used before the war when I worked on a farm in Norfolk. They are German to English of course.'

'I could use them in reverse, or try to anyway.'

'You could practice on Heiner.'

'I'm getting more used to his speech now.'

'His speech is quite good. It is his other skills and learning that are rather slow.'

'He's a good lad.'

'He likes you, David.'

Davey felt a surge of pride at this admission.

'Come into the yard,' said Christoph. 'There's something I'd like to show you.'

Christoph explained that the yard was in need of re-surfacing. The Russian prisoner had made a start on the task. Now the farmer had an opportunity to get the work completed and keep the yard free of mud over the coming winter.

Christoph walked Davey to the distant top field of the farm. Stones were heaped here and there, apparently at random.

'As you can see, this is very stony ground. What is required is a systematic approach to clearing this field so that I can use it for something productive and, at the same time, make use of the stones. In the past, we laid large stones then smaller ones on top to make as smooth surface in the yard as possible. Can you do it?'

'I've worked in a quarry. Not quite the same, but I can do it.'

'You can start in the morning. We've got the last of the potatoes to deliver today.'

'What tools will I need?'

'You tell me.'

'A wheelbarrow, a rake. That's about it. If most of the stones are on or near to the surface, I can dig for what's lower down.'

'Clear what you can first, then I will be able to see if I can plough.'

Christoph gave Davey a pair of worn leather gloves after breakfast the next morning and showed him where the tools were kept. Davey collected what he needed and wheeled the wheelbarrow to the top field.

He stood and surveyed the huge task ahead of him, overjoyed at the prospect of labouring outside for the foreseeable future. He would miss working with Heiner, but he was glad to be working on his own and less of a burden to Christoph.

Davey took the photograph of Kate and Marion out of the top pocket of his tunic, smiled back at his family, returned the photograph and hung his tunic on a fence pole.

'Ah could walk away, escape. Naebdie wid ken fi ages,' Davey said aloud. 'Where the hell would ah garn?'

Pit the Hofmann family in danger of their lives. Ah couldnae dae that.

'C'mon Davey Muir, get working. Deserve their trust,' he said.

Davey decided to ignore the efforts of Dimitri and make his own plan of action.

He made a mental picture of the field divided into strips. He marked the width of each strip by placing large stones along the grass verge at one end of the field where it ran alongside a neat hedge. The field was soon divided up into manageable sections. Davey planned to face the hedge and work backwards, piling the large stones as he went. When he reached the other end of the field, which was a long way off up a gentle slope, he would use the wheelbarrow to clear each strip of piles of stones and heap these at the starting end of each strip. The next part of his scheme would be to gather the smaller stones and make a separate heap of these at the end of each strip, much like picking potatoes.

Davey imagined Marion and Davie asking him questions when they grew up.

Whit did ee dae in the war, Daddy?

Cleared a field of stanes.

Fi whit?

That's enough questions.

'When would you like me to start on the yard?' Davey asked Christoph at the end of the first day of his mammoth task.

'I leave it up to you. I like what you are doing. When you think that you have got enough, we can load the cart and move the stones down to the yard. I'll leave you to it.'

Davey toiled in the field of stones for day after day until, by the end of October, heaps of various sized stones had built up at the end of the field.

Davey was more than content with his universe of raking, digging and shifting stones, punctuated by Anna bringing his lunch bundle. Few words were exchanged, though Davey's *'Danke Dir'* was always met with a flashing smile before Anna walked swiftly away, her heavy boots no impediment to a lightness of step.

One mild day in early November, Davey stopped what he was doing when Anna appeared, threw his gloves on the ground and wiped his hands on the front of his trousers. Instead of handing him his bundle as usual, Anna suddenly grabbed Davey's hand and held it firmly to her breast.

Davey tried to pull his hand away, but Anna held on tightly with both hands. Davey was taken aback by her urgency and fervour.

'Nein, *nein*, Anna. *Tue das nicht.*'

Anna's eyes and voice pleaded; Davey stopped trying to tug his hand away.

'Anna, *ich bin verheiratet und habe Kinder.*'

Anna's grip softened; Davey slowly withdrew his hand from her grasp. Anna muttered angry sounding words and pushed Davey hard in the chest with both hands, forceful enough to knock him backwards onto a pile of stones. She threw his food bundle onto the ground, turned, shouted something incomprehensible and walked quickly away, muttering and waving her arms above her head.

Davey, still in shock, sat where he had landed. The incident lasted no more than a few seconds, long enough to destroy his private universe of contented solitude. There would be no more laughing with Heiner after the evening meal when he practised his German on the boy in the barn; no more meals with the family; no more living an almost normal life.

Nae mair onything. God knows whit the family'll say.

Davey left his lunch where it lay scattered on the ground. He got to his feet, put on his tunic and gathered his tools ready to return to the yard. He didn't have long to wait until he saw Christoph striding quickly up the field.

Here goes. Face the music, laddy.

Davey stood next to the wheelbarrow, awaiting the inevitable outcome.

Kate's Story

Glasgow: Cadogan Street

Nothing prepared Kate for the shock of Glasgow. The sight and sound of the city overwhelmed her senses and quashed her spirit. The dark brown buildings pressed in on one another and seemed to threaten to lean over Kate whenever she ventured outside number 49. The constant rattle of trams passing by the entrance to the tenement always took her aback. Even the sky reflected the gloom of the city.

The vivid contrast with the village plagued Kate's waking hours. She became homesick only a matter of days after arriving, yearning for the whitewashed houses and longing for her family. The city deepened Kate's loneliness and despair. She felt unwelcome, unwanted and lost in regret.

It soon became apparent to Kate that Thomas was fortunate to have occupied the two-room tenement on his own. That this was out of the ordinary was brought home to her when she used the washhouse in the back court for the first time.

'Where'd Thomas find ee?' asked the only other occupant of the back court, a short, plump woman hanging out her washing.

The woman's sarcastic tone of voice upset Kate.

'Ecclefechan,' she replied.

'Where the hell's that?'

'Down south. Near Lockerbie. I'm Kate.'

'Listen, Kate. The tenements in this block are only fi families. Thomas used tae have a woman here. You're no supposed to have only two adults. Think yourself lucky, dearie, for the time being by the look of ee.'

The woman left before Kate could say anything.

Thomas was away from home for most of the week, delivering to customers. Kate had no choice but to keep the troubling revelation about Thomas to herself.

Kate challenged Thomas when he returned late on Friday afternoon. 'Whi wus the woman who used tae live here?'

Thomas put down the evening newspaper. 'Ah, who've you been talking to?'

Kate looked up from her sewing. 'She didnae give me her name. Ah tried tae be friendly, told her mine and where ah come fri.'

'Don't you bother about her. She's just a busybody.'

'Whi is she?'

'It's probably Lizzie Donaldson from the floor above. A well-known gossip,' said Thomas as he picked up his newspaper.

'No her. The woman whi lived here.'

Thomas didn't answer.

'Wis there a bairn?'

Thomas met the fury in Kate's eyes.

'Yes, there was a child. They left last year. I'm sorry you found out this way.'

'Sorry ... sorry! Is that a' ee can say. Ee bring iss here ...' Kate banged the table with both fists. 'Ee wernae garn tae tell iss, were ee?' said Kate, her voice quivering with anger.

'I would have ... I would,' pleaded Thomas.

Kate flung back her chair. 'Ah'm sleeping in the parlour the night. Dinnae ee dare come near iss. Ee hear. Ee've deceived iss, Thomas. Ah cannae garn hame and ah cannae call this hame. And ee thought that ah'd bring ma bairns tae live here in this awfy place.'

Thomas had no answer. He averted his eyes from Kate's reddening cheeks and swollen eyes.

'Ah'll fin somewhere tae garn in the moran.'

'You've only been here five minutes. You can't just go.'

'Dinnae try and stop iss. Ee've tricked iss, made a fool of iss.'

'Where'll you go?'

'The Poorhouse.'

Thomas leant across the table and gripped Kate's arm. 'You can't go there. Listen, Kate. Stay here until the baby is born. At least until then.'

Kate sighed deeply, pushing Thomas's hand away.

'You'll be safe here,' said Thomas. 'You need to be somewhere safe. I promise to leave you alone.'

And so, an uneasy truce was agreed. Kate washed and cooked and kept the tenement clean and tidy. Thomas handed over money for housekeeping and kept to his side of the arrangement: they slept apart.

*

Jean was born at five in the morning on Sunday, 16th September 1917. The Maternity Hospital allowed Kate and her baby to leave on the following Thursday.

There was no one to take Kate home. She walked to Cadogan Street, her arms aching from carrying her belongings and baby Jean. Thomas wasn't at home: he wasn't expected until the weekend.

Kate arrived home exhausted, but glad to be on her own with Jean. She fought tiredness, fed her daughter and put her down in the cot that Thomas had brought back from one of his customers.

'At least that shows some kindness,' she said as she settled her daughter. 'Whit's tae become of iss, Jean? Whit's tae become of iss?'

Jean looked up at her mother and waved her arms about. Soon she was asleep.

'Ee dinnae ken the half o' it, dae ee?'

Jean's cries woke Kate. She lifted Jean from her cot and fed her. Kate's thoughts turned to her other children every time she fed Jean, or put her down.

Ah wonder whit they're daein. They willnae be coming here.

Kate heard the door on Saturday morning.

Thomas threw his jacket on the back of a chair. 'Don't get up, Kate. Can I hold her?'

'Wait until she's been fed.'

'She's beautiful.'

'Aye, that she is.'

Thomas held Jean awkwardly.

'Pass her back noo. Ah'll pit her doon.'

Thomas sat in silence.

'Ah'll no be staying here, not noo she's wi iss.'

Thomas sat still, looking sullen.

'There's nothing ee can dae tae change ma mind,' said Kate.

Thomas picked up his jacket and left. She heard the front door go.

Probably gaen tae the pub.

Their tenuous arrangement held, keeping Kate and Jean out of the Home for Deserted Mothers that was only a few streets away.

Davey's Story

The Price of Rejection

Both men spoke at the same time.

'You first,' Christoph repeated sternly.

'I'm finished here. Will you take me back to camp now or does the truck still pass by?'

Christoph made no reply.

'I didn't do anything. I didn't lead her on,' said Davey, arms outstretched in a gesture of appeal.

'We trusted you, we all trusted you. Pack your things. I will return you to Nürnberg in the morning.'

'Now, please.'

'It is not convenient now. In the morning.'

'Can I tell you what happened?'

'I am not interested,' said Christoph, angrily. 'You have abused our trust, especially my daughter's. She must be ten years below your age. What did you think you were doing?' he shouted.

'I didn't do anything,' pleaded Davey. 'Please believe me.'

'What! Over the word of my daughter? I want you out of here by the morning,' Christoph shouted, jabbing Davey in the chest before striding off the way he had come.

Davey sat on the nearest heap of stones, drained of emotional strength, his head buried in his hands.

'C'mon, Davey Muir,' he said aloud. 'How the hell did you let that happen?'

Davey lifted the wheelbarrow and set off for the farmyard.

Ah hope ah dinnae see onyone.

Davey returned the tools and slipped into the barn, apparently unnoticed.

He lay on his bed, letting the hours go by until darkness filled the barn. He thought about the family sitting around the kitchen table.

Ah can guess whit they're saying.

'Nae good lying here ony longer,' he said quietly.

Davey's stomach rumbled loudly.

Ah can last oot until midday soup in the moran.

Davey swung his legs onto the floor, rubbed his aching forehead and fumbled beneath his bed for the candle. Its flickering light cast a yellow pool on the dusty floor of the barn.

He reached to the end of the bed for his tunic and undid the top pocket. It was empty.

He remembered that he had put Kate's photograph in the cupboard drawer; he didn't want it to get damp while his tunic was hanging on the post near where he was working in the field.

Davey slid open the drawer. Fragments of the photograph lay scattered.

'NO! Oh, no.' Davey gripped the sides of the drawer. 'How did she ken it wis there?' he said aloud.

Davey placed the pieces on the bed, pushing them together like a jigsaw.

Ah'm so sorry, Kate, so very sorry.

Kate's delicate face was almost intact in the top left piece.

Perhaps ah could stick 'em together? Ross has some glue.

Davey left the pieces where they lay and set about emptying the drawer and cupboard of his modest belongings. He left the jacket and cap given to him by Christoph where they hung on a hook behind the door of the barn next to his greatcoat.

Davey used some of the cold water that remained in the bowl to wash himself.

Ah'm no garn intae the yard tae fetch ony mair.

He packed his clothes in Didier's backpack and laid it and the torn photograph on the table before turning in for the last time at the Hoffmann's farm.

Back tae the hut in the moran then.

Davey hardly slept on his last night. Images of Anna and Kate flickered through his waking thoughts and shrouded his dreams when fitful sleep did come.

The sound of the horse and cart in the yard jolted Davey awake.

Damn, ah missed the cockcrow.

Davey dressed hurriedly just in time to hear the barn door open.

'Ah'm ready, *Herr* Hoffmann,' said Davey as he shouldered his pack. 'Ah wished she hadn't done this though.'

Davey held out the fragments of photograph before sliding them into his tunic pocket.

Christoph held out his hand without a word.

Davey showed him the pieces.

Christoph, stony-faced and still silent, handed them back, avoiding eye contact.

'Might I sit down?' he said, crossing to the table.

'It's your barn,' replied Davey.

Christoph sat on the bed, sighed deeply and leant against the wall.

'Please sit down, David,' he said.

Davey sat on the only chair and faced Christoph.

'Where can I start?' said Christoph with a sigh. 'Where indeed?' he added, as if talking to himself.

'David, Heiner saw what happened,' he said suddenly.

'Heiner?'

'He was mending the fence in the orchard.'

'But you believed Anna. You had to.'

'Heiner was very upset this morning. He didn't say anything yesterday when I told everyone that you are leaving. But this morning he cried uncontrollably.'

'Even so, ah'll away. Ah cannae stay.'

'You've slipped into dialect.'

'Best if ee start afresh with another prisoner.'

'No, David. I'm not sending you back. Anna has done wrong. That is the end of the matter. We will be sending her to her grandmother's for a while.'

'Please don't send her away. It's me you should be sending away.'

'It's just for a short while. She hasn't seen my mother for some time. It will be good for her.'

'I'm so sorry about what happened. It was so sudden. She took me unawares.'

'David, do not fret.'

'You've picked up a Scottish word.'

Christoph managed a weak smile.

'If you want to stay, please unpack and go over for some breakfast. I'm taking Anna into town now, so perhaps you should wait until we've gone.'

So that's whit the cart's fi.

Christoph got up from the bed and started for the door.

'*Herr* Hoffman, when will Anna return?'

'I don't know. We'll see. And less of the "*Herr* Hoffmann*" please. You know that you can still call me Christoph.'

Davey waited until the cart left before he crossed the yard and went into the house.

An uneasy quiet greeted Davey when he took his usual seat at the breakfast table. Agnes returned his '*Guten Morgen*' tersely; Heiner did not look up from his plate.

'*Ich gehe arbeiten*, Agnes,' said Davey when he had finished.

'*Heiner wird Dir Dein Essen bringen*,' she replied in a detached manner.

Davey changed into his old breeches and tunic, collected his tools and set off for the top field.

When he arrived and got ready to continue clearing stones, Davey hung his tunic in its usual place and stared at the exact spot where less than a day ago his future at the farm had evaporated.

'Oh, Anna. Whit have ee din?' he said aloud.

Birds had devoured most of yesterday's lunch and pecked holes in the cloth bundle.

Davey cleared the mess, shook out the soiled cloth and put it into his pocket.

'Noo, where wis ah?'

The height of the weak November sun, accompanied by a brief pang of disappointment, signalled a break for lunch.

Heiner waved as he rounded the end of the hedge.
Hope he's in a better mood.

Heiner chatted amiably as he sat next to Davey on a pile of large stones. Davey nodded as if he understood.

Suddenly, Heiner stopped chewing his hunk of bread and looked at Davey with a very serious expression.

'*Es tut uns leid*,' he said, spreading his arms wide. '*Es tut uns leid*, David' he repeated, a tone of appeal in his voice.

Ah think he's saying sorry. Nae need, son.

'*Es ist gut*, Heiner. *Ist gut.*'

Heiner's reassuring grin returned.

'*Wollen wir heute Abend Deutsch lernen?*' Davey asked.

Heiner nodded vigorously between mouthfuls of cheese.

The mood at the evening meal was more relaxed than it had been at breakfast.

Christoph nae here again.

'*Bereit*, David?' said Heiner.

'*Danke*, Agnes,' said Davey.

She held up her hand when Davey tried to gather up his utensils and spoke to Heiner who was already half way out of the door.

'*Ein gutter Junge*, Agnes,' said Davey when Heiner had left.

'*Meistens*,' she replied. '*Meistens*,' she repeated before clearing the table.

One tae look up.

'*Gute Nacht*,' said Davey.

'*Gute Nacht*, David.'

First time she's used ma name fi ages.

'A'reet, Heiner. Where were we?'

236

Heiner looked puzzled. He flipped the English-to-German phrase book open where they had left off two evenings ago.

'Our first lesson since … '

Heiner looked blankly at Davey.

'Sorry, son. *Du bist der Boss.*'

Heiner started at the top of the page of the section with the heading *Das Wetter*, pronouncing each phrase and inviting Davey to follow.

'*Es ist heiß,*' said Heiner.

'*Es its heiß,*' repeated Davey. 'It is hot.'

'*Es ist kalt.*'

'That's an easy one. It is cold, I mean *es ist kalt,*' said Davey.

After a few more weather phrases, Heiner turned to a section that they had worked on a few weeks previously: *Family*.

He closed the book and tested Davey by pointing to himself.

'Ah, we've done this before. Heiner, *Sohn von* Agnes *und* Christoph. Agnes, *Mutter von* Heiner. Christoph, *Vater von* Heiner'

Heiner looked pleased.

'Christoph, *Vater von Anna.*'

'Anna, *Shwester von* … '

Heiner's face fell at the mention of his sister.

'*Ach nein,*' said Davey. 'Let's do something else.'

They turned to the section on useful phrases. Heiner pointed to Davey, then to himself.

He wants me to …

'*Guten Morgen* is good morning.'

Heiner made a good attempt. '*Einfach,*' he added.

'*Gute Nacht* is good night,' said Davey.

'*Einfach.* Gud … night,' replied Heiner.

'One more. *Wie geht's* is how are you.'

'How … are … you?' said Heiner.

'Very good,' replied Davey. '*Sehr gut.*'

Davey closed the book, pointed to his wrist and yawned expansively.

Heiner found it very funny that there was no watch, but he took the hint.

'Gud … night … David,' said Heiner, pausing at the door of the barn.

'*Sehr gut*, Heiner. Good night.'

Davey opened the book and repeated aloud the words and phrases he had practised with Heiner.

There'll come a time when ah'm a faither tae groan up bairns.

He looked up '*meistens*' in the dictionary section: *mostly*.

A knock on the barn door interrupted Davey's verbal exercises. A weary looking Christoph appeared. Davey closed the book.

'Don't let me stop you, David,' he said, sitting heavily with a sigh. 'Your first lesson since … How are you two getting on with the book?'

'I'm slow, but I'm picking up bits and pieces. He's a grand wee teacher. Three times a week with Heiner is good. Leaves me time to practise on my own.'

'I wonder if I can find a better chair,' said Christoph distractedly. 'Or another chair,' he added.

He seems troubled.

Davey leant forward intently, hoping to turn the conversation to more serious matters. 'Christoph, there's something that I'd like to ask you. It'll be Christmas soon. I imagine that you take time off work. There might be less work to do on the farm. Will I be returned to camp?'

238

'No. We had prisoners here last Christmas.'

'In that case, there's something I'd like to make. There's several pieces of spare wood in the workshop. I won't want much.'

'Help yourself. You know where the tools are.'

'I can fix that chair while I'm at it. Easy enough to stop it wobbling.'

'You know woodwork as well as farm work? We are indeed fortunate to have you here.'

Christoph sighed again and stared at the wall before turning to face Davey.

'I think we know each other well enough to be honest with one another.'

Davey nodded.

I wonder whit's coming.

'To be honest with you, David. Keeping the farm going, doing business where I can is getting more difficult. I'm neglecting my family.'

Business on the side?

'Sending Anna away and trying to be a father to Heiner – Agnes just gets on with it. She is strong, stronger than me.'

Christoph paused, a shadow of sadness passed across his features.

'Keeping the farm going and holding my family together … ' Christoph trailed off, as if talking to himself. 'Heiner can be difficult. You haven't seen how he can be. And as for my wayward daughter,' he said with a resigned shrug.

'That's partly my fault,' said Davey.

'No. Agnes and me agreed to send her away for a while. She'll learn.'

Christoph placed his hands on his knees, straightened his back and looked more cheerful.

'You will let me know if Heiner loses his temper, or misbehaves?'

'I will.'

Perhaps a' he wanted wis a man-to-man chat?

Christoph stood to leave the barn.

'We all want this stupid war to be over. The naval blockade is hurting the whole country. People are suffering. There are food shortages.'

'Not here yet though,' said Davey.

'We're fortunate that we can feed ourselves and make a living from what we do here, with your help – don't forget that. Goodnight, David.'

And his other workers.

Davey filled the steel bowl with hot water and treated himself to a thorough stand-up wash. He also washed a shirt and some underwear before he turned in.

Ah'll start the moran's night.

Davey lit a candle and sorted through the oddments of wood that were scattered around the benches of the farm's workshop until he had made a pile of knot-free pieces large enough for what he had in mind. He earmarked a few that he could practice on. If he worked every day after work and after his German lessons, he would finish in time.

Davey hid each piece in the barn when he was satisfied that it was perfected, sanded and attractively treated with some wood stain that he found amongst the tins and bottles on one of the shelves. He responded vaguely when Christoph asked him what he was making.

'*Ein Geheimnis*,' he replied, looking around the kitchen table during the evening meal.

The family exchanged glances and conversation that Davey didn't follow, with the exception of the word for 'secret'.

A Family Christmas

Davey continued his feverish work for several weeks. He had to take care not to upset Heiner who showed an interest in following Davey to the workshop after his German lessons.

'*Ein Geheimnis*,' said Davey touching his nose in the hope that the gesture meant the same in Germany. '*Das ist geheim*,' added Davey in the hope that drawing the boy into a conspiracy would work.

'*Sehr gut*, David,' said Heiner after each occasion when he tried to follow Davey. '*Du gewinnst*,' he added, touching the side of his nose and winking for extra effect.

Davey made a box out of lightweight wood when the work was finished, lightly stained it and arranged for the top and front of the box to be easily removed.

His anxiety grew as Christmas Eve approached. He could not throw off the feeling that he was encroaching upon the Hoffmann family. He was an outsider and would be in the way.

Camp Christmas wis easy. P'raps ah'll just stay in the barn.

Work on the farm continued up to Christmas Eve. Davey was spreading a bed of small stones on a patch in the yard when Christoph approached.

'The yard is looking much better than last winter. You have done a very good job.'

Davey stopped tamping down the stones with his homemade wooden tool.

'I've seen you use that before,' said Christoph. 'Good idea.'

'I can get a good solid surface with this.'

'The yard is nearly finished,' said Christoph.

'Almost. The field is clear. It might be ready to plough soon,' said Davey.

'You haven't found the whole thing boring?'

'No. I like working on my own. You gave me a job to do and it's almost done. What happens now? Back to camp?'

'No, David; I need you here. I couldn't get a local or an immigrant to work as hard as you do. You are my best worker. You know I can't afford to pay you. Some of the farmers in this part of Germany are struggling to make a living for their families. I couldn't do without you, but I am embarrassed that you are free labour, slave labour to some.'

'Bed and board is good enough for me, *Herr* Hoffmann.'

'How many times … please address me by my first name,' said Christoph with a smile. 'The real reason I have sought you out is to invite you to our Christmas Eve supper.'

It took a moment for Davey to answer. 'You and your family are very kind. I couldn't possibly intrude on your celebrations.'

'I insist. Anna has returned. Our family is together and we all request your presence.'

Anna's back!

'But… '

'I insist.'

'Then I accept. And thank you, all of you.'

'You can thank us later. I hear that your German is coming on.'

'I wouldn't say that. I've been practising. Heiner has managed to teach me even though he doesn't understand English. We've muddled along somehow.'

'Why don't you pack up now. Give yourself time to get ready. It'll be dark in an hour.'

Get ready! With whit?

Davey spent the remainder of the afternoon cleaning his boots and brushing dust off his trousers. He put on his recently washed spare shirt, Heiner's cast-off jacket and made every effort to make himself look presentable. He trimmed his moustache and beard with a pair of scissors that Agnes had let him use after Christoph suggested that she cut his hair.

Davey looked in the mirror that he had made by polishing the lid of an old tin. 'Davey Muir, ee'll hae tae dae,' he said aloud. 'Four Christmases away fri hame. How mony mair?'

One of the previous occupants of the barn had left a worn-out hairbrush. Davey had washed it thoroughly following its discovery. He used it to brush his hair back from his forehead before he picked up his wooden box and stepped into the yard.

The light from the kitchen window cast a yellow glow. Davey stood for a moment, reflecting on the many days he had spent resurfacing the yard.

Ah hope it lasts.

The evening had grown cold. The grey clouds of the morning had given way to reveal a bright moon and constellations familiar to Davey.

Ah wonder if Kate is looking at the same stars. Ah wonder whit she is daein the night?

Davey clutched the box tightly, crossed the yard and knocked.

Anna opened the door. '*Komm, bitte,*' she said, looking unashamedly at Davey.

Davey left his boots in the passage and entered the kitchen. Forgotten aromas of Christmas flooded his senses, reminiscent of home. The room smelled strongly of roasting, mingled with rich fruit. Davey dabbed at the corner of his mouth with his handkerchief.

'*Frohe Weihnachten,*' chorused the Hoffmann family.

Davey went from one family member to the next wishing each, '*Frohe Weihnachten*'. Anna held his gaze the longest. There was a look in her eyes that reassured Davey and troubled him at the same time.

Heiner said, 'Merry Christmas, David.'

'Merry Christmas to you too, Heiner.'

Davey went over to the side table where he had set down the box. He cleared his throat, '*Das ist mein Geschenk für die Familie.*' Davey opened the lid and lowered the front of the box. '*Es ist ein —*'

'We can see what it is,' exclaimed Christoph.

Everyone was talking at once; Davey could not make out what anyone was saying. The family stood around the open box, pointing and commenting excitedly, occasionally glancing at Davey who was standing at the other side of the room.

Anna crossed the kitchen and grasped Davey's hand in hers, '*Die ist so schön.*'

'It is indeed very beautiful, David,' said Christoph. 'We call a nativity scene "*Weihnachtskrippe*": Christmas crib. We will treasure this. It will come out every Christmas. After the war, we will think of you.'

'The only thing I could give you for Christmas is something I could make,' said Davey.

'It must have taken … it did take you a long time. I can remember when you started. You are good with wood: the detail … '

'I've had lots of practise at home.'

'Let us sit,' announced Christoph.

Davey looked around the kitchen while Anna and Agnes ladled vegetable soup into bowls. A fire blazed in the grate, sprigs of holly adorned the mantelshelf and a modest Christmas tree in one corner of the room sheltered a few presents beneath its decorated branches.

Ah bet they dinnae hae much tae give tae each other.

The next dish comprised roast chicken and roast potatoes.

They must've killed yin o' their ain.

This delicious course was followed by a kind of fruitcake that was new to Davey. Anna's gestures showed that she had made it.

Davey showed his appreciation, '*Das ist ein serh guter kuchen.*'

Anna laughed at Davey's pronunciation in a way that was not mocking, but was warm and friendly.

Christoph produced a bottle after the meal. 'This is a fruit liqueur made by Agnes. A kind of schnapps. I suggest a small one. You probably haven't touched alcohol for a very long time. You should be careful.'

'I haven't touched a drop in over three years.'

'I think we can risk a small one. Sip it slowly.'

Each member of the family proposed a toast. Davey joined in raising his glass to each one, not minding what he was wishing for. He gathered that Christoph's toast included wishing those gathered

246

together a Happy Christmas: he heard the word *'Weihnachten'* several times.

At length, a languid silence fell across the table as all eyes turned to Davey.

Oh, oh. Ma turn.

'Freiden nicht Kreig.' Nods and murmurs of approval accompanied slow sips of Agnes's liqueur in response to Davey's wish for peace. *'Danke für alles,'* added Davey. Appreciative voices again greeted Davey's stabs at expressing himself in German.

They seem tae appreciate ma efforts.

'I don't know how she's done it, but Agnes has got hold of some real coffee,' said Christoph when the toasts had been completed.

Agnes filled china mugs from a white enamel pot.

'It's filtered in the pot, in a lined bag,' explained Christoph.

'We only drink tea at home. Coffee is too expensive,' said Davey. 'I've had more coffee over here than in my whole life.'

'What does this one taste like?' asked Christoph.

Davey carefully sipped the dark liquid. It smelt slightly nutty. 'It tastes a bit like the Christmas cake that my ma makes. I've never tasted coffee as good as this.'

'Es ist sehr gut,' said Davey to Agnes.

Agnes smiled.

After the meal, the family clustered around the nativity scene again, Anna picking up items and repeating their German word for Davey's benefit.

Ah'll never remember a' these.

Only Heiner remained at his place at the table, dejection replacing his usual happy countenance.

Christoph glanced knowingly at Davey, who guessed what was upsetting the boy.

Ah hope ah dinnae get this wrong after a' the practise.

'Heiner, *ich werde Dich holtzarbeiten lehren.*'

Heiner's smile returned as he said something to his father.

'That's a very kind offer, David. He's never shown an aptitude for practical things other than the work here. Do you think he'll learn?'

'Let's see. We'll start with something easy. I think he'll impress you. Heiner teaches me German. I teach him woodwork.'

Davey showed the family how to close the front and top of the nativity scene before taking his leave.

'*Danke Euch allen, danke.*'

Another round of handshakes and a final exchange of '*Frohe Weinachten*' accompanied Davey to the front door. He looked back at the house when he reached the barn.

'Ah wonder if the others on fairms get this treatment?' he said aloud.

Whit wis yer Christmas like, Kate?

Kate's Story

News from Home

Kate wrote very few letters to Chrissie. She had difficulty expressing the numbness that clouded her life with Thomas. She wrote about mundane matters until Jean was born: afterwards, her letters became mournful.

'Ah'm away tae the post,' she told Thomas as she gathered up Jean.

'What do you tell your sister about me?' he said.

'Dinnae worry. Ah dinnae talk about ee,' replied Kate, as she buttoned up her worn out overcoat.

'It's cold. Is Jean wrapped up?'

'Ee can see she is,' said Kate over her shoulder, on her way out of the door to the stairs.

'We'll tell her we had a miserable Christmas, Jean.' said Kate on the way down, 'The worst Christmas of ma whole life.'

Cadogan Street
Glasgow
January 7th '18

Dearest Chrissie.

I hope you all had a good Christmas and I hope that Marion and Davie are well. I miss them terribly, especially this Christmas. And what a miserable Christmas and Hogmanay it was, mostly on my own as Thomas had to work extra providing for the pubs and hotels.

It was my birthday today. I didn't tell Thomas. Twenty-three today and my life is in ruins. Davey has gone and my two are miles away.

Thomas wants me to stay but I can't. I feel trapped. If I stay, Jean will be looked after. Thomas provides for all three of us. If I come home, how will I look after Jean, Marion and Davie? And how can I face the village. The shame of it all.

Perhaps I could stay in Lockerbie or Annan, close enough to the Fechan to make a fresh start. Would you make some enquiries for me please. There might be more work in the town.

Oh, Chrissie. How will I get my family together again?

I'll close now. Write again soon.

Love,
Kate.

In turn, Chrissie didn't write often; she thought that news from home would upset her sister.

Kate received two letters on the same day in early April. Her sister had never sent two together. She dithered about which one to open first.

Commercial Place
The Fechan
April 20th '18

Dear Kate.

You must come home. Father has been wounded and is in hospital in France.

Can you come as soon as possible? Mother is in a terrible state.

Love,
Chrissie.

p.s. P O for ticket enclosed.

The other letter, written the day before, made no mention of the news about their father.

Kate packed her homemade carpetbag and put Jean in her cot while she wrote a note for Thomas.

Ah'll tell him no tae come efter iss.

Kate walked to Argyle Street railway station, with her carpetbag over her left shoulder, leaving both arms free to carry Jean. There was just over an hour to wait for the next train to Carlisle.

The noise and smoke in the station concourse made Jean cry. Kate found a Women Only waiting room, fed Jean and willed the minutes to bring her closer to escape from the city.

Kate could see the clock that hung from the high roof of the concourse. She moved to another seat in the hope that time would pass quickly if she couldn't see the large clock face. She moved back to her original seat when she realised that she couldn't hear the announcements.

'Alright, love?' asked an elderly woman.

'Fine, thanks. Ah'm waiting fi the Cairle … oh, ah should be garn.'

'Take care, love.' The woman held the door open. 'And the wee un.'

Kate thanked the woman and made her way through the bustle of the concourse.

Grey suburbs gave way to fields and low hills, interrupted by names of stations halting temporarily outside the carriage window. Each station put distance between Kate and her short, troubled life with Thomas. She wanted to look ahead and let the train take her, never to return.

Jean slept in her mother's lap for most of the journey. Kate wondered how Davie and Marion would respond to her and to their sister Jean. Despite making a clean break from Cadogan Street, new worries crept into Kate's mind. She fretted how she would look after three children. Thomas had given her money; now she had no financial means. Underlying all these worries, Kate felt ill at ease about what village folk would think of her.

The journey gave Kate time to reflect on her year away from her home and family. She promised herself that she would never leave the children or the village again. The agony of being an absent mother would soon be over.

Another station prompted Kate to shut out her apprehension and see where she was: Lockerbie – only a few minutes more.

Jean stirred and wriggled in her mother's lap as the train drew to a halt.

We're hame, Jean.

Kate let the window down and turned the outside door handle, stepped onto the platform at Ecclefechan station before reaching into the carriage for her bag. She waited until the train could be heard no longer.

Kate stood on the deserted platform. Her chest felt tight and her head ached.

'Well, Jean, let's the two o' iss face them a',' Kate said aloud.

A warm breeze accompanied Kate as she walked along the Lockerbie to Carlisle Road towards Ecclefechan. Familiar fields and the smells of nearby farms cleared her senses, driving out the images and noise of Glasgow. Kate hoped that memories of her brief life away from home would soon recede. She had left the village as a widow with hope of a new life with Thomas, to find her trust in him cruelly dashed; she returned determined to remain a widow.

Kate hesitated at the top of the hill that led into the High Street. The comfort of recognition and familiarity held her gaze. Someone went into the hotel. The knot of elderly men gathered, as usual, outside the corner shop. Everything looked unchanged, hiding the loss of young men like her husband who would never be seen in the High Street taking their turn to linger on the corner in their old age.

Home beckoned mother and child.

Davey's Story

Master to the Apprentice

There were a few maintenance jobs to do during the Christmas period, after which time the work and routine on the farm soon returned to normal and Davey was fully occupied.

Heiner proved to be a willing pupil. Davey showed him how to look after his father's tools and demonstrated how to use planes, chisels, and the spoke shave. After a few lessons practising the basics of woodwork, Davey drew a diagram of a large wooden spoon on the dusty floor.

'*Für Deine Mutter*,' Davey told him.

Heiner beamed with delight.

Davey selected a suitable piece of wood for Heiner to practise shaping the spoon. He practised over and over again during the next few evenings, abandoning several attempts. Heiner's patience and tenacity delighted Davey. Having an eager pupil made an unexpected addition to life on the farm.

By late January, Heiner had reached the stage when he had to gouge a concave depression in the end of his piece of wood. Davey showed him how to achieve the most difficult part of the task, insisting that Heiner practise on some blocks of wood with chisels of various sizes.

When Davey felt that Heiner was ready, he supervised him on the delicate and tricky task of shaping the end of the piece of wood. Heiner looked disappointed to begin with. Removing wood proved to be a slow and frustrating process. Davey encouraged him to chisel out small pieces at a time until, after several sessions, a sufficiently concave depression emerged from the end of the spoon's long handle.

Davey made a smoothing cloth by gluing sand onto pieces of sacking. Heiner rubbed the surface of the spoon until his fingers were red and raw. He would not stop until he was satisfied that the concave part was perfectly smooth.

Davey looked on from what he was doing on the other side of the workbench.

Whit a worker!

The remaining task was to knock the corners off the reverse side of the spoon and smooth that part. Heiner carefully and painstakingly chiselled away at unwanted wood, then went to work with the sand cloths until the back of the spoon looked perfect.

Man and boy worked in near silence most evenings bent over their work, the sound of tools on wood sending motes of sawdust floating in the candlelight.

One evening when Davey was repairing some rake handles, Heiner put down his sanding cloth and held up his spoon, turning it over and stroking its surfaces. Davey stopped what he was doing.

It's taken him weeks. Whit a grand lad.

Heiner handed his finished work to Davey.

'*Sehr, sehr gut,* Heiner. *Sehr gute Arbeit. Sehr gut gemacht.*'

Heiner grinned broadly in response to his teacher's praise.

Davey's design had deliberately left a square end for hanging the spoon and a flat narrow handle to make it straightforward to fashion. Davey showed Heiner how to make a hole in spare pieces of wood. Heiner practised a few times before turning his attention to the end of the spoon. Time spent with a round file completed the task.

Heiner could barely contain his impatience while the light wood stain dried. He and Davey tidied the workshop and swept the floor of sawdust to take Heiner's mind off the spoon hanging tantalisingly on a nail from one of the beams. Heiner kept looking at his spoon while he and Davey cleaned and put tools away and tipped sawdust into the oil drum in the corner of the workshop.

'*Noch nicht*, Heiner, *nein*,' said Davey just in time to stop the boy from reaching up to touch the spoon too soon.

When sufficient drying time had elapsed, Davey put Heiner out of his misery. '*Ist es fertig.*'

Heiner touched the curved rim of the spoon gingerly. He turned to Davey, '*Es ist trocken?*'

Must mean 'dry'.

'*Gut.*'

Heiner turned this work over and over, smiling to himself.

Ee can be very proud, laddy. That wis no an easy piece tae start wi.

'*Komm mit mir*,' said Heiner.

Davey shook his head.

'*Bitte*, David.'

Davey shook his head again.

'*Bitte*, David, *bitte.*'

Heiner was on the verge of tears. Davey gave in and followed Heiner across the yard. The house was in darkness save for the usual warm glow from the kitchen window.

It had snowed while they had been in the workshop. The light from the kitchen cast a blade of orange light on a thin coating of the first snow of 1918. Davey and Heiner left their boots in the passage as usual.

Davey lingered in the doorway of the kitchen while Heiner presented his mother with the fruits of his many hours of labour. Agnes put her sewing down and looked from Heiner to the spoon, then at Heiner again. Anna put her sewing down too. Everyone waited for Agnes to say something.

Agnes's radiant smile matched the joy on Anna's face and the broad grin that spread across Heiner's features. The only word Davey understood readily was 'Papa' when Agnes held Heiner's hands in hers. All three of the family were talking at once, taking turns to examine the spoon filling the room with laughter and tears.

Davey watched this tender scene unfold with pride, intent on slipping away unnoticed.

Agnes and Anna were calling to him: he heard his name amongst the excited chatter and gestures for him to enter the kitchen.

'*Alles* Heiner's *Arbeit. Alles* Heiner,' pleaded Davey.

Later that evening, Christoph entered the barn.

'There's still just the one chair,' said Davey. 'Without its wobble though.'

'You've done wonders with my son, David. I've seen the spoon. I've never been able to interest him in anything intricate or detailed. Perhaps I've under-estimated his abilities.'

'He's a good learner. I was amazed at his patience.'

'Well, you have succeeded where I have not,' said Christoph, a distinct note of regret evident in his voice. 'You will make a good father. How old is your son now?'

'He was born while I was training. He'd be getting on for three now.'

'And you've never seen him?'

'No.'

'I can't imagine how that feels. Can't imagine,' Christoph added quietly.

'I'll see him one day, when it's over,' said Davey. 'I'll teach him woodwork.'

Davey's attempt at distracting Christoph from his mood of lingering disappointment failed.

'And how to lift tatties ... potatoes,' he added.

Christoph managed a half-hearted smile. 'That day might come sooner than you think. The war is looking bad for Germany, David. The naval blockade is having a devastating impact on the whole country. Food shortages are getting worse, particularly in the towns and cities.'

'And I'm an extra mouth to feed,' put in Davey. 'And it's my side that's doing the blockading.'

'We're blocking your ports too,' said Christoph. 'Both our countries rely on imports from America. Anyway, it's not your fault and I've no wish to return you to camp if that is what you are thinking. Are you willing to see out the summer and then see where we are?'

263

'Of course; I've said many times that living and working here is a mighty piece of luck for me. The war will be over one day. Until that time comes, I wish to stay and help you and your family. I see it as my duty as a soldier.'

'For no wages.'

'I don't expect any. How could I as a prisoner of war? I don't care about wages. I have food and a roof over my head.'

'Food: I was coming to that,' said Christoph. 'We will have to cut down, as a family I mean. We have sufficient potatoes and turnips for a few months, aside from what I sell to the army and in the … the market. Flour is getting harder to purchase though. We have stocks for perhaps a few weeks, and our dairy production is enough for the five of us with some spare to sell. As you know, immigrant labour has practically dried up. I still have to rely on local women and the older men.

'There, that's the situation as I see it. I can't see how my country can continue to wage this war for another year.'

Christoph fell silent and stared at the floor of the barn. An awkward quiet descended between the two men, broken by Christoph seeming to emerge as if from a trance. He stood abruptly; Davey followed suit.

'I've been lucky too, David. You coming here has been vital for the farm, particularly this year. It's going to be a difficult one.'

'Heiner and me will work all the hours God sends,' said Davey. 'He is a grand lad, really.'

'I know. Father and son don't always get on. We'll get through this. My family will get through this dreadful and wasteful war.'

Christoph made to leave.

'Before you go, can I make a suggestion?'

'What is it?' asked Christoph.

'A way to make flour go further.'

'What is?'

'Tattie scones.'

'What?'

'Scottish potato scones. You mix flour with mashed potato. It'll make your flour go further. I've watched my mother and my wife make them many times.'

'Would you show Agnes in the morning? Goodnight, David.'

Davey experimented with a small batch. He didn't use much butter, so he tried milk instead. After a few failures, he settled upon a satisfactory method. Agnes wrote down Davey's recipe and made a large scone on the hotplate of her wood-burning stove. When the scone had cooled, Agnes cut triangular slices as Davey had showed her and everyone tried them, with the exception of Christoph who had gone to Erlangen with the horse and cart. The reaction from Agnes, Anna, and Heiner was unanimous.

They like 'em.

Bread was made less frequently in the kitchen after the introduction of Davey's version of Scottish tattie scones to the Hoffmann household.

∗

In the weeks that followed, Heiner repaired and made new milking stools for the dairy. Christoph produced a brace and bit drill from somewhere, enhancing Heiner's skills in the workshop. Sometimes the boy would have to be told to leave what he was making and return to his duties on the farm.

Davey worried that he might have over-indulged Heiner. His reluctance to keep up his farm work annoyed his father and Davey felt responsible. The last thing he wanted was to have the boy banned from the workshop.

One morning in March, Davey heard harsh words coming from the open kitchen door. Heiner strode into the yard, almost knocking Davey over.

'Heiner, *warte*,' he called out to the retreating boy. '*Bitte*.'

Heiner sat on an upturned wooden crate at the other side of the yard, head in his hands.

Christoph emerged from the house, the look on his face spoke of his anguish.

Davey held up his hands. 'Before you say anything, this is my fault. I've over-indulged him.'

Christoph's angry look relaxed a little. 'Don't blame yourself, David. Heiner can be difficult at times. I need his pair of hands though, as I do yours. I am unlikely to be able to hire any Polish workers this summer. The bulk of the work will be in the hands of the three of us.'

Christoph looked across to where Heiner was sitting, then he faced Davey, 'Damn this war for what it is doing to my country and to my family.'

'Let's come to an arrangement, like before Christmas,' said Davey. 'Limit the time he can spend in the workshop. Say, some evenings and a bit of the weekend. I'll stick to the same times. That might work.'

Christoph nodded. 'I'll talk to him later. What is today's work?'

'We've got more fences to mend. Are you ploughing later?'

'We must prepare for sowing this month and the next. Food shortages will be worse this year.'

Davey had never seen Christoph look so worried.

How much mair can he feed an extra mouth?

'You could ask for more prisoners.'

'I couldn't feed them, David. I'm afraid more work will come your way, and Heiner. He's getting stronger and more useful.'

'I'll take him up with me,' said Davey.

'Thank you. He responds to you. He's annoyed with me.'

'Grand, we'll away up to the top field.'

Davey left Christoph and approached Heiner. The boy looked up at Davey; he had been crying.

'*Lass uns gehen,*' suggested Davey.

Heiner stood, dried his eyes with the sleeve of his shirt, glanced towards the house and said, '*Ja,* boss.'

Davey put his arm around the boy's shoulders as they set off to the store to gather the day's tools. 'C'mon lad, we've got work to do for your father.'

Heiner looked puzzled.

'*Arbeit für Vater, für den Hof. Du und ich.*'

Heiner muttered something that Davey didn't understand, smiled and began sorting out the tools that they needed for the day's work.

That's ma boy; cheerful again.

'*Komm,* David. *Du und ich. Lass uns arbeiten. Vater braucht uns.*'

267

Davey and Heiner set off to the fields under a pallid sun, holding out its promise of warmer days to come, heralds of the sun moving north to the summer.

Kate's Story

Home Again

Commercial Row appeared quiet. Kate wondered where the children were. She hurried down the hill as best she could, taking care not to jiggle Jean in her rush to give voice to the reason that gave her a means to leave Thomas: Kate was desperately anxious for news of her father.

She was halfway down the hill when she saw her sister close the door of her old home. Chrissie saw her, ran up the hill and tried to throw her arms around her sister.

'Mind the bairn. She'll be squashed.'

Chrissie pulled away, her eyes red and glistening.

'Oh, Kate ... Kate. Thank God ee're here. Ye didnae write.'

'Ah came just as soon as ah read your letter. How is faither?'

Chrissie didn't reply; her tears turned into sobs.

'Chrissie?'

Still no reply.

Chrissie's weeping almost came to a stop.

'C'mon, we cannae talk oot here. Let's garn in,' she said in a strangled voice.

Their mother was in the back kitchen, giving Davie and Marion their tea. Jane Johnstone looked up from cutting bread; the shock of seeing her prodigal daughter loosened her grip on the knife. The children stopped eating and stared at Kate.

Kate passed Jean to Chrissie, dropped her bag on the kitchen floor and gazed at her children. 'My, how ee've grown. Just look at ee.'

Marion cried when Kate stroked her cheek and kissed the top of her head.

Davie pulled away when Kate made to kiss him. 'Hello, son,' whispered Kate.

'It'll be a wee while yet afore they get used tae ee,' suggested Chrissie.

'Finish yer tea,' said Jane. 'We'll no be lang.'

The women gathered in the front parlour, away from the children. Kate hugged her mother while Chrissie held Jean.

'Have ee told her?' said Jane.

Chrissie shook her head.

'Faither has passed, Kate,' said her mother quietly, as she drew away from Kate.

Kate's hands covered her open mouth; an audible breath squeezed between her fingers. She fell into an armchair, consumed with shuddering sobs.

Chrissie held her niece until her sister's heaving chest calmed.

'First Davey, noo Faither. Damn this bloody stupid war,' Kate shouted. 'Damn it tae hell.'

Jean started crying. Chrissie jiggled her in her arms.

'It's a' right, pet. Shh noo, dinnae greet.'

'Oor men've gaen,' said their mother. 'But there's a new life – a lassie.'

'Aye,' said Chrissie. 'She's lovely. Your Aunty Chrissie has got ee.'

The women spent the rest of the afternoon talking until they were exhausted, sharing their feelings until private grief replaced its outward expression.

Kate slept in her own bed that night, a deep, long sleep that held the promise that she could take up her old life. There would be many difficulties ahead: she could think about the practicalities in the days to come.

Davey's Story

Last Days

In early September, Christoph brought rumours of Germany's impending defeat. Davey strove to hide his feelings from the rest of the family, torn between sadness and excitement upon hearing this news. As the rumours grew, he yearned for home with hope rather than with certainty.

The Hoffmann family were subdued in Davey's presence at mealtimes after listening to what Christoph told them. Davey was ill prepared to contemplate missing them: they had taken him under their protection and had treated him with genuine affection.

Despite the tension in the household, Davey continued to work with his full commitment. Not once, since Davey first was told of the likely outcome of the war, did he or Christoph broach the subject of what would happen to him in the event of Germany's defeat. Everyone tried to carry on with life on the farm.

One evening in late September after the evening meal, Christoph sought out Davey in the barn. He was sewing a tear in his well-worn trousers.

'Agnes would have done that for you.'

'She has enough to do without mending my clothes.'

'You are a very capable man, David. I can't sew.'

'I've had to be. I come from a large family. You have to learn to look after yourself. Agnes let me have some sewing bits and pieces. I'd run out of what was in my kit bag.'

Christoph watched Davey at his domestic work.

'Last year's potato crop was good. The winter before you came was a failure in most of Germany,' said Christoph apropos, apparently, of nothing at all.

'And this year?'

'I'm not optimistic. Seed potatoes are hard to come by. It's selling the crop that is the problem. As you know, I supply the camps at Nürnberg and Erlangen. When the war is over, I'll have to find new customers. The country is in chaos, David. The war has crippled us.'

Davey struggled to find words to console Christoph.

'Germany is on the point of losing. What the immediate future holds, I don't know.'

'I hope things work out for you, for your family and the farm,' said Davey.

Christoph's look of despondency grew deeper. 'The Kaiser has left the country, fled to the Netherlands, I believe. And, to make matters worse, there is revolution in parts of the country and an influenza epidemic.'

Davey was at a loss to respond.

'I've spoken to Herr Fischer. Arrangements for your repatriation are uncertain at the moment. I'll let you know when I hear anything more.'

Christoph got to his feet and made to leave. Davey stood and extended his right hand. They shook with a warmth and firmness that confirmed the friendship that flowed from one to the other.

'I'm sorry about the war,' said Davey. 'Sorry about what it's done to your country. Goodness knows how much damage it has done to both our countries.'

'At least you know that you will be going home.'

Davey smiled weakly and nodded. Christoph's despair had robbed him of words.

'Goodnight, David.' Christoph let go of Davey's hand, turned and left the barn.

Davey sat on the bed, unable to finish patching his trousers, his mind a jumble of questions and emotions.

*

A few weeks later, when Christoph had been away from the farm since early morning, Davey felt that something might have been discussed amongst the family before he took his place for the evening meal. There was an uneasy quiet in the kitchen.

Davey accepted a mug of ersatz coffee from Agnes and waited for Christoph to say something. Agnes, Anna and Heiner looked anxiously at Davey. After a lengthy silence, during which everyone distracted themselves by blowing on and sipping their mugs of coffee, Christoph cleared his throat.

'David, it is official,' he said. 'Germany has lost the war. An armistice will be signed in a few days' time. Hostilities will cease at eleven in the morning on 11th November. I've told the family. You are free to go.'

Davey stared at his half empty mug, his stomach churning at the thought of leaving.

When he felt he could meet the intense looks from around the table, Davey said, 'Could I stay until the eleventh? I don't want to go back to camp, even for a few days.'

Christoph translated then said, 'I think that would be best. I can't imagine what is going to happen in the camps when the war is over. We could leave here early on the morning of the eleventh. I'll take you back.'

Sleep didn't come easily that night. The reality of leaving the family he had spent a year with was something Davey knew would happen eventually, but its inevitability brought with it a feeling of intense sadness. He conjured images of Kate and tried to imagine Marion four years older.

She'll not know iss.

The son he had never seen would be more than three years of age.

Wull he look like iss?

Davey's mind simmered with confusion. In a few days' time, he would have to face another reality, leave the comfort and safety of the farm and his agreeable isolation and return to camp with no idea how or when he would be sent home.

Eventually, sleep overcame his troubled mind as the pale blades of dawn slid into the barn.

It wasn't until the evening of 10th November that Christoph brought further news. Davey was gathering his few belongings and stowing them in Didier's backpack.

'May I suggest that you don't wear your greatcoat and backpack until we get there. The more you look like a civilian, the better. Some people will be hostile to you, David. It pays to be careful. Please keep the cap and wear Heiner's old jacket.

'I have received news from my contacts in the army. The German authorities are to be given the responsibility of organising trains to move prisoners of war out of Germany with the assistance of the Red Cross. The railway network has broken down, so how this will be done remains to be seen.'

'Thanks for letting me know. I don't know what to expect when I get back to camp. Not that I'm looking forward to that place.'

'I can't keep you here, David. I wouldn't know how to get you onto a train. You'll be better off with those in charge in camp.'

Whee'll that be?

'Until the morning, David.'

Davey watched the retreating figure leave the barn, returned to his packing then went to bed for the last time on the Hoffmann's farm.

There was little talk at breakfast the following morning. Agnes had made a fresh potato scone. At the end of the meal, she wrapped what was left in some brown paper and gave it to Davey. He retrieved his backpack from where he had left it near the door and stowed the piece of scone.

'*Vielen Dank*, Agnes.'

Agnes nodded, turned away from Davey and set about some unnecessary and noisy tidying up.

Anna was next with a gift. She had embroidered a 'D' on the corner of a white handkerchief.

'*Vielen Dank*, Anna.'

Davey carefully folded the handkerchief and slipped it into his trouser pocket.

Heiner stepped forward and handed a small wooden box to Davey. He demonstrated how its lid slid open while Davey held the box, revealing a number of coins and notes inside.

'You never know when you'll need some money on your way home,' said Christoph.

Davey gazed at the box; it was beautifully made, with perfect joints. '*Von* Heiner' was painted on the inside of the lid. His voice cracked as he thanked the boy.

When did he dae this?

Davey looked from face to face, utter sorrow left him bereft and unable to speak. He took a deep breath, found his voice and said, '*Dank Euch allen, danke.*'

Agnes was still facing away from Davey. 'Agnes,' he said. 'Agnes, *danke und auf Wiedersehein.*' Agnes turned and returned Davey's embrace.

Heiner was next. 'Goodbye, Heiner.'

'Goodbye, David,' he replied, sobbing as he too returned Davey's embrace.

Anna was last, scarcely able to speak through her tears. She managed to say, 'Goodbye, David,' as she hugged him fiercely.

Christoph had left discreetly and was waiting in the yard with the horse and cart.

Davey put Heiner's box in the top of his backpack while the family looked on, everyone in tears. His resolve broke and tears sprang from his eyes as he bade them a final farewell at the door of the kitchen.

He hung his backpack over his left shoulder, collected his greatcoat from the hook in the passage and closed the door behind him. He stood in the yard and looked about him, to imprint a picture of what had been his home for the past year firmly in his mind.

He turned to look back at the house. The kitchen window framed three faces. The finality of this image pierced his heart and held him in its grip, pleading with him to stay.

'Goodbye,' he mouthed, tore himself away and climbed up next to Christoph who, without a word, shook the reins.

As the cart moved slowly out of the yard, Davey looked behind and waved in the direction of the kitchen window. Three arms waved back at him in the reflection of the outside world until they dissolved as trees and sky overcame Davey's last sight of Agnes, Anna and Heiner.

Ah'll never see 'em again.

The cart turned the corner of the yard and started down the track towards the lane, pushing the farmhouse out of view behind the outbuildings.

Davey stared ahead, remembering the first day he began life at the Hoffmanns' farm a year ago. He saw himself waiting at the end of the lane as Christoph commanded his horse to turn right towards Nürnberg.

He had arrived as a prisoner of war, weakened from poor food, assigned to another work detail in the expectation that it would lessen the tedium of the weariness of camp life. He left as a member of the Hoffmann family with his strength and dignity restored.

He had volunteered in the knowledge that he would be trained to kill German soldiers; he ended the war part of a German family.

Davey glanced across at Christoph.

How different he is from Kurtz.

Davey fingered his beard.

Ye're supposed tae be clean-shaven in the airmy.

Christoph drew the horse and cart to a halt at a place in the forest where the lane passed through a clearing. 'Today is a very sad day for me too,' he said. 'You have become one of the family. I am not sure that is supposed to happen in war.'

'I'll never forget that,' said Davey. 'I hated Germans after they left me for dead. When I came to your house, it was different. You were different. I felt no hatred. It's as if the war had had no effect on us. I know it has, but you know what I mean.'

'I do. We're just two working men, David. Thrown together under unusual circumstances.'

'Aye, a desk job isn't for me,' said Davey. 'I've done manual work since I left school. I love being outside.'

'Me too,' said Christoph, with a smile. '*Los,*' he commanded, shaking the reins.

'Before we go into town, there's something I'd like to talk to you about. I didn't want to tell you in front of the others. They were too upset this morning.'

'Alright,' said Davey.

'Agnes and I have always disapproved of what the Kaiser has done to our country. Now that he has gone and the war is over, we can't see a future for us here.'

Whit can he mean?

'Perhaps when the army returns,' continued Christoph, 'the revolution will be put down. I don't know. Then it depends on what your side will do with us. Are we to be governed by them?'

Davey continued to look puzzled.

'The point that I am trying to get to, David, is this. We have had several family conferences, as you might say. And we have kept you out of all this.'

Ah, houses – nearly there.

'We've decided to leave Germany.'

'What?'

'Yes. We might return one day, but in the aftermath of the war we are resolved to sell the farm. It could take a while. I was hoping that Heiner would run it one day.'

'Where will you go?'

'Australia.'

'Australia!'

'Yes. To carry on farming.'

Davey looked back. The farmhouse had disappeared, eclipsed by the forest.

'It could take months before we are ready to go.'

'I don't know what to say.'

'It will be a terrible wrench to leave our friends and relatives, and our country.'

'Anna and Heiner are young. They'll be fine.'

'They are the most enthusiastic to leave! There's one more thing to tell you. We would like you to come with us.'

Davey stared at Christoph, deprived of speech for the second time that day.

'I know that this is rather sudden, David.'

'Sudden! You mean leave Scotland, do what you're doing – leaving your country. I don't think that my family would agree to anything like that.'

'I'm sorry to burden you with this at the last minute. It's what Agnes and the others agreed.'

'I'm so very grateful for your offer, but you know it's impossible. We couldn't carry on as before. Heiner and me working together. There'd be Kate and our two. That's two families to support. What you ask is impossible.'

'Look, nearly there — ' Christoph broke off. 'What's going on at the gate? I'll stop here.' Christoph pulled on the reins and turned to face Davey. 'I knew what you would say, but I had to ask. You understand that, don't you? For the sake of the others.'

'Please don't think that I'm not grateful. I am.'

'The offer is still open if you ever change your mind ...'

Davey was distracted by the commotion at the gate to the camp. 'While I was there, all I ever thought about was getting out —'

'And now we can't see how to get in,' said Christoph. 'The guards look overwhelmed. Wait here, David.'

Christoph got down from the box seat and approached the guards. Davey could see him pointing in his direction while the guards gestured towards the noisy mob near the gate.

Christoph climbed back into the box seat. 'These men have walked here from nearby farms and factories.'

'Returning work details,' said Davey. 'Why can't they get in?'

Christoph shook his head. 'This is a ridiculous situation. Where are they supposed to go? Where are *you* supposed to go?'

Finally, the gate opened and the large group of men filed into the camp.

'I'd better go,' said Davey.

Both men got down from the cart and shook hands. 'Goodbye, David. We part as friends, I hope.'

'Whatever happens, I will always hold you and your family in my heart. *Viel Glück und auf Weidersehen.*'

'*Auf Weidersehen*, David and good luck to you too.'

Christoph climbed back into the box seat, raised his hand to Davey and shook the reins into action. Davey only had a moment to watch the retreating cart before he tagged onto the rear of the returning prisoners.

'*Warte bitte,*' he said to the guards as they made to close the gate. They responded to Davey's request and let him through, closing the gate behind him.

Davey joined the returning prisoners gathered at the rear of what looked like a roll call.

A bit late fi a roll call.

'Onyone got the time?' asked Davey.

The church bells opposite the entrance to the camp rang out half past the hour.

'There's yer answer, mate,' someone in front replied.

'Whit's happening?' Davey asked the prisoner standing to his left. 'Christ, it's Perkins. Ah didnae recognise ee.'

'I didn't recognise you either,' replied Perkins. 'You haven't bothered to shave then.'

'Whit's garn on, Perks?'

'Rumour is this special roll call has been called by the Kommandant. What happens after the hour is up is anyone's guess.'

'How lang have ee been here?' asked Davey.

'Just got here. There's a bunch of blokes from factories with us. They just walked out. No one stopped them.'

'Where's the rest of the fairm workers?'

'Don't know. I haven't seen any of 'em, apart from you.'

'Ah've only just got here. Ma boss brought me in. Ah could see that ee couldnae get in.'

'The guards don't know what to do,' said Perkins. 'Hey, look behind you.'

The guards who were on the gate had disappeared, nor were there any guards in the watchtowers.

Davey and Perkins exchanged puzzled glances.

'Whit's garn on up front?'

'Hah, a short-arse like you can't see. I can get you a box to stand on if you like.'

'Ah havenae heard that yin for ages. Just tell iss.'

'We're a long way back, but I can see Germans.'

The church hour bell struck three quarters of the hour.

Kommandant Fischer strode out of his office in his breeches with his swagger stick tucked under one arm. He ascended his makeshift podium and armed himself with a megaphone. The noisy chatter of several thousand prisoners of war slowly faded and an expectant silence descended upon the parade ground.

'Gentlemen,' Kommandant Fischer began.

A tremendous cheer erupted and flowed back and forth along the ranks of men.

'Makes a change from "*Schweinhund*",' observed the man in front of Davey.

Kommandant Fischer held up his hand. It was several minutes before he could continue with his address. 'Gentlemen,' he repeated, this time through his interpreter who also held a megaphone. 'In a few minutes time, the war will be over.'

Another tumultuous cheer soared skywards.

The Kommandant didn't have much to say. He advised everyone to stay in camp and await instructions. 'You will soon be going home,' he added.

This was the end of his short address, which elicited a final roar from the assembled ex-prisoners.

The ranks of men began to break up and mill about. There was much backslapping, sporadic cheering and hurling of caps in the air.

Davey remained where he had been standing. 'Wis that it, Perks?'

'What more did you expect him to say?'

'Ah dinnae ken. Something aboot how and when we garn hame.'

'We're still in the army. Lots of hanging about, remember?'

'It must be nearly —'

The church clock struck the hour. Another thunderous cheer erupted and drowned out the next ten bells. The sky danced with hats and caps and men hugged unashamedly. Everyone seemed to be shouting incomprehensibly in a raw, animal release of pent up energy and emotion.

'Someone else is trying to speak,' hollered Perkins.

It took several minutes for the senior British NCO to get their attention.

'Gentlemen, gentlemen!' he shouted through a megaphone until the assembled men had calmed down enough for him to be heard. 'I won't detain you for long. We and our French counterparts will meet with Herr Fischer later this morning. I urge you not to leave the camp. Some citizens will be hostile. Our daily routine should continue as normal. We await instructions from the Allied Forces and the German authorities as to our repatriation. I hope you understand. The Armistice has only just been signed. We don't know what will happen next. Can I ask that we assemble at noon tomorrow in order for the camp committee to keep you informed?

'One more thing. As some of you know, there has been an outbreak of typhus in the Russian compound. This has been quarantined and is under our guard.

'Finally, camp numbers have been swollen by the return of work details. Not all have returned as yet. The committee will address the problem of accommodation for these men as a matter of urgency. Thank you, and carry on.'

'How're they going to contain something like typhus?' said Perkins.

'And where are we supposed tae stay?' said Davey. 'D'ye get the impression the camp is full without iss?'

Perkins shrugged. 'I'm off to my old hut. See you later.'

As Davey made his way through the crowd, several prisoners looked askance as he wound his way amongst them. He felt their silence and suspicion as he approached and passed by.

Must be ma civvies and beard.

Davey quickened his pace up the hill to his former hut.

'It's Farmer Muir,' yelled Dusty Miller as Davey approached. Several men were sitting outside on the bench that was positioned under the window.

'We rented out yer bed, Davey,' said Phil Davies. 'You didn't come back.'

Nae room then.

'What'll you do?' asked Dusty.

'Ah dinnae ken. There's loads of iss. We were trying tae get into camp earlier. How mad is that? Wanting in.'

Davey stayed and chatted for a while before moving on. 'Ah'll away and talk tae the committee.'

'That useless bunch. They haven't a clue what's going on,' said Phil.

'Understandable, the uncertainty ah mean,' suggested Davey. 'They've got thoosands o' iss tae get hame. Just imagine how mony camps there are like this yin. We could be here for ages.'

'Cheer up, Davey,' urged Dusty. 'We'll be home soon enough.'

'Ah'll away and see whit ah can fin' oot.'

Davey knocked on the open door of the NCO's hut and waited.

'Come,' called a voice.

A group of NCOs were relaxing at the hut's central table, drinking tea and eating biscuits. The remains of several Red Cross parcels were scattered about the table.

Sergeant Williams occupied the seat opposite the door.

'What can we do for you, soldier?' he asked. 'Actually, before you answer, you don't look like one. What's the meaning of the beard and hair? And your clothes? You look like a civvy, apart from your French overcoat.'

'Ah've been billeted on a fairm for the past year, sarge. Nae razor, but the farmer's wife trimmed ma hair occasionally.'

'What else did she do for you, private?' asked the sergeant, leaning forward in his chair and pointing at Davey to a chorus of laughter.

'Lost your tongue, private? What's your name?'

'Private Muir, sarge.'

'That's sergeant to you, Muir.'

Davey didn't reply.

'Hey, aren't you the Jock who argued with me the first day you arrived?' said Williams, leaning back in his chair. 'I didn't recognise you at first.'

Davey stayed silent.

'Well, Private Muir, it's clear that you've had a cushy time. Just look at you. Well fed, I'll be bound.'

Davey stood his ground, fuming inwardly. 'Whit's garn tae happen tae us returnees? There were loads of iss ootside the gate earlier.'

'The camp's full, Muir.'

'Where dae we sleep until we're sent hame?'

'We're working on it.'

'How and when will we fin oot?'

'You ask a lot of questions, Muir.'

'And you fellas have a lot o' responsibilities.'

'You trying to tell us our job?'

'I'm saying there are more work details to come back. We'll need food and shelter, sergeant.'

'Listen, I don't need an uppity Jock coming in here making demands.' The sergeant's chair scraped on the floor of the hut.

Davey held the gaze of the sergeant. The two men glared at one another in the threatening silence. The sergeant was the first to look away as he sat down and scraped his chair towards the table.

'Ye insulted ma boss's wife,' announced Davey.

'It was a joke, Muir.'

'Didnae sound like a joke tae me.'

'Look, Muir. We're all on the same side here. Let's keep calm.'

'Apologise.'

The menacing silence returned.

'I'll do no such thing.'

'C'mon, soldier, forget it,' said one of the other NCOs.

'I'll nae forget it. These people were kind tae me. Ah came back here and … By the way, d'ye realise that the gairds have disappeared. Good luck with keeping order. Ye've got thoosands of hungry men oot there.'

'Telling us our job again.'

'Ah'm finished here. Ye still owe me an apology, *sarge*, and ah dinnae give a jobbie whit rank ee are.'

Davey shot a defiant look around the room, turned and left the hut.

Once outside, Davey drew a deep breath of crisp November air.

And those eejits are in charge!

Davey's next call was Ross's hut.

'He's not here any more,' said one of its occupants. 'He was sent to Ingolstadt.'

'Ah wis there,' said Davey.

'The fort, not the men's camp, so we heard. He tried to escape from here, twice.'

That's ma boy.

Davey stayed and chatted for a few minutes before calling on his French pals. They too were disenchanted with the lack of information.

'It's early days,' suggested Davey. 'Naebdy seems tae ken whit's garn tae happen. Ah hope yer senior staff are mair clued up than oors.'

Gallic shrugs greeted Davey's optimism.

Ah forgot tae stop speaking Fechan.

'We would offer you a bed, but we're full,' said Pierre with an additional shrug.

'Thanks anyway,' said Davey. '*Bon chance.*'

Handshakes all round sent Davey onto the parade ground, where men vomited and staggered around near their huts.

Where'd they fin drink?

The remnants of Red Cross parcels littered the ground outside huts on the hill.

They cannae tak the food.

The parcel store was unguarded and ransacked by the time Davey got there.

'This is disgraceful,' announced a soldier standing by the door of the storeroom.

'Ma God, look at a' these,' said Davey.

'The Germans have been hoarding our parcels,' the soldier continued. 'The men have taken revenge, so it seems.'

'There must be hunnerds left,' observed Davey.

'There won't be for long if the men carry on like this. This place needs to be guarded.'

'By us?'

'All the Germans have deserted their posts.'

Davey spotted the stripes on the soldier's tunic.

'Things are bound tae get oot o' hand,' observed Davey.

'Maybe, but we've got to get a grip. I don't even know if the gate is being guarded. We don't want hordes of men tramping around town. Could get ugly with the locals.'

'We were told not tae garn oot,' said Davey.

'True, but how much notice … look, I'll leave you to it, soldier.' He gave Davey a quizzical look up and down and left.

Davey spotted a German guard's kit bag in an adjoining room, emptied it of its contents of clothes, none of which he wanted, with the intention of filling it with items discarded from open parcels; he didn't touch unopened ones. Davey filled the kit bag with packets of tea, tins of biscuits, tins of cocoa, and bars of soap. He hoisted the bulky kit bag over one shoulder and returned to the parade ground. Scores of men were running towards the Russian compound.

Typhus! They've got tae keep 'em oot.

Davey went back into the German quarters.

There must be another way oot.

The living quarters of German officers and guards had been ransacked, furniture upended and paper scattered everywhere.

Davey guessed that everything of value had been taken. Undaunted, he went from room to room in the aftermath of the inmates' whirlwind of revenge. He came across a large tin of coffee in a kitchen, prised open the tin and revelled in the aroma of real coffee. The tin was added to the contents of the kit bag.

Finding nothing else worth taking in the kitchen and adjoining canteen, Davey continued his systematic search of the Germans' living and sleeping quarters, trying doors and looking out of any window that faced away from the parade ground. At length, he saw what he was looking for – an entrance to the camp that would have been unknown to the inmates. Building material lay in piles against the outside wall.

Ah wonder if Ross escaped fri here.

He forced the window open and was on the point of throwing out the kit bag when he heard a commotion in a nearby room. A narrow corridor led to the source of the raised voices, English voices interspersed with indistinct German.

Davey entered a large office, by the look of the furniture. A German guard cowered in a corner, sitting on the floor with his hands covering his face. Three inmates stood over him, one holding a pistol. Their threats ceased the instant Davey came through the door.

'Whit's garn on here?' said Davey.

The guard dropped his hands at the sound of Davey's voice.

Kurtz!

'Kurtz!'

'You know him,' said the pistol-waving soldier.

'Oh, aye. Ah ken him a'reet.'

'He didn't get away quick enough,' said the soldier.

'And ee plan to dae whit?' said Davey.

'What d'you think?'

'So ee reckon committing murder is a'reet noo is it. The war's over, in case ee didnae notice.'

'Look, mate. What's it got to do with you?'

'It's got a lot tae dae wi me. Ah'm a witness.'

'What! You'd report this? Who to?'

'Ah would. So ee'll have tae shoot me too.'

The three men exchanged glances. The one with the pistol turned to face Davey.

'You don't think he deserves it then?'

296

'It's no for ee tae decide is it.'

'So what do you suggest we do with him?'

'Were ony of ee wounded before ee were captured?'

'What?'

'Wounded. Were ony of ee wounded?'

The men looked at one another; all shook their heads.

'No, we weren't. What's that got to do with anything?'

'His airmy damn near shot ma right leg off and yin shot me in the guts when ah was lying wounded, shot iss as ah lay there. Ah was left fi days.'

'Christ that's awful, mate.'

'If onyone wants revenge, it's me. Ah've earned it.'

'Do you know how to use one of these?'

'Er, how dae ee ... ?' said Davey.

'Standard issue Mauser. You flip this back and then ... '

'A'reet, looks easy enough. Is it loaded?'

Davey held out his hand.

The soldier with the pistol hesitated.

Davey curled and uncurled his fingers. 'C'mon,' he said.

The soldier handed the pistol to Davey. 'It's loaded,' he said.

Davey held the pistol and pointed it casually at Kurtz whimpering in the corner.

'Look, fellas,' said Davey, 'ee dinnae need tae witness this. Why don't ee scarper? Dinnae tell a soul whit's occurred here. Neither wull ah. We havenae seen each other or him – a'reet?'

Davey waited until the three men left the room, then he waited for several minutes more. The building took on an eerie silence, as if listening to the faint thrum of voices coming from the parade ground and bearing witness to the continued snivels and sobs of the hapless guard.

'*Nun*, Kurtz. *Jetz had ich Dich.*'

The German replied with even louder whines of fear, smothered by his hands.

Kate's Story

Armistice

A special service was arranged at the church in Ecclefechan at ten-thirty on Monday, 11th November 1918. Chrissie had volunteered to look after the children while Kate and their mother attended.

In the moments leading up to eleven o'clock, the vicar drew attention to those who had lost menfolk.

'Aye,' whispered Jane.

Kate put her arm around her mother and marvelled at her strength, doubting her own as the congregation fell silent, listening as the church clock struck eleven. Bowed heads shielded inner feelings as the sound of celebration drifted into the church moments after the clock had signalled the end of the war.

The vicar had a kind word to say to everyone as the congregation filed out. To many he expressed his sympathy.

'I am very sorry to hear of your loss, Mrs Johnstone and of yours, Mrs Muir,' he said when Kate and Jane stepped into the post-war light a few minutes after eleven.

The two women thanked the vicar and joined the throng of women and elderly men exchanging handshakes and greetings in front of the church.

Several people approached Kate and Jane and offered commiserations. Everyone in the village seemed to know which families had lost someone.

The gathering outside the church dispersed, mostly in the direction of the High Street. It looked to Kate and Jane that every house had emptied onto the road outside the hotel. Children were scampering around the legs of couples dancing to a piper: women with women, and women with the older men. Bottles of beer were held aloft and people were singing *Auld Lang Syne* and *Loch Lomond*, and other songs.

When the piper had exhausted his repertoire, he started at the beginning and played them all over again to the delight of the revellers in the street. Dancing, singing and drinking continued for most of the afternoon in the street and in the bar of the hotel.

Kate, Chrissie and their mother watched the dancing and joined in the singing for a while.

'Garn ower and hae a drink, Mother,' urged Kate. 'And ee Chrissie. Jean's getting heavy. Ah'll garn and put her doon.'

Kate closed her front door. The muffled sounds of celebration in the street were not enough to bring so much as a tinge of joy. Armistice Day had brought with it a feeling of agonising grief and a stark reminder of loss.

Marion and Davie went with their grandmother; Kate sat with Jean cradled in her arms. 'Ee havenae got a faither, ma little one,' she said aloud.

Jean closed her eyes and slept in Kate's lap.

Kate had a lot to be thankful for. Her mother had lived in her house while she had been in Glasgow, looked after her two children and paid the rent. She could not have asked for more. Now her mother was a widow too.

Davey had been gone for four years. What had been a dull ache of sadness at the loss of her husband of barely one year had been amplified by a fresh wave of sorrow at the loss of her father.

Jean continued to sleep in her mother's lap. The revelry in the street dimmed with the onset of dusk. Armistice Day in Ecclefechan drew to a close.

'Davey wis a guid maun,' whispered Kate to Jean. 'He wid hae been a guid faither to ee, right enough.'

Kate rocked Jean gently in her arms as the gloom of the parlour grew around them and its chill deepened. She put Jean in her basket, made up the fire and watched the coals throw a yellow light into the room. Kate replaced the poker, wiped her hands on her apron and took down Davey's photograph from its place on the mantelpiece.

Kate gazed at the image until her eyes moistened, blurring Davey's kind face. She replaced the photo and dried her eyes on a clean corner of her apron.

'Aye, Davey, ee'll never see the bairns grow up.'

Davey's Story

A Fateful Day

'*Shh, shh,*' Davey pleaded, his finger to his lips. '*Shh, sei still.*' Davey made calming movements with his hands as he sat on the floor a few feet away from Kurtz.

The guard slowly dropped his hands again, his sobs subsiding, his breathing slowing.

'*Sei still,*' said Davey, using his hands again.

The German nodded, keeping his eye on the pistol.

How'd they get it off him?

'*Wo is der Ausgang?*' Davey used his hands to point first to Kurtz then to himself.

Kurtz cast an anxious glance over his shoulder as Davey followed him along the corridor. Davey responded with a flick of the pistol.

They reached a door without incident or interruption. The small window above it told Davey that it was a way out of the building.

Davey followed Kurtz into the yard he had seen earlier. Another flick of the wrist sent Kurtz towards the entrance to the yard. A padlock lay on the ground.

My, they did leave in a hurry.

Well, if onyone sees this, tae bad.

'*Halt,*' said Davey. '*Dreh Dich.*'

Kurtz, trembling and whimpering, turned to face Davey, unable to take his eyes off the pistol.

Davey raised his arm, aiming at Kurtz who sank to his knees, muttering incomprehensibly, hands covering his face again.

Davey let two rounds take their course. He paused, then fired once more.

Kurtz turned to see three trickles of cement forming a neat pile on the ground beneath the wall.

'*Steh auf, los,*' ordered Davey.

Kurtz staggered to his feet.

'*Jetzt geh,*' said Davey, gesturing with the pistol towards the open gate.

Kurtz stared at Davey, a wild look on his face, his mouth moving soundlessly.

'*Los, geh,*' commanded Davey.

The two men faced one another. What had taken a few minutes would stay with them, perhaps in secret, for the rest of their lives.

Kurtz stepped slowly towards the gate and turned. '*Danke,*' he mouthed, before he slipped away and was gone.

Davey hurled the pistol into a corner of the yard.

He returned to the German quarters, retrieved the kit bag and made his way back to the yard. He took off his greatcoat and hung it over his backpack.

He adjusted the position of the heavy kit bag on his shoulder and stepped through the open gate, half expecting to be challenged: nothing happened.

There are pals ah would have liked tae say goodbye tae, but ah'm away.

He found himself in a narrow lane that ran alongside a high wall to the rear of the German quarters of the camp. The only watchtower in view was unmanned.

Yesterday ah would hae been shot at.

From his view of the church tower, Davey judged that he had emerged from the camp at right angles to the high fence that included the main entrance. He could see small groups of prisoners passing in and out.

They're no supposed tae garn intae toon.

Davey set off in the opposite direction. In the gathering dusk he passed unnoticed as a local, a mien assisted by his beard and worker's cap and jacket.

It was still dark when Davey reached the end of the lane to the Hoffmann's farm. He started up the track cautiously until the farmhouse and outbuildings came into view; the house was in darkness.

Davey removed his boots before entering the yard. He stepped noiselessly across to the front door, carefully placed the kit bag next to the front step, retraced his steps and collected his boots. He made his way slowly down the track until the stones beneath his feet hindered his progress.

Nae need tae run this time.

Davey sat on a patch of grass at the edge of the track, put his boots on and looked back at the silhouette of the house. He took a deep breath to quieten the thudding in his chest and relieve the tightness in his throat.

Several deep breaths later, Davey felt ready to leave the farm, this time for good. Home beckoned, though he didn't know how or when he would get there.

Just as he turned away, a movement at the top of the track made Davey turn back: a figure was running towards him, nightdress flapping wildly.

Anna leapt into Davey's outstretched arms, pressing against him with unnerving strength. The fierce grip of her arms around his neck almost made him cry out. He held her, this time not resisting her ardour and guiding hands. He held her until her gasping breath subsided and she loosened her grip and faced him. Tears rivered her cheeks.

'*Vergiss uns nicht,*' she pleaded.

'*Natürlich nicht,*' Davey replied.

'*Ich werde dich vermissen.*'

'I'll miss you too, Anna.'

'*Ich liebe dich,*' she whispered.

Anna stopped Davey's reply with a finger to his lips, took her hand away and kissed him hard on the mouth, then softly. She turned and walked slowly towards the house.

Davey watched the retreating figure until she left his sight, unable to move in either direction along the farm track. Forwards would take him to a place where he would start a new life; the other direction would take him home to his family.

'Fin a guid maun, Anna,' he said aloud.

Ah must garn … ah must garn.

With a long sigh, Davey strode quickly down the track, turned left along the road to Erlangen, and walked away from the Hoffmann's farm.

For the first time in his life, Davey felt invisible forces pulling him in two directions. 'C'mon, David Muir, buckle up,' he said aloud. 'Get gaen.'

Despite his defiant words, Davey's plodding pace gave voice to the confusion and hurt that he felt. He felt his eyes moisten and he had to keep swallowing hard. He could still feel Anna's clinging body.

Ah've no ken sadness like this afore.

310

He stood in the lane several times, turning as if to go back before turning again, walking away from the farm until his willpower failed and he stopped again. After several minutes of faltering, he overcame his indecision and forced himself to keep going. This time he didn't look back.

Davey's pace quickened as he approached the outskirts of Erlangen. He had been to the town several times with Christoph to make deliveries to the railway station. On one occasion, Christoph pointed out the whereabouts of the small prisoner of war camp on the edge of town.

Slivers of a wan dawn crept across the sky, lifting the town into the pale light of day. Davey quickened his pace further. He had wanted to arrive at the camp under cover of darkness, taking advantage of the deserted streets. He was only just in time. Townsfolk going about their early business cast suspicious glances as he hurried across the centre of town.

It was almost fully light when Davey reached the main gate of the camp. He was ready with answers for the British soldier on duty.

Going Home

Davey stayed in Erlangen camp for about a month. He shaved off his beard and had his hair cut by an English soldier who was a barber before the war.

Reluctantly, Davey abandoned the clothes given to him by Christoph and acquired tunic and breeches from the NCO committee.

Ah need tae feel like a soldier tae garn hame.

Returning farm workers were housed in the former quarters of the German guards, but food was scarce and their diet poor compared with life on the farms. Although Davey was in good health, as a result of spending over a year at the Hoffmann's farm, he and his fellow returnees found it difficult reverting to a camp diet. Fortunately, their stay at Erlangen camp did not last long.

A month after the Armistice, the German Red Cross arranged train transport. Davey was assigned to a train leaving Erlangen on 15th December. Carriages were comfortable and the former prisoners were given hot drinks, sandwiches and soup by Red Cross workers at several stations during their long, overnight journey.

Early the next day, the train drew up alongside the docks in Danzig, next to a Danish Red Cross hospital ship. Women and children held out their hands as the soldiers disembarked and lined up at the foot of the gangplanks.

Why're they haein tae beg?

Many of the soldiers handed over Red Cross parcels. Davey had some biscuits and chocolate in his backpack and gave them to a pitiful looking young woman; her rags of clothes hung from her skinny frame.

The woman handed the food to a child who was half-hidden behind her. The woman grasped Davey's hand and said something that he took to be 'thank you' in a language that he did not recognise, her voice breaking and quivering.

Davey gave her his remaining German money. 'Ah'll no need this,' he said as he closed the woman's fingers over the coins in her palm. 'Ah'm sorry, ah've nae mair,' he added, shaking his head.

The woman touched Davey's cheek with her other palm, then spoke to the child. Davey left them and joined the straggling line of men at the foot of the nearest gangplank.

Davey found a space near the rail from where he could look down at what was happening on the dockside. The woman and the child stood on the edge of the crowd, waving and smiling. The little girl blew him a kiss.

Davey waved in return.

The crowd of women and children began to drift away after the last of the soldiers embarked.

'Guid luck,' Davey said aloud as he watched the retreating figures. Just as he was on the point of leaving the rail, the child turned and looked in his direction and sent him a final wave.

Danish Red Cross officials moved amongst the soldiers, directing them to the large canteen and to cabins. Davey was allocated an outside cabin with two bunk beds and a shower cubicle. A Red Cross worker entered Davey's full name on a clipboard and, in perfect English, wished him a good journey

'How lang wull we be on board?' asked Davey.

'About five days if the weather holds. We will reach Copenhagen tonight, then cross to Leith.'

'Leith! Scotland! Thank you.'

'You can obtain breakfast on the deck below. You won't mind sharing in here?'

'Not at a'. This is a' grand,' replied Davey.

His cabin was on the starboard side. Davey peered out of the porthole. Sea and sky filled the circular view, the line where they met rolled gently up and down, mesmerising Davey towards drowsiness.

As he lay on the lower bunk, the door of the cabin opened just as the ship's engines changed their throbbing tone.

'Looks like we're away, pal,' observed a lanky Scotsman.

'Aye, Scotland next stop,' replied Davey. 'I'm Davey Muir.'

'Hamish Sutherland,' replied his cabin mate, grasping Davey's outstretched hand. 'A'body calls iss Mish.'

A pang of guilt shot through Davey's body.

Ah havenae thought aboot Hamish for ages.

'D'ye mind the top bunk?' asked Davey.

'Nae bother, pal.'

Mish flung a grubby pack onto the top bunk. 'Have ee had breakfast?'

The aroma of bacon frying in the noisy canteen drove some of the men to excess. Davey forced himself to be restrained at meal times on the ship. Too many men found that they couldn't stomach good food after years in prisoner of war camps.

Mish took Davey's advice; both men ate a modest breakfast of bacon and eggs, but didn't go up for seconds.

After a 'good feed' as Mish put it, Davey went up on deck, relishing the freshness of the cool sea air. A few circuits of the upper deck brought on a wave of tiredness. He hadn't slept much on the long train journey, so he returned to his cabin and fell into a deep sleep the instant he lay down.

Davey woke up to the sound of Mish snoring loudly on the top bunk. The porthole formed a black disc on the wall of the cabin. A line of lights appeared faintly across its centre.

We cannae be there a'ready.

'Whit can ee see?' Mish said suddenly.

'Lights,' replied Davey. 'Where are we?'

'Copenhagen,' replied Mish. 'How's yer geography?'

'Denmark?'

'Aye, yer right. We take on supplies apparently. Mair food for one thing.' Mish lay down again. 'Aye, they'll need a lot o' food for a' these hungry buggers.'

'Ah'm away up on deck,' said Davey.

Mish mumbled something on his way back to sleep.

Davey joined a large group of men standing at the rails in the chill night air. The sparkling lights looked like a string of jewels laid out on a black velvet cloth that drew nearer, transfixing those around him into a reverential silence as the ship edged closer to its docking place.

'It's a strange thing,' said the soldier standing next to Davey, breaking the quiet. 'We left England to go and fight in France and here we are in Sweden.'

'Denmark, ye eejit,' came a reply from nearby.

Laughter enriched the prospect of arrival at the city with the magic lights.

Davey and Mish were woken at first light the following morning by an announcement heard over public address: all men were to assemble on deck.

A Danish padre took to a microphone and, in English, announced that a Corporal Arthur Jones had died during the night.

The padre read Psalm 23 and invited the assembled soldiers to say the Lord's Prayer.

As the body slid ceremoniously over the side of the ship to be engulfed by the sea, Davey thought about the men he had trained and fought alongside. An image of Angus and Hamish leaped out of his memory.

A silence descended upon the assembled men as a loud splash signalled the end of the short service.

So near, so near.

The men filed away, subdued and thoughtful. Barely a word was heard in the canteen at breakfast.

The hospital ship left Copenhagen later that evening for the final part of its journey. On the fourth evening

316

after leaving Denmark, the ship laid off Leith dock until the following morning.

Davey and his fellow former prisoners of war reached Scottish soil on Sunday, 22nd December.

A Scots band played and marched up and down as the ship slid into dock, to the yells and cheers of men leaning over the rails. Davey half-heartedly joined in the cheering as he looked down at the kilted musicians marching towards the foot of the gangplank, playing on to greet the returning prisoners as they disembarked.

In the midst of cheering men and joyful music, an unfamiliar numbness enfolded Davey as he stepped from the end of the gangplank onto Scottish soil.

A group of women lined up at the foot of the gangplank thrust photographs towards the disembarking soldiers.

'Have ee seen him?' came appeal after appeal as the returning prisoners shuffled slowly past the line of women towards the open door of a large warehouse.

They look as distressed as the women at Danzig.

Davey stumbled as he passed the last of the women. He looked at the photograph she held out to him; he shook his head.

'Are ee a'right, pal?' came a voice behind him.

'Aye, fine noo,' replied Davey.

Red Cross nurses and uniformed soldiers bustled about, organising refreshments at a series of long tables. After a late breakfast, the men lined up in front of other tables behind which sat soldiers filling in forms.

Davey's turn came after a long wait, standing around chatting to men near him in his line. A lance corporal recorded Davey's details and informed him that he must report to his barracks in Berwick-upon-Tweed. He issued Davey with a rail warrant and sent him to the next stage in the process – the issue of new clothes.

'Berwick! Why no hame?'

'This is the procedure.'

'Seems daft tae me.'

'Ah'm just daein ma job, soldier. Change at Edinburgh. Over there next.'

Davey pleaded with the soldier issuing clothes to let him keep his boots, greatcoat and backpack. Davey's earnest appeal fell upon deaf ears until a sergeant approached, having heard the heated exchange and took control of the situation.

'You realise that you're still in the army, private,' he told him. 'We have our orders.'

'Aye, ah ken. Ah was given these efter a French soldier in the bed next tae me passed. Ah've worn 'em ever since.'

'Alright, you can keep the boots. We don't have any of your size anyway. They look almost worn through. You must give up the French coat though. You're in the British Army.'

'Thanks, sergeant.'

Sorry Didier.

'Put your prison uniform on the pile over there and collect a uniform and a set of clothes. There's changing rooms and washrooms at the back. You can get a shower and a shave. When you're done, report back here.'

Davey reported back, looking like a regular soldier.

'That's better, private. Backpack belong tae the Frenchman?'

'Aye. They gave iss his kit efter he died of his wounds.'

'You were wounded, then.'

'Aye, badly.'

'Sounds like you had it rough, private.'

Davey replied with a brief nod.

'You can keep the pack.'

'Ah might get some new boots at Berwick,' suggested Davey.

'Keep these if you can. Worn out or no. It's where they came from that's more important.'

'Thanks, sergeant.'

'Wait there,' said the sergeant.

The sergeant returned with Davey's greatcoat rolled up tightly under his arm.

'Don't put this on until you're out of sight. I don't know what they will say at Berwick mind.'

'Thanks again, sergeant.'

'There aren't any other from your battalion off your ship, so you'll be on your own returning to barracks. You should be there by this afternoon.'

'Why dae ah hae tae garn tae barracks?'

'Army procedure. You'll not be there long. There'll be paperwork to do. Good luck, private.'

Davey was given instructions how to walk to Leith railway station. He was relieved to be alone, walking away from the army officialdom that had taken up most of the morning. Now, despite his army uniform, he felt free.

Davey's presence walking through the town drew little attention from the citizens of Leith.

They must be yissed tae this.

Davey reached the imposing structure of Leith Central railway station after about half an hour's walk from the docks. As he reached the top of the stairs that led to the platforms above street level, he saw a group of soldiers and joined them.

'Were ee off the Danish boat?' asked one.

'Aye, I've tae report to Berwick. You?'

'I just want to go home,' replied another.

'Ah'll no miss the airmy,' said the first soldier. 'Hanging aboot tae the very last.'

Further conversation centred upon moaning about the army and their treatment since they disembarked.

'After the ballyhoo with the band, I got the impression that we were a bit of a nuisance,' said one of the men. 'You know, just returning prisoners rather than soldiers. The things we could have told 'em.'

'It was heartbreaking, those women,' said Davey.

'Aye, there'll be a lot of us still missing. There but … Here's our train.'

Leith was a dead-end station, so their train drew up just short of the buffers. Passengers alighting merely glanced at the group of soldiers waiting to get aboard.

The short journey to Waverley was sufficient to establish names and destinations in England and Scotland. Handshakes and good luck wishes were exchanged on the platform in Edinburgh before the group dispersed in search of onward trains.

'See ee at the next yin,' quipped Alastair as he shook hands firmly.

'Ah bloody hope not,' replied Davey. 'Ah'm staying hame if there's another yin.'

*

The final few miles of the journey to Berwick clung to the coast. Davey peered out to sea, his thoughts and feelings drifting and shifting as the town came into view, radiating waves of familiarity as if he had been away for a matter of days rather than years.

As in Leith, Davey's presence at Berwick station and along the route of the short walk to his battalion's barracks drew little attention from passers-by.

They have nae idea whit's happened tae iss.

Davey explained to the sentry why he had been sent to Berwick before he passed under the imposing archway and entered the barracks, wondering what he was supposed to do. The parade ground was almost deserted. A few soldiers moved between buildings, oblivious to his indecision. After standing just inside the archway for a few moments, he made his way to where he thought he remembered seeing offices when he first came.

He knocked on a door marked 'Major Weir'.

'Come in,' came a loud voice from within.

Davey entered, saluted and announced himself.

The major sifted amongst a pile of papers on his desk, looking up from time to time at the man standing before him until he found what he had been looking for.

'Muir, you say.'

'Yes, sir.'

'Initial?'

'D, sir. David.'

The officer traced his finger down a list.

'Ah, found you. Good God, man, you were captured in nineteen fifteen! We lost track of you after Loos, Private Muir.'

'Ah wis shot and lay for a few days, sir.'

321

'A few days! You were lucky to survive.'

'Yes, sir. Ah wis treated in a French hospital.'

'French,' the officer repeated. 'You've got one of their coats,' he said as if to himself. 'Look, Private Muir, there is a procedure for this. Are you alone?'

'Yes, sir. We came into Leith from Denmark this morning. Ah'm the only returning KOSB off the ship.'

The Major stared at Davey, looked at his list again, then looked hard at Davey with a shake of his head.

'Welcome back, Private Muir.'

'Thank you, sir. Whit happens noo? Ah wis told at Leith tae report here.'

'You're still a soldier in the King's Own until such time … I'm going to hand you over to someone who will deal with the preliminaries. You'll be given three months furlough, starting tomorrow.'

Davey felt his chest tighten.

'Thank you, sir.'

'That's the procedure. You can go home in the morning. Please follow me.'

The major took Davey along the corridor, opened the door to another office, leant in and said, 'Sergeant, take care of this one will you.'

Before he entered the room, Davey addressed the major, 'Sir, your list: did many of us return after Loos?'

The major shook his head. 'There are still names on my list unaccounted for. You're a lucky man, private. You can go in now.'

Sergeant Gibson looked up from his paperwork and stared open-mouthed at Davey.

'Can ah sit doon, sergeant?' Davey asked.

Sergeant Gibson continued to gape at the man standing in front of his desk.

'Sergeant?'

'Er ... yes, of course. Please take a seat.'

Davey sat and faced Sergeant Gibson.

'Private Muir, isn't it?'

'Ye remember iss, then?'

'Of course ... of course I remember you. I didn't think ... '

'That ah wid survive. Wull here ah am, sergeant.'

'No, I mean ... what happened to you?'

'Taken prisoner at Loos, after a hell of a fight.'

'My God, hats off to you, Private Muir.'

'Ee didnae garn over?'

'No. I spent the war training, like I did with your lot,' he said. 'I couldn't have done what you did,' he continued after a long pause. 'And a prisoner for all that time ... '

Sergeant Gibson shook his head, picked up his pen and got to work.

Davey spent the next hour in the sergeant's office, answering questions and filling in forms.

'That's all for now, Private Muir. There'll be more when you return from leave. Here's your rail warrant. You can catch a Carlisle train in the morning. I'll show you where you can sleep tonight.'

The sergeant stood and extended his right hand. 'Well done, Private Muir.'

The two men exchanged handshakes.

Davey was bombarded with questions from serving soldiers for the next few hours. Most had fought with the 7th or the 8th until Armistice Day; returning prisoners were on leave.

Davey disliked being the centre of attention. He felt self-conscious about being the only former prisoner of war in barracks. At length, his fellow soldiers got tired of asking Davey about life in captivity.

'Well, a' be glad tae get hame,' remarked a Glaswegian. 'We've got leave soon, in time for Christmas.'

Davey lay on his bunk; he had barely given any thought to Christmas. His mind flew back to last Christmas, conjuring images of the smiling faces of the Hoffmann household and the intense gaze of Anna.

It would be Christmas Eve on Tuesday; today was Sunday. Davey would be going home on Monday, 23rd December. He had nothing to give Kate, Marion, and Davie: nothing but himself.

Davey lay awake trying to picture what his children would look like after his years away from home.

They willnae ken iss.

This realisation repeated in Davey's mind, until he heard a distant clock strike three. He didn't hear the clock any more that night. The next thing he became aware of were soldiers getting up and moving about.

After a breakfast of tea, toast and jam, Davey showed his orders to the sentry at the archway and set off for the station. He didn't have long to wait for the train that would take a northerly route via Lockerbie to Carlisle. He shared a carriage with civilians who politely acknowledged the presence of a soldier without speaking to him.

Davey dozed for most of the journey. The Carlisle train didn't stop at Ecclefechan, so he alighted at Lockerbie, looking forward to the six-mile walk to the Fechan as an opportunity to prepare himself.

Exiting the station brought Davey into Bridge Street. Instead of taking the Carlisle road south out of town, he crossed the bridge over the railway line and walked towards the first row of terraces beyond the bridge. He knocked on the door of number three, his pulse racing. He was on the point of turning to leave when he heard footsteps. Davey stood away from the front step; he could feel the rhythm of his heartbeat in his throat.

A middle-aged woman opened the door, wiping here hands on a faded apron.

'Mrs MacFadyen?' asked Davey.

'Aye, that's me,' replied the woman.

'Ah'm Davey Muir. Ah wis wi Hamish in — '

'Ye'd better come in, son.'

Davey followed Mrs MacFadyen into the kitchen at the rear of the house. Baking utensils covered most of the table; the sweet aroma of baking filled the room.

'Are ee making a scone?'

'Aye. When wis the last time ee had yin? Will ee no sit doon?'

Davey sat down; Hamish's mother stood by the sink, wiping her hands on her apron.

'Hamish didnae come home, Davey. He's deid, son.'

Davey opened his mouth to speak, but he made no sound, stifled by the pounding in his head that made him feel dizzy.

Hamish's mother placed a tumbler in front of Davey and poured some whisky.

'Slowly, son.'

Davey sipped the honey-coloured liquid, savouring a burning sensation almost lost from memory.

'Ah tried tae look oot for him, Mrs MacFadyen, Ah really tried.'

'Ah know, son. Ye did yer best.'

'Ah'm so sorry, Mrs MacFadyen. Ah should've brought him back.'

'It's no your fault, Davey. Dinnae blame yersel.'

Davey stared into his whisky, unable to look Hamish's mother in the eye.

'Ah'll come and see ee when ah'm settled. Ah'm just on ma way hame tae the Fechan.'

'Have ee got someone waiting for ee?'

'Aye, ah dae. Ah'll away just noo.'

'Thanks for calling. All the best, son.'

Davey re-crossed the railway bridge and turned onto the Carlisle road. He walked quickly, breathing heavily from the effort, forcing his body to a physical extreme to absorb the news about Hamish.

As soon as he found a suitable place to recover from the shock, he sat on a wall at the front of a white cottage on the outskirts of Lockerbie. He closed his eyes and let his breathing return to normal. Images of Hamish crowded in.

'That's private, pal. Ee cannae sit there.'

The man's voice jerked Davey out of his state of distress.

'Sorry, ah was just resting,' Davey said to the retreating occupant of the cottage as he opened his front door and went back inside.

'Just garn,' Davey called loudly.

Miserable bugger.

Davey felt better after letting off steam. He set off at a fast pace along the Carlisle road towards Ecclefechan. The sweet familiarity of the hills and farms between Lockerbie and the Fechan lifted his sprits. The outline of Burnswark Hill, sharpened by the chill afternoon air, signalled his approach and drew him closer to home.

He hesitated at the turn from the main road to the centre of the village. Four years of absence fell away as he stood at the top of the hill. A surge of relief and hope tugged at him as he convinced himself of his whereabouts, filling his eyes with the overwhelming attachment he felt to the scene of normality that was laid out before him, waiting for him to step back into his former life.

His French army boots announced his return as he walked down the hill into the slumberous, wintering village.

Kate and Davey's Story

Bonds were Broken

Kate had got out of the habit of looking up the hill every time she crossed the road between the hotel and her home.

On the Monday afternoon before Christmas, she carried a basket of dirty linen to be laundered in the shared wash house at the rear of the row of terraced houses.

Halfway across the road, Kate heard something: the noise of boots scuffing the stony road made her look; a voice calling her name made her look; arms waving frantically made her look.

She saw him, striding down the hill.

Kate's basket fell from her grasp and toppled over. She ran towards him, a cry somewhere between a scream and a keening howl bearing his name split the tranquillity of the lazy afternoon.

Several villagers stood and watched as the two figures stood motionless a few feet apart from one another, as if rigid with shock.

Davey quietly called her name again and spread his arms wide.

Kate shuddered and sobbed violently, her head buried in Davey's shoulder.

'Shh, shh noo,' he said.

Kate's shaking slowly calmed to a tremble as Davey held her firmly.

'Ah cannae hear ee,' he said. 'Ah cannae tell whit ee are saying.'

Kate pulled away, her face flushed and wet with tears.

'Ah thought that ee wis deid,' she wailed. 'Ah thought that ee wis deid … deid,' her whimpering voice trailed away, dissolving into a convulsion of weeping.

Davey held her close to him.

'Shh. Dinnae greet noo. I'm hame. C'mon. We cannae stand oot here.'

Davey picked up Kate's basket and followed her into the front room.

'Where're the bairns?' he asked Kate.

'Davie is next door with Chrissie. Marion is in the back kitchen.'

Marion looked up from where she was scribbling with a crayon on a large piece of paper on the kitchen table, a puzzled expression met Davey as his daughter looked from him to her mother and back again.

'How old are ee?' said Davey.

Marion didn't answer.

'It's a'reet. Tell him,' said Kate.

'Ah'm four and a half,' she replied, still looking rather perplexed. 'Have ee come tae visit?'

'Aye.'

'That's ma sister.' Marion pointed to a wooden cot.

Davey bent down to look under the table.

'Kate?'

'Oh, Davey … Davey,' spluttered Kate.

'Well?'

Gasping and crying robbed Kate of speech.

'Whi's the bairn?'

Kate fled into the front room.

'It's a'reet, Mummy's upset,' Davey said to Marion. 'Ah'll see tae her. Dinnae worry.'

Davey sat opposite Kate. Her body shook from weeping, her breathing shallow and rasping. She wrung her hands in her lap and couldn't look at Davey.

He waited until her breathing returned to normal. She cast fearful glances at him, looking away the instant their eyes met.

'Ye'll hae tae tell iss, Kate.'

'Ye'll be so angry with me.'

'Go on, tell iss.'

'They said ee were missing. Then there was nothing ... nothing! Ah thought ah wis a widow. The shock of seeing ee ... ah've never felt the like. Can ee imagine?'

'Ah cannae.'

'Ah didnae stay wi him fi lang. He wasnae a guid maun. Noo ye're back, ee'll never forgive iss.'

'Whit's done is done, Kate. The bairn's greetin.'

Kate brought Jean into the front room.

'Is Marion a'reet?'

'Aye.'

'Gie her tae me.'

Kate handed Jean to Davey.

'Ye remember how tae hold a bairn.'

'Aye, ah dae.'

Davey gazed at Jean; she stopped crying and peered up at him.

'Whit's her name?'

'Jean.'

'Hello, Jean,' he said. 'Ah'm yer faither.'

The End

Davey and Kate

In the back garden of 2 Ashgrove Crescent, Ecclefechan,
in the early 1950s.

Kate with Marion and Davie

Probably taken towards the end of 1915

My mother, Jean, and five of her siblings

Jean is standing top left, aged ten or eleven. Marion is
seated, with Davie standing behind her.

Characters

Members of the Muir Family

David ('Davey') Muir I was 12 years of age when my grandfather died in 1959.

Catherine ('Kate') Johnstone I remember my grandmother more clearly than my grandfather. I was 34 years of age when she died in 1981.

Jean Burnie Johnstone My dear mother died in 2013. She was the third of ten children born by her mother.

Davie Muir I have no record or recollection when my uncle Davie died.

Marion Muir My auntie Marion died in January 1976.

Chrissie My grandmother had a sister called Christina, usually known as Teen. I don't remember much about her, although I came into contact with Teen during my childhood holidays in Ecclefechan. The character of Chrissie is loosely based upon Christina.

Jane Johnstone was Catherine's mother.

Thomas Hiddleston was Catherine's father. Sapper Thomas Hiddleston, my great grandfather, died of his wounds in hospital in the spring of 1918 following his repatriation from the Western Front.

Other Real Characters

Thomas McDermott was Jean's father. Despite extensive and exhaustive genealogical research by Gordon McPhail (see acknowledgements), Thomas remains a mystery. Apart from his name, address and occupation entered on my mother's birth certificate, nothing more about him could be determined.

Doctor Wigniolle I took the liberty of using a real character in the part of the story when my grandfather was hospitalised in Saint Clotilde, in the town of Douai. This French hospital was taken over by the German authorities in late 1915.

I hope that I have done justice to Dr Wigniolle and his staff. I wrote him as a sympathetic, caring and gifted surgeon. My grandfather was very fortunate to be cared for at Saint Clotilde.

All other characters are fictional and it should be noted that there was no Company E in the 7th KOSB.

In the process of fictionalising the stories of Davey and Kate, it was critically important to strive for authenticity and accuracy. This was particularly paramount for Davey's part of the story, which spans the period between volunteering and repatriation. Consequently, many written and orally recorded resources were consulted in undertaking research. The principal elements of this material are referred to in the following sections.

Acknowledgements

This book has been several years in the making, from research to publication. Throughout that period, very many individuals have provided me with help, advice and given their time in order to assist me in bringing the story to fruition. I am greatly indebted to all of them for their willingness, kindness, selfless generosity and support.

First and foremost, a special expression of gratitude goes to my wife, Annette. Her unfaltering love, support and encouragement throughout have kept me going, and her timely ideas have often helped to resolve many a plot problem or stumbling block.

Beta Readers

Huge thanks go to my wife, Annette; Wanda Pierpoint-Jones; David Wake (and for his formatting help); and Andy Conway. Annette read an early draft and also read the final draft. I am particularly indebted to David and Andy of New Street Authors (newstreetauthors.com) for their inspiring ideas and suggestions, as well as for their editing skills.

Professional Editing

I am very grateful to my wonderful editor, Sarah Abel. Sarah's meticulous editing has proved invaluable.

Cover Design

A huge thank you goes to David Wake for his brilliant cover design, which incorporates a photograph of my grandfather and an image of the battle of Loos, and to Andy Conway for his creative input to the design of the front cover. A particular thanks also to Andy for his enticing back cover blurb and for coming up with the inspiring title of the book.

Family Recollections

I was fortunate to have a number of lengthy telephone conversations with my uncle Hiddleston before he died in 2017. It was during one of these conversations that he told me that his mother thought that she was a widow (after Davey was reported missing). On another occasion, my uncle told me that his father was billeted on a farm towards the end of the war and that the family wanted him to stay.

My cousin, Peter McGeer, was a reliable source of Muir family history: thank you Peter.

I am grateful to Deborah, Don and Maureen McKenzie, friends of my uncle Hiddleston when he lived in Canada. The McKenzie family sent me valuable material, including the photograph of my grandfather that has been incorporated into the front cover of the book.

The family also sent me the Dead Man's Penny struck for Thomas Hiddleston. (A Dead Man's Penny is a brass plaque, about five inches in diameter, issued to the family of all soldiers who were killed in the First World War.)

Ancestry Research

I am particularly indebted to Peter Payne. This book might never have got off the ground without his skill and diligence in researching my grandfather's war records. His reading and interpretation of these records gave me a framework upon which to build the story of my grandfather's POW experience.

Wendy Whiteley, for her work in investigating the Muir family tree.

Gordon McPhail (www.ancestrydoctor.com) for his thorough search for information about Thomas McDermott.

Face-to-Face Meetings

Davey's Story

I am very grateful to Dr Emily Mayhew of Imperial College London for spending time with me discussing the nature and treatment of the kind of wounds inflicted upon my grandfather during the battle of Loos.

Emily suggested that an X-ray, taken when Davey was elderly, which showed a fragment of metal in his stomach, was consistent with the body's way of dealing with such a foreign body by encasing it in fat. This is likely to explain why a fragment of bullet remained undetected in Davey's body until it showed up several decades after the end of the war.

I am very thankful to Ian Martin, Archivist of the King's Own Scottish Borderers (KOSB) Regimental Museum. The museum is housed in Berwick Barracks, Berwick-upon-Tweed. Ian accorded me the rare privilege of reading the KOSB War Diary. This unique document recorded events contemporaneously leading up to and during the battle of Loos on a daily basis and, as such, formed a critical primary source.

Visits

Kate's Story

I am very grateful to the staff at the Tenement House, Glasgow. The National Trust for Scotland manages this museum. My visit gave me a valuable insight into the kind of property that my grandmother lived in with Thomas McDermott in Glasgow.

Davey's Story

My wife and I visited Loos-en-Gohelle in May 2012. We tried to find Hill 70 and remain reasonably convinced that we saw the ridge from a distance, across (private) land that would have prohibited closer scrutiny. We were also kindly and unexpectedly invited to visit a small two-room museum in the centre of the village.

Visiting the scene of the battle of Loos and thinking about my grandfather's part in it was a very affecting experience.

Other Acknowledgements

Kate's Story

Thanks go to Katie Flanagan, Special Collections Librarian, Brunel University London. Katie provided access to railway timetables that were in place when Kate returned to Ecclefechan from Glasgow. These, together with other resources, also enabled me to explore the route that David Muir was likely to have taken when he returned home from Leith and when he went AWOL during training.

Davey's Story

I am appreciative of the translation from German made by Sarah Wuerfel of my grandfather's war records held by the International Committee of the Red Cross (ICRC). These records give the date of his transfer from Saint Clotilde to Ingolstadt POW camp, as well as the dates for subsequent transfers. These records also give very brief details about my grandfather's leg wounds.

Thanks go to Sebastian Remus, an historian based in Germany. Sebastian undertook extensive research into the Battle of Loos from the German side's point of view. Sebastian also painstakingly checked and corrected the German dialogue, a task for which I am particularly grateful.

Thanks also go to Cathy Gibbs, Library Assistant (Archives), Dumfries and Galloway Council, for her exploration of the local press archives.

Thomas Hiddleston

Thanks again to Peter Payne for his work on examining the war record of my great grandfather.

I am very obliged to Jane Evans, for her valuable help in locating my great grandfather's war grave. Standing before his headstone in the war graves cemetery on a sunny day in June 2017 was a very moving experience.

Historical Notes

Davey's Story

Davey's story is based upon very few known facts and events. Thanks to Peter Payne, I know in which regiment my grandfather served, the date of his capture at the battle of Loos, and the periods of time he spent in Ingolstadt and Nürnberg POW camps.

I have also unearthed uncorroborated evidence that Davey spent a period of time in a third POW camp immediately prior to the Armistice. This evidence does not give the dates of this period. This third POW camp is not mentioned in his official war record and does not appear in his International Committee of the Red Cross (ICRC) records.

I have endeavoured to use these few facts to weave an entirely fictional narrative that begins with Davey enlisting.

Davey at the Front

Accounts of soldiers fighting at the Western Front emphasised the drudgery and squalor of life in the trenches when there was no fighting, and drew a stark comparison with the burst of activity when troops climbed out of the trenches – usually known as 'going over the top' – to engage the Germans face-to-face.

I have tried to reflect what a number of soldiers reported as 'a lot of hanging around' in Davey's experience of days spent behind the lines and at the Front itself prior to the battle of Loos.

Davey's Wounds

German Red Cross and ICRC documents record Davey's leg wound but not his stomach wound. The latter was recorded only in his (British) war record.

I have made the reasonable assumption that my grandfather's leg wound was as a result of machine gun fire on the downward slope of Hill 70 on the first day of the battle of Loos. This is where a number of soldiers of the 7th KOSB were wounded between the German first and second lines.

I have taken the liberty of envisaging that his stomach wound was inflicted when he lay wounded. That this happened to a number of soldiers is a statement of fact.

Davey's Prisoner of War Experience

POW experience in WW1 is less documented compared with WW2. There are a number of books written by officers, but very few accounts from the lesser ranks. A number of books were consulted in order to gain an understanding of life as a POW in WW1, as well as orally recorded testimonies. (See Key Resources section.)

The tedium of life as a POW in WW1 comes across in the resources that I have used. Consequently I have tried to reflect the likely mundanity of Davey's life as a prisoner of war, an existence relieved to some extent by work usually in local industry or agriculture.

Incidents such as those involving the guard Kurtz are fictitious.

Davey's POW Camps

Very little could be found by way of descriptions of Ingolstadt and Nürnberg camps, apart from a relatively brief one of Ingolstadt, which I made use of. I made the assumption that Nürnberg camp was similar in layout to Ingolstadt.

Richard van Emden's book, *Prisoners of the Kaiser*, includes several photographs of camps; these proved highly valuable in terms of researching the life of a POW.

The Battle of Loos

I made an extensive study of this major battle, one of the largest of WW1. This research was made possible by a number of books and other resources (see the next section).

Key Resources

A complete list of resources – websites in particular – would be too lengthy and unwieldy to be included here; instead, only key resources are mentioned.

If any reader has a question about any aspect of the book, historical or otherwise, they are very welcome to leave me a message on the contact page of my website.

https://davidmuir.website

I will endeavour to reply quickly.

Principal Websites

The Imperial War Museum: iwm.org.uk

The IWM proved to be a highly valuable source of spoken testimonies of soldiers and POWs. I focussed mainly upon the latter; it is in this section of the museum's archive of recorded interviews with soldiers that I came upon a number of accounts of POWs billeted (unguarded) at farms. It was the discovery of this vital information that gave credence to my uncle Hiddleston's remark that his father worked on a farm. (There was even one case where a prisoner stayed at the farm after the war, taking the place of the [absent?] farmer.)

The International Committee of the Red Cross (ICRC): icrc.org

David Muir's record is held in the ICRC archives. These give brief details of his (leg) wound and the dates of transfer from camp to camp.

The KOSB: kosb.co.uk

Douai: The town of Douai's website that included some information and photographs of wounded prisoners arriving at Saint Clotilde has been removed since I carried out some research into the hospital's role in the war.

The National Trust for Scotland: nts.org.uk

This site includes material about the tenement house in Glasgow.

Feature Films

They Shall Not Grow Old, directed by Peter Jackson, released in 2018.

Peter Jackson's astonishing film adds sound and colour to black and white (silent) footage of WW1 soldiers, from enlisting, training and journeying to the Front. As a large troop of soldiers makes its way towards front line trenches, the frame opens out and sound and colour are added in spectacular fashion. The remainder of the film examines life behind the Front and in the front-line trenches in sufficient detail to inform Davey's Story with accuracy and authenticity.

The only event that is not included in the film is what happens when soldiers climb out of their trenches, cross no-man's-land and encounter German guns and troops. This part of the film is told by drawings of hand-to-hand fighting, accompanied by the spoken commentary of soldiers who experienced what is depicted in the black and white still images.

1917, directed by Sam Mendes, released in 2019.

The film was inspired by fragment of stories told to Sam Mendes by his grandfather. As such, I was interested in the depiction of events, details of clothing, trench construction and so on when watching this brilliant film. The film helped to underpin the validity of a number of details written for scenes in Davey's Story.

La Grande Illusion, directed by Jean Renoir, released in 1937.

Renoir's film focuses upon a group of French officers held prisoner in WW1. I watched the film merely to see if there were any specific details about French POWs that might prove useful.

Books: Specific

Soldier's wounds and their treatment; transport of wounded soldiers:

Emily Mayhew, *Wounded: A New History of the Western Front in World War 1* (Oxford University Press, 2014).

A French surgeon's experience of treating wounds:

Georges Duhamel, *The New Book of Martyrs,* (Aeterna Publishing, 2011).

In the absence of finding any books about the medical treatment of captured British soldiers, the following book about two military hospitals in France and, more notably, in London, gave me an insight into the treatment of wounded solders in hospitals ran by the British military authorities. It is of great significance that Endell Street hospital was run entirely by women.

Wendy Moore, *Endell Street, The Trailblazing Women Who Ran World War One's Most Remarkable Military Hospital* (Atlantic Books, 2020).

POW experience:

Max Arthur, *The Road Home* (Phoenix, 2010).

George Connes, *A POW's Memoir of the First World War* (Berg, 2004).

Richard van Emden, *Prisoners of the Kaiser: The last POWs of the Great War* (Pen & Sword Military, 2009).

James W. Gerard, *My Four Years in Germany* (The Echo Library, 2008).

H. G. Gilliland, *My German Prisons* (BiblioLife, no date of publication is given in my edition).

F. W. Harvey, *Comrades in Captivity* (Douglas McLean Publishing, 2010).

Robert Jackson, *The Prisoners: 1914–18* (Routledge, 1989).

John Lewis-Stempel, *The War Behind the Wire* (Weidenfeld & Nicholson 2014).

John Yarnall, *Barbed Wire Disease: British and German Prisoners of War, 1914–1919* (The History Press, 2011).

The KOSB:

Captain Stair Gillon, *The K.O.S.B. in the Great War* (Naval and Military Press, 2009).

The Battle of Loos:

Author unknown, *A Border Battalion* (Forgotten Books, 2012).

Peter Doyle, *LOOS 1915* (The History Press, 2012).

Nick Lloyd, *LOOS 1915* (Tempus Publishing, 2006).

Books: General

A number of other books were consulted that covered the experience of soldiers fighting at the Front in France in WW1.

Illustrated Books

John Griffiths, *Old Berwick* (Stenlake Publishing, 2014).

Heather F. C. Lyall, *Vanishing Glasgow* (Aberdeen University Library, 1991).

Paul Pattison, *Berwick Barracks and Fortifications* (English Heritage, 2011).

Jim Walker, *Images of England: Berwick-upon-Tweed* (Tempus Publishing, 1998).

About the Author

Photograph by Gareth Davies

David Muir was born in Scotland in 1947 and attended a number of boarding schools in the English Midlands. After a spell trying to be a schoolteacher, he spent over twenty years as a lecturer in one of the new universities in the West Midlands region, where he wrote a number of technical books on computing. Having now retired, he spends time writing fiction, a blog and poetry. He lives with his wife in Solihull.

David Muir's website: davidmuir.website

Also by David Muir

Finding Sarah

David Muir's second novel, *Finding Sarah*, is available as an e-book and a paperback from Amazon.

Reviews

'I enjoyed this novel. David Muir here treads between tragic romantic saga and literary detective fiction as we follow a romance and its repercussions through several generations, a large part of it through rediscovered letters and diaries. From Birmingham to Skipton in the Yorkshire Dales to the Gower, South Wales, and from 1970 to the present day and beyond, this is broad in its reach and genuinely moving in places. A real step up in this writer's output.'

'[This novel is] a gentle and sensitively written story of a forbidden love affair with consequences that gradually unfold throughout the course of the book. The female characters are interesting and have depth and strength, and the agony and ecstasy of a love affair in it's early stages is convincingly portrayed.'

'A most enjoyable novel. I particularly liked the style of the book, written from different viewpoints, a flowing narrative which is quite engaging, and the author's meticulous attention to detail.

'Above all, this story is about emotions, love, envy, jealousy, their interaction and control of attitudes and behaviour, and the subsequent, perhaps inevitable, consequences.

'I very much recommend this book, perhaps as a holiday read. It is so different to the author's first book, which I would also recommend, and now very much look forward to reading his next book.'

Visions of Whereafter

David Muir's first novel, *Visions of Whereafter*, is available as an e-book and a paperback from Amazon.

Reviews

'David uses an unusual literary device to introduce us to his heroes - famous names from the near and distant past. I enjoyed this very much. I also enjoyed the final chapter - a conclusion that I did not see coming. A great read!'

Printed in Great Britain
by Amazon